THE
PROMISE

ROBERT
CRAIS

THE
PROMISE

First published in Great Britain in 2015 by Orion Books,
an imprint of The Orion Publishing Group Ltd
Carmelite House, 50 Victoria Embankment,
London EC4Y 0DZ

An Hachette UK company

1 3 5 7 9 10 8 6 4 2

A CIP catalogue record for this book is
available from the British Library.

ISBN (Hardback) 978 1 4091 2715 4
ISBN (Export Trade paperback) 978 1 4091 2991 2
ISBN (Ebook) 978 1 4091 2992 9

Printed and bound in Australia by Griffin Press

The Orion Publishing Group's policy is to use papers
that are natural, renewable and recyclable products and made
from wood grown in sustainable forests. The logging and
manufacturing processes are expected to conform to the
environmental regulations of the country of origin.

www.orionbooks.co.uk

for Randy Sherman
pilot, surgeon, partner, and friend
no man better to have at your six
or flying the lead.

The Drop House

1

Mr. Rollins

THE WOMAN STOOD in the far corner of the dimly lit room, hiding in shadows like a fish in gray water. She was small, round, and dumpy. The fringed leather jacket probably made her seem rounder, but she'd never been a looker. She reminded Mr. Rollins of an overripe peach, and the peach was clearly afraid.

A steady rain fell from the overcast night. The dingy, one-bedroom bungalow west of Echo Park reeked of bleach and ammonia, but the windows were closed, the shades were down, and the doors were locked. A single yellow twenty-five-watt lamp provided the only light. The chemical smell gave Mr. Rollins a headache, but he could not open the windows. They were screwed shut.

Rollins wasn't his real name, but the man and the woman probably weren't using their true names, either. Amy and Charles. Amy hadn't said three words since they arrived. Charles did the talking and Charles was getting impatient.

"How long does this take?"

The chemist's answer was resentful.

"Two minutes, dude. Relax. Science takes time."

The chemist was a juiced-up, sleeved-out rock pile hunched over the coffee table. A hiker's LED headlamp blazed on his forehead. He was heating the contents of a glass jar with a small torch while watching two meters that looked like swollen TV remotes. Rollins had found him cooking meth eight years ago and used him often.

Charles was a trim man in his forties with neat brown hair and the tight build of a tennis player. Mr. Rollins had made three buys off Charles in the past year, and all had gone well. This was why Mr. Rollins let him bring the woman, only now, seeing her, Rollins wondered why she wanted to come. She damned near pissed herself when Rollins searched her and made them put on the gloves. He made everyone who entered the house wear vinyl gloves. Rollins did not allow food or drinks. No one could chew gum or smoke cigarettes. The list was pretty long. Mr. Rollins had rules.

He smiled as he adjusted his gloves.

"They make your hands sweat, don't they, Amy? I know it's a pain, but we're almost finished."

Charles answered for her.

"She's fine. Tell your man to finish up so we can get out of here."

The chemist mumbled without looking up.

"Fuck off."

Rollins smiled at Amy again and glanced at the round plastic container beside the chemist. It was filled with a material that looked like yogurt and felt like modeling clay.

"Where'd you get this?"

Charles stepped on her answer again.

"I told you where we got it."

Rollins considered pushing his pistol up Charles's ass and popping a cap, but he did not let his feelings show.

"I'm just making conversation. Amy seems nervous."

Charles glanced at Amy.

"She's fine."

Amy's voice was whisper-soft when she finally spoke.

"I made it."

The chemist snorted.

"Yeah. Right."

Then the chemist sat up and gazed at Rollins.

"Whoever made it did a righteous job. It's the real deal, brother."

Charles crossed his arms. Smug.

"You see?"

Rollins was impressed. The material in the Tupperware was not easy to come by. Charles claimed the woman had two hundred kilograms.

"What about tags?"

The chemist turned off the torch and unplugged the meters.

"Ethylene test shows zero. I'll know parts per million when I run a samp at home, but the stuff is clean, bro. No tags. Untraceable."

Rollins thanked the chemist, who packed his equipment into a green backpack and let himself out through the kitchen. A light winter shower pattered the roof.

Charles said, "So now what? Are we in business?"

Rollins sealed the lid on the Tupperware.

"The buyer will test it himself. If his results are the same, we're golden."

Amy spoke again and this time she sounded anxious.

"I'll make more for the right buyer. I can make all they want."

Charles took her arm, trying to turn her away.

"Let's see their money first."

Amy did not move.

"I have to meet them, you know. That's a requirement."

"Not now."

Charles steered her toward the front door like a shopping cart. Rollins quickly stopped them.

"Back door, Charles. Never the front."

Charles swung the woman around and aimed her toward the kitchen. After insisting she come, Charles couldn't get her out of the house fast enough.

Rollins opened the back door and asked for their gloves. He gave Amy a gentle smile.

"Buyers don't like to be met, but they'll make an exception for you, Amy. I promise."

She seemed ready to cry, but Charles pulled her out and they disappeared into the rain.

Rollins locked the kitchen door and hurried to the front door, where he peered through a peephole. When Charles and Amy reached the street, he returned to the kitchen and opened the back door to air the place out. The tiny backyard was dark and hidden from neighbors by overgrown bushes and a sprawling avocado tree.

Rollins stood in the door breathing air that didn't stink of ammonia and called his buyer.

"Good news."

A coded way of saying the tests were positive.

"Very good. I will send someone."

"Tonight."

"Yes. Now."

"You have the other things here, too. I've told you for a week to come get this stuff."

"I am sending someone."

"I want it gone. All of it."

"He will take it."

Rollins put the Tupperware in the bedroom with the other things and returned to the kitchen. He still wore his gloves and would wear them until he left. He took a one-liter spray bottle from beneath the sink and sprayed bleach on the kitchen counters and floor and door. He sprayed the coffee table where the chemist had done his work and the stool on which the chemist had sat. He sprayed the living room floor and the doorjamb between the kitchen and living room. Rollins believed the bleach would destroy the enzymes and oils left in finger-prints or spit and erase DNA evidence. He wasn't convinced this was true, but it seemed sensible, so he bleached out the house whenever he used it.

When Mr. Rollins acquired the house, he made several changes to better serve his needs, like screwing shut the windows and installing peepholes. Nothing fancy, nothing expensive, and nothing to attract the neighbors' attention, none of whom knew him, had met him or, hopefully, seen him. Rollins did only enough maintenance to prevent the house from becoming an eyesore. He let people stay from time to time, never anyone he personally knew and only long enough so the neighbors would think the house was a rental. Mr. Rollins had not built a fortress when he acquired the house, just a place of relative safety from which to do his crime.

Rollins put away the bleach, returned to the living room, and turned off the lamp. He sat in the darkness, nose burning as he lis-tened to the rain.

9:42 P.M.

2142 hours.

1742 Zulu Time.

Mr. Rollins hated to wait, but there was big money at stake if Charles and Amy were real. Rollins wondered if Charles beat her. He seemed like the type. She seemed like the type, too. Rollins's older sister married a man who abused her for years until Rollins killed him.

Rollins checked the time again.

9:51.

Rollins put his pistol on the couch. He rested his hand on the gun, checked the time, and closed his eyes.

9:53.

The rain stopped.

10:14.

Someone knocked at the front door.

Rollins jerked to his feet and moved quickly into the kitchen. The buyer's man would never use the front door. That was a rule. Everyone used the back.

Rollins quietly closed and locked the kitchen door as knocking came from the front.

Knock knock knock.

Rollins slipped off his shoes and hurried to the front.

Knock knock knock.

Mr. Rollins peered through the peephole and saw an adult male in a dark rain shell. The hood was back and the unzipped shell exposed a loud patterned shirt. Average height, Anglo, dark hair. The man pressed the bell, but the bell didn't work, so he knocked again.

Rollins held his pistol close as he watched.

The man waited a few seconds and finally walked away.

Rollins watched for another two minutes. Cars passed and a couple went by huddled beneath an umbrella even though the rain no longer fell. The world appeared normal, but a siren wailed in the distance. Rollins had a bad feeling.

10:32.

Rollins phoned the buyer again.

"The person you sent, he knows to go to the back?"

"Yes. Of course. He has been there before."

"If you sent someone, he didn't show."

"Hold on. I will find out."

A second siren was screaming. Closer.

The man's voice returned.

"He should have been there. This is not right."

"I'm jammed up here, man. I want to leave."

"Bring the material to me. Not here. Someone will meet you by MacArthur Park, there on the northeast corner."

Rollins felt a flash of anger, but kept his voice cool. Rollins had made a fortune off this man and stood to make more.

"You know the rules, Eli. I'm not driving around with your things in my car. Come get this crap."

Rollins was pocketing his phone when he heard a wet crunch in the yard and pounding on the back door.

Rollins hurried to the kitchen, checked the peephole, and saw a face he recognized. Carlos, Caesar, something like that. His eyes were bright and he was breathing hard when Rollins opened the door.

Rollins scratched gloves from his pocket.

"Put on the gloves, you idiot."

Carlos ignored the gloves and ran to the living room, trailing mud and grass. He peeked out the nearest window, bare fingers touching the shade. A helicopter passed overhead so low the little house shook.

"Fuck your gloves. You hear that? The police are on me, bro. Ain't this fuckin' cool? I smoked their blue ass!"

The helicopter rumbled away, but circled the area.

Rollins felt a burst of fear. Thoughts of mud, grass, and finger-prints on the shade vanished. He touched aside the shade and saw a blazing searchlight sweep the next street.

"You brought the police."

Carlos turned away, laughing.

"I lost them, bro. I could be anywhere."

Rollins felt as if his head were filling with angry maggots. The helicopter orbited overhead, lighting up the shades. The chop of the rotor moved away and slowly circled.

"How the fuck did this happen?"

"They made my face. I got warrants, y'know? Relax."

Carlos flopped onto the couch, giggling, wired on adrenaline and chemicals. His muddy shoes were on the cushions.

"They don't know where I am. They gonna roll over us and keep right on rollin'."

Rollins gathered his thoughts. The house was now lost. The goods in the bedroom were history. The mud and the grass no longer mattered. Rollins could not allow himself to be found here with the material in the bedroom and this giggling idiot on the couch. Rollins accepted these facts and the acceptance brought calm.

The pistol was no good to him now. Rollins returned to the cabinet where he kept the bleach and took out a rusted, fourteen-inch pipe wrench. The wrench easily weighed three or four pounds.

Carlos was still stretched on the couch when Mr. Rollins went back to the living room. He strode directly to Carlos without saying a word and brought the wrench down hard. He felt the head go on the first blow, but gave it two more. Rollins dropped the wrench and put on a fresh pair of gloves. He pressed the pistol into Carlos's hands, both hands so it would look like Carlos had handled the gun, and dropped it beside the wrench. If Rollins was picked up, he did not want a gun in his possession.

The helicopter passed again. The shades flashed into blinding white rectangles and once more filled with black.

Rollins trotted to the front door and looked through the peephole. A police officer passed on the sidewalk and another spoke with people across the street. Rollins closed his eyes. He took slow, measured breaths as he counted to one hundred. He put his eye to the peephole again. The policemen were gone.

Rollins returned to the kitchen. He wore a dark sport coat and slacks. There would be blood splatter, but the blood would be difficult to see at night on the dark fabric. He had a nylon rain shell, but decided not to put it on. The sport coat was better. The police were looking for a young Latin guy in a black T-shirt, not an older, well-dressed Anglo. His car was several blocks away. If Rollins could get away from the house and beyond the police perimeter, he still might survive.

The light returned and slid away again.

Rollins moved in the moment of darkness. He opened the kitchen door, peeled off his gloves, and stepped out. A cop and a German shepherd were in the backyard. The dog was a deep-chested brute with angry eyes and fangs like daggers. The cop shouted as the dog charged.

2

Elvis Cole

MERYL LAWRENCE GAVE ME three things on that rainy night when she hired me to find Amy Breslyn. She gave me an address in Echo Park, two thousand dollars in cash, and a corporate personnel file with so much information about her missing friend it could have been compiled by the NSA. It probably was. She gave me these three things, but nothing else. Everything else was secret.

The Echo Park address was four or five years old and probably no longer useful, but it was on my way home. Twenty minutes before ten that same night—fifty-two minutes after I agreed to find Amy Breslyn—I parked beneath a streetlight during a soft, feathery rain, one block from the Echo Park house. I would have parked closer, but no other spots were available. A fire hydrant saved me.

A teenage girl chased a young boy past the window of a house across from me. Next door, a middle-aged woman in purple tights pedaled an exercise bike. Behind me, a balding man laughed at a television as large as a wall. Nine forty was early. Every house on the block was alive with life except the house I came to find. It was dark and lonely and promised to be a waste of time.

I was watching the purple woman when my phone rang.

"Elvis Cole Detective Agency. We do it in the rain."

Humor. I am my own best audience.

Meryl Lawrence's voice was quiet within the darkness.

"I found her house key. I guess it fell off the console. It was under my front seat."

I had met with Meryl Lawrence in her car behind Vroman's Bookstore in Pasadena. She hired me in a parking lot because Ms. Lawrence did not want to be seen with me. She paid me in cash because she wanted no record of our association. Like so much about Amy Breslyn, my relationship with Meryl Lawrence was Top Secret.

I said, "Good work. Now I won't have to climb down her chimney."

"Are you coming back? I'll give you the key and her alarm code."

"Not tonight. I'm at Lerner's house."

Her voice perked up.

"Has he seen her?"

"Haven't spoken to him yet. I'm waiting for the rain to stop."

"Oh."

She sounded deflated. The address belonged to an aspiring writer named Thomas Lerner. Lerner and Amy's son, Jacob, grew up together. After college, Lerner wanted to be a writer, so he rented the Echo Park house for cheap and set about typing. Jacob Breslyn went to work as a journalist and happily traveled the world until he and thirteen other people were killed by a terrorist blast in Nigeria. Amy changed after Jacob died, Meryl told me. Amy withdrew and was never the same. Now, sixteen months after Jacob's death, Amy had simply walked away, vanished, disappeared, over and out, gone. Meryl did not know if Amy had kept in touch with Lerner or if he still lived at the Echo Park address, but if anyone knew Amy's secrets, Meryl felt it would be Amy's last and only link to her son.

"It doesn't look like anyone's home. If he's here, I'll see what he knows. If he moved, maybe I can find out how to reach him."

"Ask if she mentioned a boyfriend."

She had gone on about the boyfriend in Vroman's parking lot. Meryl Lawrence had never met the man, didn't know his name, and couldn't describe him, but she was one hundred percent convinced a man was behind Amy's disappearance. Sometimes you just have to let them vent.

"I'll ask."

"I only met Thomas the one time, but he should remember. Tell him I haven't been able to reach her, so I'm worried, but don't tell him I hired you, and please for God's sake don't mention anything else I've told you."

"I know how to handle it."

"I know you know, but I want to make sure you understand. Everything I told you is strictly off-limits."

"If I understood any better, it would be tattooed on my head."

Meryl Lawrence swore me to secrecy because she was afraid. She was a senior executive for a company called Woodson Energy Solutions, where Amy Breslyn had been a chemical production engineer for fourteen years. They manufactured fuels for the Department of Defense, which meant their work was classified. The first thing she asked when we met was if the word 'confidential' on my business card truly meant confidential.

I told her, "Yes, ma'am, it does."

"Swear to me. Swear you won't breathe a word."

"I promise."

Four days earlier, Amy Breslyn had taken a leave of absence without explanation and with no advance warning. She did so by email. Meryl and her bosses tried to reach Amy, but their calls and texts were not returned. A day later, Meryl went to Amy's home. Amy was gone, but nothing seemed amiss. The following day, Meryl discovered four hundred sixty thousand dollars missing from Amy's department. Meryl kept this discovery secret. She believed her friend had been coerced, and hoped to handle the situation without involving the authorities. She hired me off the books and without her company's knowledge. She also refused to give me access to Amy's office, corporate email, and any information related to Amy Breslyn's work. Security.

"I'll get the key from you in the morning. Want to meet in the same place?"

"Oh my God, no. It's too chancy. I have to be in West Hollywood tomorrow. Pick a place, and plan on meeting me at seven."

I suggested a parking lot at the corner of Fairfax and Sunset. Meryl Lawrence liked parking lots.

"All right, tomorrow at seven unless I hear otherwise. Maybe you can settle this tonight and save us the trouble."

From the look of the dead little house, I doubted it.

"Is it still raining?"

"Yes."

"If you do it in the rain, get out of your car and find her."

One hour into the job and I was already getting attitude.

I fingered through Amy Breslyn's file by the hazy glow of the streetlight. Her corporate portrait showed a round woman with light brown hair, a soft face, and the sad eyes of someone who lost her only child for reasons no sane person could understand. If she wore makeup, I could not see it. She was as anonymous as a blur in a crowd except for the fact this particular blur possessed a Ph.D. in chemical engineering from UCLA. I tucked her picture into my pocket.

When the rain stopped a few minutes later, I walked up the street and went to Lerner's door. A porch lamp hung beside the door, but the bulb was as dark as the rest of the house. I knocked, waited a few seconds, and knocked again. I pressed the buzzer, but the bell didn't work any better than the lamp. Lovely.

I knocked some more, then went back to my car.

Twelve minutes later I was deciding whether to wait or return in the morning when an LAPD helicopter thundered overhead so low it rattled my car. Its searchlight crawled across the nearby houses, making their newly wet roofs shimmer. I craned my head to watch. A flashing radio car suddenly filled the street three blocks ahead and more lights flashed in my mirror. A second black-and-white crowded the intersection one block behind me. The helicopter boomed over again, raking the ground with its light. I twisted and turned. Whatever was happening was happening fast. More radio cars joined the first two, strobing the houses with red and blue flashes as a small army of uniformed officers dismounted to block the street.

The people who lived in the houses appeared in their windows or came outside to watch. I got out of my car and watched along with them. The Los Angeles Police Department was surrounding their neighborhood like a gathering thunderstorm.

A short man in a faded sweatshirt came to the door of the house behind me and called out with a Spanish accent.

"What they doin'?"

"Setting up a perimeter. I think they're looking for someone."

He joined me on the sidewalk. A woman holding a baby took his place in the door.

The helicopter flew in a lazy circle three or four blocks wide, burning the earth with its searchlight. We stood below in a brilliant white pool so bright we squinted, but then the pool was gone.

The man hooked his thumbs in his pockets.

"We got too much crime 'round here. I got babies in my house."

I pointed at Lerner's.

"The dark house on the next block. Does Thomas Lerner live there?"

He stared at the house.

"Who?"

"Young guy. Anglo. He'd be twenty-eight or twenty-nine, something like that. Thomas Lerner."

He shook his head before I finished.

"We been here three years and there ain't no Lermer guy there."

"Lerner."

"Was some black chicks when we moved in, but they gone. A Filipino dude stayed there for a few weeks and we had a man from El Salvador, but that was a couple years ago. Nobody livin' there now."

The news wasn't all bad. If the property was a rental before, during, and after Lerner lived there, the landlord might have a forwarding address or Lerner's rental application. The rental app would give me the names and addresses of employers, references, and maybe even Lerner's parents. Finding him would be easy.

Several officers were working their way toward us, going from door to door. An officer with dark hair came up the sidewalk. Sergeant stripes were pinned to his collar and his name tag read ALVIN.

I said, "What's going on?"

"Suspect pursuit. Latin male, twenty-five to thirty. He's wearing a black T-shirt with a skull on the front. You guys see anyone like that run through here?"

We told him we hadn't.

The homeowner said, "What he do?"

"Homicide warrant. We spotted him over on Vermont, and chased him this way. We're pretty sure he went to ground here in the neighborhood."

The homeowner glanced at his wife and lowered his voice.

"We got babies, sir. I don't want no shootin' out here."

"Lock your doors and windows, okay? We'll find him. We've got the eye in the sky, the manpower, and a dog coming out. Stay inside and you'll be fine."

The man hurried back to his house.

I said, "People coming home from work or getting back from dinner or whatever, are you guys going to let them in?"

"Yeah, no problem, but not after they turn loose the dog. If a dog is running around, we won't let anyone in."

I glanced toward the black-and-whites blocking the intersection.

"How about leaving? Can I get out?"

"You can, but we have to finish the door-knocks. We'll free up someone to move the cars as soon as we can."

"Okay, Officer. Thanks."

It was going to be a long night.

A few minutes after I settled into my car, the helicopter broadcast a recorded announcement. The recording warned residents a police K-9 dog was going to be released and told the suspect this was his last chance to give up. I heard barking, but it sounded far away.

The cops finally finished their door-knocks and drifted back to the intersection. I spotted Alvin, decided it was a good time to leave, and was putting my key in the ignition when a man came out of Thomas Lerner's house. I could not see his face and I did not see a black T-shirt, but everything about the way he moved told me he was wrong. He did not stroll casually from his house the way a person would or pause to look at the helicopter or amble out to the street. He stayed close to the house, masked by broken shadows and clearly trying to hide. I got out of my car for a better look, but lost him in the darkness. Then lights flashed in the trees behind his house and the dog barked fierce and close. The shadows moved, and the man ran away from me into the neighboring yard.

I shouted and waved at the cops behind me.

"Alvin! Runner! OVER HERE!"

Alvin shouted back, but I was already chasing the man and running hard.

The man veered hard across the street and passed through a pool of faint light. I saw a dark sport coat and dark pants and maybe dark hair, but then he was gone between the houses. Alvin was shouting. I was gaining ground when I reached Lerner's house, but an officer in tactical gear charged into the front yard. He shouted, too, and he aimed a pistol.

I stopped cold and threw my hands in the air.

"A man came out. There! He ran across the street."

The tactical cop shouted past his pistol.

"STOP! Do not MOVE!"

I didn't move. Somewhere behind me, Alvin shouted I was a civilian and the tactical cop ran back behind the house. Alvin and two other cops reached me. The other cops kept running, but Alvin grabbed my arm.

"Dude, what the hell? You want to get shot?"

"Man came out of this house. He ran across the street."

"Was it our guy? Long hair? Latin in a black T-shirt?"

"I thought so, but I don't know. Short hair. He was wearing a sport coat."

Alvin radioed that officers were in foot pursuit of a man seen leaving the address and gave them the general direction. The helicopter pulled into a tight orbit overhead, then banked away to hunt. Its whup-whup-whup was deafening.

Alvin shouted over the roar.

"So you decided to play hero?"

"I didn't decide anything, Alvin. I saw him and I thought he was your guy. He ran and you were a block behind me. It seemed like the thing to do."

Alvin suddenly lifted his radio and glanced at the house.

"We got him."

"The guy I was chasing?"

He tipped his radio toward Lerner's house.

"No, numbnuts. The guy you thought you were chasing. Our one-eighty-seven suspect. He was in there, too, and his running days are over."

I stared at Thomas Lerner's house and felt a greasy prickle across my chest. I pictured myself knocking with a body on the other side of the door. I pictured myself with a murderer inches away.

"Your fugitive was in this house?"

"Still is. Looks like the asshole you saw killed him."

Alvin started away, but I didn't move.

"Alvin, I'm looking for a guy who used to live here. I knocked on the door twenty minutes ago."

Alvin studied me like he didn't understand.

"I didn't go in. I knocked a couple of times, no one answered, so I went back to my car. I was about to leave when you guys rolled up."

Alvin asked to see my identification. I handed him my driver's license and investigator's license. The investigator's ticket made him frown.

"Okay, Mr. Cole, stand by. They'll want to talk to you."

Alvin radioed again and had trouble getting an answer. The helicopter orbited back and speared Lerner's house with its light. Alvin's radio exploded with overlapping transmissions. He darkened at something he heard, abruptly took my arm, and steered me toward the perimeter.

"Let's move. They're sending someone."

Alvin changed in that single moment. The officers grouped at their cars changed. The houses and yards and night clouds above us all changed as the air crackled with frantic tension.

Alvin towed me down the center of the street as if we couldn't walk fast enough. The officers who had been on the perimeter only minutes ago hurried from their posts to spread through the neighborhood, once more knocking on doors, their faces brittle and anxious.

"What's going on, Alvin? What's happening?"

Alvin broke into a jog, so I jogged along with him.

People were directed from their homes as we passed. Some hesitated. Others lurched to the street. The cops moved faster and their voices grew louder. Their eyes seemed wider and brighter.

"Why are these people leaving their homes, damnit?"

Alvin picked up the pace.

When we reached the intersection, a middle-aged male detective in a tired gray suit and a female detective in a navy pants suit were waiting by a dark blue unmarked sedan. A uniform command officer stood nearby, but paid no attention.

Alvin said, "This is him."

The male detective lifted his jacket to show me his badge.

"Bob Redmon, Mr. Cole. Rampart Detectives. This is Detective Furth. We'd like you to come with us."

Furth barely glanced at me. She was watching the men and women, teenagers and children flow across the perimeter, some angry and sullen, others nervous and scared. They formed a growing crowd that spread along the sidewalk.

I said, "Tell me what's going on, Redmon. Why are you pulling these people out of their houses?"

Redmon ignored my question.

"While it's fresh, you know? Shouldn't take long."

"Are you arresting me?"

He opened the sedan's rear door and motioned me in.

"We'll give you a lift back."

"My car's a block away."

Furth spoke for the first time, showing her strain.

"Get in the car or we'll lock your ass up. C'mon, Bobby, I want to get out of here."

I asked them again.

"Why are you evacuating these people?"

Redmon simply held the door until I got in. Furth and Redmon got in after me and Furth started the engine.

A loud siren whooped on the far side of the intersection. A large black Suburban topped with blue flashers arrived and nosed through the intersection. It was an ominous vehicle with words on its side that answered my question.

Furth eased forward, going slow because of the crowd. I stared at the Suburban. Somewhere above, the helicopter's whup-whup-whup matched the beat of my heart. When I was in the Army, it was a comforting sound. The heavy pulse of rotors meant someone was coming to save your life.

I did not tell the police my true reason for being there. I did not mention Amy Breslyn. Not yet, not then, but everything might have been different if I had.

Meryl Lawrence had told me little about Amy Breslyn, but now those facts seemed to have a new and dangerous meaning.

I promised Meryl Lawrence to keep Amy's secrets mine, so I kept them. And many, I still keep.

We passed the black Suburban with its silent, flashing lights. The people on the sidewalk were gripped by the sight of it like mice entranced by a snake. I was gripped, too. The words on the Suburban explained why we were being evacuated.

BOMB SQUAD.

3

LAPD K-9 Officer Scott James

A LIGHT, INTERMITTENT RAIN sprinkled Scott James as the Air Support helicopter passed overhead, blinding him with its searchlight. Scott shielded his partner's eyes.

"Remind me to bring our sunglasses next time."

The thirty-million-candlepower Nightsun was impressive, but Scott knew the helicopter's high-magnification cameras and FLIR heat imager gave the Air Support crew a much better view than their searchlight. Police officers, dogs, car engines, and anything producing a heat signature would glow on their monitor. Their eye-in-the-sky imager was the next best thing to X-ray vision, but it wasn't infallible.

"When they need superpowers, they call K-9. Right, Maggie?"

Maggie licked his fingers and circled his legs.

Maggie was an eighty-five-pound black-and-tan German shep- herd. Nothing filled her with joy more than playtime with Scott. Playtime tonight would be searching for a fugitive murder suspect named Carlos Etana.

Scott was strapping into his ballistic vest when Paul Budress approached from the command post. Budress was one of the K-9 Platoon's senior assistant trainers.

"A woman saw a guy matching Etana's description. Might be we have a scent trail."

"Outstanding. The guys here?"

Maggie would be the only dog released, but Budress and two other handlers would assist with the search. Civilians and regular patrol officers had been cleared from the area.

Budress spit a squirt of tobacco juice.

"Waiting inside."

"Let's get the party started."

Scott clipped Maggie's lead and followed Budress into the search area. The streets and yards were deserted, but people stood in their windows, holding up small children to see the police dog as a prerecorded message broadcast from the helicopter echoed over the neighborhood. The message asked residents to remain in their homes and warned the suspect he had one minute to surrender before a dog would be released. The broadcast was so loud Scott was reminded of the scene in *Apocalypse Now* when "Ride of the Valkyries" boomed from American helicopters as they destroyed a VC village. This was the second time the warning was broadcast, both in Spanish and English.

Budress plugged his ears.

"How many warnings do you need before we charge you with felony stupid?"

Evanski and Peters were waiting in a driveway around the next corner. Scott raised a hand, and the two handlers led them up the drive.

Evanski related what she learned from a witness.

"Lady said a Latin male ran up the drive here and over this fence. Long hair, black shirt with a skull. Definitely our guy."

The four officers unshipped their flashlights as they reached a low chain-link fence threaded with ivy and climbing roses. Freshly torn leaves and broken stems littered the ground and hung in the vines. Scott studied the yard behind the fence and saw muddy divots where someone scrambled for traction. This was an advantage he had not expected.

Maggie was trained to source nonspecific human scent, but the search for a nonspecific scent was methodical and slow. Scott had to direct her from yard to yard around each house and garage, and make sure she sniffed all the places a person could hide. A specific scent changed his plan. If Maggie could whiff Etana's specific scent, Scott wouldn't need to direct her from house to house. Maggie would follow Etana's scent cone directly to her prey.

"Looks pretty good. You guys ready?"

"Bring it on, brother."

Scott abruptly slapped his knees and ruffed Maggie's head. A high squeaky voice meant praise and play. A command voice was firm and strong. Scott made the squeaky voice.

"You wanna get some, Maggie-girl? Wanna catch us a bad guy?"

Maggie wiggled and rolled against him. She jumped away and bounded back. This was the hunt and the hunt was play. Maggie wanted to play.

Scott stood tall and deepened his voice.

"Down."

Maggie dropped to her belly. Her ears pricked forward, and she stared into his eyes. This was their start position in training.

Scott pointed sharply at the gate.

"Maggie, smell. Smell him, girl. Smell."

Maggie followed his gesture and moved to the ivy.

Scott studied her behavior and body language as she sniffed the leaves and the earth beneath the vines and the air surrounding the plants. Maggie understood Scott wanted her to identify and seek the strongest human scent in the area to which he pointed. When she flattened her tail and pawed the fence, Scott knew she had the scent. He drew his pistol, opened the gate, and followed her.

"Maggie, find'm. Seek."

Budress and the others came after and spread to the sides in a loose V. The Nightsun passed over, painted them with light, then moved away, plunging them into darkness.

Maggie did not need their flashlights or the airship. She trotted directly past a rusted swing set, through a hedge, and into the next yard.

Evanski said, "She's on it! Look at her!"

Maggie followed the scent trail through the next yard and into an adjoining yard, where she suddenly seemed to lose the track, but then her nose came up and she found herself blocked by a fence. Scott checked the far side for dogs and hazards, then lifted her over and followed. The narrow passage forced Budress and the others into a single file and spread them behind.

Budress called.

"Slow it down."

Scott followed Maggie through a carport and more shrubs, then beneath a large metal awning, and through more hedges into a small yard canopied by a drooping avocado tree. Scott faced a small clap-board house huddled beneath the tree. No lights burned in the win-dows, and the wide-spread tree draped the house with shadows.

Scott flashed his light at the house just as a nicely dressed man stepped out. The man was a middle-aged Anglo with fair skin and close-cropped hair, wearing slacks and a sport coat. He jumped with surprise, and Maggie charged forward, barking.

Scott immediately called her off.

"Maggie, out! *Out!*"

Maggie returned to his side, but the man was obviously shaken.

"What the hell? What are you doing back here?"

"Please step inside, sir. We have a fugitive in the area."

"What's going on with this helicopter? It's driving me crazy."

"Go inside, sir. Please."

The man grimaced, but stepped back into his house.

Scott heard the door lock, and stroked Maggie's back.

"He scared the hell out of me, too."

Budress crunched through the hedge, followed quickly by Evanski and Peters.

"Who's the voice?"

"Civilian. We scared him."

Budress let fly with a squirt.

"C'mon, get her back on the hunt."

Scott walked Maggie back to the hedges and pointed at the ground.

"Smell it, girl. Smell. Seek seek seek."

Maggie ran to the door and barked.

Scott called her back.

"Not that guy, baby. The *other* guy."

He directed her to the scent again and told her to seek.

Maggie charged directly back to the door.

Scott felt a buzz of adrenaline.

"Paul, he's here. Etana's inside."

Scott called Maggie to quiet her barking and took a position beside the door. Budress radioed their situation as Peters and Evanski moved to the corners of the house.

Scott hammered the door.

"Sir, open the door. Police. Please open the door."

The man didn't respond.

Scott flashed his light through a gap between the window and the shade. A young male in a black T-shirt was sprawled on a couch. A white skull design was visible on his shirt, but part of the skull gleamed red, and his face was a crushed mix of blood, bone, and hair.

Scott's heart rate spiked as he keyed his radio.

"Suspect down in the house, in need of assistance. A second suspect is inside, Anglo male, fifty, sport coat."

Even as Scott made the call, he realized the man in the sport coat might have ducked out the front door.

"Paul, the front!"

Scott reached the front yard as the man in the sport coat raced across the street, but someone shouted from the opposite direction and Scott saw a second man running toward him with three officers in pursuit. Scott raised his gun, and the second man skidded to a stop, waving toward the man in the sport coat.

"A man came out! There! He ran across the street!"

Scott shouted over him, praying the guy wouldn't do something stupid.

"Stop! Do not MOVE!"

Then one of the officers chasing him shouted.

"He's a civilian. The guy's a *civilian!*"

Scott jerked his pistol to the side, and ran back to Budress.

"The dude I saw took off. Officers in pursuit."

Budress flashed his light through the window and moved to the door.

"Screw him. This guy's dead or dying. We gotta go in."

Budress heaved back and kicked hard above the knob. The door flew open and Scott released his dog.

"Get'm, baby. Get'm."

Maggie surged into the house.

Scott went in behind her, gun up and ready. He cleared the kitchen and moved into the living room. Maggie pulled up short at the body, barking to let Scott know she had found her prey.

Budress kicked a pistol away from the body.

"Keep moving. Clear the house."

Scott directed Maggie into a hall. A bathroom and a small bedroom were open, but a door at the end of the hall was closed.

Maggie took passing sniffs at the bath and bedroom, but slowed at the closed door. She seemed to study the door for a moment, then sank to her belly and gazed at the door. Scott saw her nostrils work, but she didn't bark as she would if someone was in the room.

Budress said, "Front rooms are clear. What's she got?"

"Dunno. What's with the smell? Chemicals?"

"Bleach. It's killing my eyes."

Scott moved closer. Maggie glanced at him proudly and wagged her tail, but stayed on her belly. Scott had never seen her alert this way.

Budress shouted.

"Police. Open the door and step out. Do it *now*."

Scott pressed his ear to the door but heard nothing. He shrugged. Budress pointed at the door, and nodded.

Scott threw open the door and lit up the room.

Behind him, Budress whispered.

"Clip her, man. Do not let her go in."

Scott clipped Maggie's lead, then keyed his mike.

"We're in the house. Do not approach our location. I say again, do not approach."

The incident commander's voice crackled from their radios.

"What the hell? Say your situation."

Scott wasn't quite sure how to say it.

"Explosives. There's enough explosives in here to blow up the neighborhood."

Scott glanced at Budress, who motioned him back.

"Back away, Scott. Let's back the hell out of here."

Scott backed from the room with his dog.

4

Mr. Rollins

THE ON-AGAIN-OFF-AGAIN RAIN speckled his windshield with diamonds. The windows fogged with steam from his body, so he cranked the defroster full blast. It did nothing to wash the stink of bleach from his nose.

Mr. Rollins sat in his car three blocks outside the perimeter, wiping rain from his face as he worked to contain his fear. It was important to play this out in a way that solved his problem.

"You sent an idiot, Eli. The police followed him to my house."

"Wait. Carlos?"

"Your idiot brought the police to my house. They have him. He's probably ratting us out."

"You are high."

"Pray I'm high."

Eli's voice grew sharper and his accent more pronounced.

"Say something I understand. What you are talking about?"

Mr. Rollins watched the helicopter slice the dark with its saber only a few blocks away. They were still hunting, only now they hunted for him.

Eli's voice was cold.

"I am not saying this twice. Put Carlos on the phone."

Eli was a dangerous man, but Mr. Rollins did not fear him. Under his own name and others, Rollins had committed robberies, armed robberies, and interstate hijackings before he realized he could make more money buying and selling what others had stolen. He had three felony convictions in his past, and had served two stints in prison. He had murdered seven people including his brother-in-law, and each time he met a buyer or seller, he was prepared to do murder again. But now, he tempered his voice.

He planned the play and worked the plan. Always.

Rules.

"I can't, Eli. *Listen to me.* The police have him."

"You are serious?"

"The police were chasing him. On foot, the helicopter, dogs. He was bleeding and talking crazy. I think he's dead. I barely got away."

"You are serious."

No longer a question.

"The house is gone. I can never go back or use it again. Everything in the house is gone. The cops have everything."

Now Eli sounded worried. Worried was good.

"I need these things."

"Send someone better than Carlos next time."

"These dates will not wait. We have a timeline."

"Everything's gone, Eli. I didn't ask Carlos to bring the fucking police."

Rollins stopped talking so Eli could crunch the numbers. Eli had fallen behind his timeline and would keep falling unless he replaced the things he lost and acquired the materials he still needed. He would need Mr. Rollins to do this and time was running out.

Neither spoke for almost a minute, then Eli gave ground.

"What of the material you tested tonight?"

"What of it?"

"It is as the seller described?"

"My chemist says yes. He's going to run more tests, but it's real, Eli. Can't be traced to a manufacturer, distributor, or contractor."

"Such a thing does not exist."

"The chemist says yes."

Eli hesitated, thinking.

"They can deliver this now?"

"You're kidding yourself. They're going to see what happened on the news and totally blow me off. This deal is history."

"Convince them. I will buy all they have."

"Eli, honestly, I have bigger problems than this right now."

"What?"

"A K-9 officer saw me. He shined a light in my face and we had a conversation. He can put me at the house."

Eli was silent again, which Mr. Rollins sensed was a good sign. Eli was crunching more numbers and would reach the inevitable solution.

"You would recognize him if you see him?"

"Yes. Absolutely."

"I suggest we can each help the other. How much material remains with the chemist?"

"Quarter of a pound, something like that. Not much."

"Enough to solve your problem if you solve mine."

"I hear you."

"You will speak with the sellers?"

"Yes."

"I need this done quickly."

"Me too. My problem has to be solved right away."

"It will happen tomorrow."

Mr. Rollins lowered his phone. He watched the helicopter circle, then made a gun with his hand and tracked it. He could turn the helicopter into flaming garbage with the things he left in the house.

Rollins eased into traffic and drove slowly away. He made up a list and recited it.

Go slow.

Stay in the right lane.

Brake early.

L.A. drivers suck in the rain.

Making rules gave him order and following those rules gave him peace. His most important rule was one of the first he learned. Never leave a witness.

The only person who could tie him to the house was a flatfoot with a dog. Not even a real cop. A clown with a dog.

The clown had to go.

5

Elvis Cole

REDMON'S PHONE BUZZED when we were a block from Rampart Station. He said nothing as he listened, then lowered his phone and glanced over his shoulder.

"Detour. They want you downtown."

Furth slapped the wheel.

"This totally blows."

I said, "Who's they?"

"Major Crimes."

Furth made a big sigh.

"Anything good, they grab. Pricks."

The Major Crimes Division was a special investigative group based in the Police Administration Building along with the other elite detective groups. MCD caught hot, fast headline cases ranging from multiple homicides to celebrity victims to crimes with the potential to threaten the public safety. MCD detectives caught way more nightly news time than a divisional dick like Furth would ever see. They also wore nicer clothes. MCD was the big time.

I said, "Don't give up hope, Furth. You might end up running the place."

Furth burned me in the rearview but her eyes softened.

"Could happen."

The Police Administration Building was a beautiful glass-and-concrete building with a triangular atrium that looked like the prow of a crystal ship. The cops who worked there called it the Boat. The opposite side looked like a Borg mothership.

Furth stayed with the car while Redmon took me up. I never saw her again.

The Major Crimes squad room was large, bright, and filled with partitioned cubicles. Conference rooms lined an inner wall. Offices with views lined the outer wall. One office was open but the others were closed. Three of the cubicles were currently occupied, and three detectives stood by the open office.

Redmon said, "Here we go. The show."

A tall, slim male detective with receding blond hair came forward to meet us. He wore tan slacks and a blue pin-striped shirt with suspenders. Redmon hooked his thumb at me.

"This is him."

Redmon turned, and left without another word. I never saw Redmon again, either.

The new guy smiled and put out a hand the size of a king crab.

"Brad Carter. You're Mr. Cole?"

"Yes, sir. Elvis Cole."

He clutched my hand like a king crab, too.

"Thanks for coming. Let's talk in here."

He guided me toward a conference room.

"Coffee or tea? Earl Grey. It's my private stash."

"I'm good. Thanks."

"Need the bathroom?"

The world's most hospitable cop.

"No, thanks. I'm fine."

The conference room was small, but pleasant, with an oval table and a glass wall. Drapes were drawn to cover the glass. Carter told me to pick a seat and took a chair across from me. He left the door open.

"Would you identify yourself for me, and let me see your DL?"

I rattled off my name and address, and showed him my driver's license and my California private investigator's license. He put them aside as if he planned to keep them, then recited the Echo Park address.

"Okay, Mr. Cole. At or about eleven tonight, you saw a man leave this residence?"

"Yes, sir. I did."

"I'm told you chased him."

"Yes, sir. Was he caught?"

"Not yet, but we'll find him. Can you describe him for me?"

I described the man in the sport coat to Carter exactly as I had described him to Alvin. He scratched at a notebook a couple of times, but mostly he watched me, and mostly he stared at my mouth, as if he needed to read my lips to understand what I was saying.

"Not a lot to work with, but it is what it is. Would you recognize him if you saw him again?"

"I didn't see his face. He was too far away, and it was dark. I can't even say if his sport coat was dark gray or dark blue or dark purple."

He jotted another note.

"All right. So tell me, why did you chase him?"

"An officer named Alvin told me a homicide suspect was in the area. The way this guy crept out of the house, I thought he was probably the suspect. I was closest, so I alerted the officers and tried to catch him. I might've been able to run him down, but I don't know. An officer ran out from behind the house, pointed a gun at me, and that was that."

"This was Officer Alvin?"

"No, a K-9 officer. He had a dog. Alvin and the other officers were behind me."

Carter's phone buzzed with an incoming text. He read it, picked up my licenses, and pushed to his feet.

"I'll make copies of these, and get them back to you. You sure you don't want something? Coffee or tea?"

"How about an answer. What happened tonight?"

Carter shook his head like he didn't know what I was talking about.

I said, "The neighborhood was evacuated. The Bomb Squad showed up. What was in the house?"

"I'll be back in a few. Wait here."

Carter closed the door and left me for over an hour. I got up at the thirty-minute mark. Locked. I didn't bother to check it again. Carter would speak with Alvin. He would check my story through incoming field reports and on-scene investigators, and wouldn't return until he had more questions or no questions.

One hour and twenty-six minutes after he left, Carter returned with an attractive African-American woman wearing jeans and a blazer. She carried a cup in one hand and a silver laptop in the other. Carter had a cup, too, but it was hidden by his enormous, crab-sized hand.

The woman introduced herself as Detective Glory Stiles and flashed a beautiful smile.

"Man, crazy night. Is this off the hook or what? Sorry you had to wait."

"Worth the wait, seeing you."

The smile amped a thousand watts.

"My! Aren't you the charmer?"

"They call me Mr. Charm."

Glory Stiles was a tall woman with close-cropped natural hair and immaculate bright blue nails. Carter returned to his original seat and Stiles took a seat nearby. I glimpsed a flick of gold on her right thumbnail when she opened the laptop, but couldn't make out what it was.

Carter was different. The offers of tea were history. His expression was stern with conviction, and designed to intimidate. It's a look I've seen before, and seen done better.

He said, "Okay, Mr. Charm. Tell me again about the man you chased. Describe him."

"I just described him."

"Maybe you remembered something while you were waiting. Start at the beginning."

I smiled nicely and leaned toward him.

"Tell you what, Carter, I've been here for hours. You want to arrest me, get to it."

Glory Stiles said, "Now there's no reason to be like that."

I didn't look at Stiles. I stared at Carter.

"You want me to sit here, tell me what happened tonight."

Carter sipped his tea.

"A man was murdered."

"Not that. Why did the Bomb Squad roll out?"

Carter sipped more tea and did not answer. Glory Stiles answered for him.

"Explosive materials were found with the body, Mr. Cole. We

don't have a full account as yet, but they are being removed and disposed of. It's a dangerous situation."

I nodded, thinking about Amy Breslyn and her government contract work.

Carter stared over the top of his cup.

"Maybe Mr. Cole can give us an account."

"I don't know anything about it."

Glory Stiles said, "I know Detective Carter already asked, but I'm going to ask, too. What were you doing there, and why on God's beautiful Earth did you chase this man?"

I told them I was looking for a writer named Thomas Lerner. I had not mentioned him before and did not like putting Lerner on their radar, but sooner or later they would learn I asked about Lerner from the neighbor, and might already know. Carter gave no reaction. Glory Stiles took notes by typing, and her fingers blurred over the keys. I had never seen anyone talk and type at the same time, but she did, as if she had two brains. It was a hell of a thing to see. I repeated my conversation with the neighbor, and our conversation with Alvin, and again described when and how I saw the man in a sport coat exit the house. I used the word 'furtive.'

Carter said, "So you were in your car while the officers did the door-knocks."

"Yeah. I asked Alvin if I could leave, but he told me they didn't have anyone to move the cars."

Carter appeared to believe me, which meant they had already spoken to Alvin.

"You see anyone enter or leave the house besides the man you chased?"

"No."

Stiles asked the next question as she typed.

"When you were at the door, did you hear anything inside? Voices or noise or whatever?"

"Nothing. I knocked a couple of times. I tried the bell. It didn't work."

Stiles glanced briefly at Carter. Someone had told them the bell didn't work.

Carter leaned forward.

"Did you smell anything?"

"Like what?"

"You tell me. You either smelled something or you didn't."

I wondered if this had something to do with the explosives, and shook my head.

"No."

Carter leaned back as if he doubted me.

"Who was it you went there to see?"

"Thomas Lerner."

"Did someone hire you to find him?"

"No."

"You're a private investigator."

"I wasn't working. I wanted to see if he'd like to collaborate."

Glory Stiles spoke as she typed.

"No shit! Now wouldn't that be cool?"

Bright and bubbly, but she didn't believe a word.

"How do you know Mr. Lerner?"

We were getting down to it, and the ice was thin. I had painted a target on Thomas Lerner and the more we talked about him the larger the target would grow. Carter would want to find him just to check out my story, and pretty soon I'd be in a race to find him first.

"We met at the Times Festival of Books four or five years ago. He wanted to ask about my work, so we swapped contact info. He never called. A few days ago, I found his info and gave him a call. The phone was no good, so I tried the address."

I looked from Stiles to Carter.

"That's it."

"Could we have the phone number?"

I put an edge in my voice, like my patience was thin.

"Tossed it when it turned up bad. Why would I keep it? Had the address, so I gave it a shot."

"Tonight."

I had copied Lerner's address onto my business card. I dug the card from my pocket and slapped it onto the table.

"Yeah, tonight. And if not tonight, it would've been tomorrow or the day after or next month, but I picked tonight and here I am stuck with you, only guess what, Carter? The me being stuck part is over."

I stood.

"I'm done and I'm leaving."

Carter slowly turned the card, read it, and left it on the table. I snatched it back. He wasn't angry or threatening. He looked patient.

"Sorry for the inconvenience, Mr. Cole. I'm sure we'll talk again."

He stood and went to the door.

"Finish up, Glory. I'll get a ride for Mr. Cole."

Glory Stiles closed her computer and stood as he left.

"Okay, Mr. Cole, I'm going to print a written statement documenting what you've told us. I'd like you to read it, and if you believe it to be a true and accurate representation of what you told us, we'd like you to sign it. That okay?"

It wasn't okay, but I went along. The police almost never asked a witness to sign a statement. They preferred to incorporate witness statements in their reports, which were signed by them and not the witness. This allowed more wiggle room for the prosecutor if the case went to trial. If a witness signed, every error of fact or difference in testimony became red meat for the defense.

I followed Stiles and her laptop out to the squad room.

"Hang here for a sec, and I'll be right back."

She left me hanging and quickly crossed the room. Carter had joined two detectives outside an office. One of the two glanced at me and stepped inside.

Three hours after Redmon and Furth delivered me, the Major Crimes squad room was now crowded and busy. A dozen detectives who looked like they would rather be home in bed were working in cubicles or locked in conversations with uniform officers who floated listlessly along the walls.

An officer at a nearby desk sat with his legs out and arms crossed. He was watching me as if he'd had a long day and it was going to be longer.

He said, "Dude, you're lucky you're alive."

I didn't know what he was talking about.

"Have we met?"

"Kinda. You're the guy who chased our runaway. I almost shot you."

I saw the K-9 patch on his shoulder, and finally recognized him.

"Thanks for not shooting me."

"Too much paperwork."

He leaned forward and offered his hand.

"That wasn't the smartest move, getting involved, but thanks for trying to help."

We shook as Glory Stiles reappeared. She led me to a nearby empty desk and told me to read the document. It was only two pages long, but it was an accurate representation of my statements. Even the facts that were lies. I signed and handed it back.

"Okay, Mr. Cole, that wraps it up. We appreciate your cooperation."

"Carter has a funny way of showing it."

"We'll probably want to speak with you again. That okay?"

"Not if I see you coming."

She flashed the brilliant smile.

"Then I guess we'll just have to sneak up on you, now won't we? Your ride is outside. I'll take you down."

Carter watched as I left. His eyes held no malice, but I knew I would see him again.

An older officer with a short gray buzz drove me back to my car. The clouds broke open a final time, hammering us with a downpour so fierce the wipers were useless. The officer squinted into the oncoming rain, but did not slow. He could not possibly see the way ahead, but he did not stop.

Neither did I.

The Client

6

Elvis Cole

THE SKIES WERE CLEARING the next morning when I faced Meryl Lawrence across the front seat of her Lexus. The parking lot was on the southwest corner of Sunset and Fairfax, hidden behind a chain pharmacy and a diner known for its breakfast. Meryl Lawrence was pleased with the privacy when she arrived, but angry and shaken when I told her what happened.

"Are you crazy? Why did you get involved?"

"It seemed like a good idea at the time."

"It wasn't. It was a *terrible* idea!"

She dug her phone from her purse. Deep lines creased her face, cutting her skin into armored plates.

"Is it on the news? It'll be on the news."

"Check the *Times* website. You'll see it."

She typed with both thumbs, frantic and fast, staring at her phone.

"Did you tell them I hired you? What did you say about Amy?"

"Nothing. I didn't mention you or Amy or your company, okay? Relax."

She typed faster. Her eyes wide. Her chest rose and fell.

I touched her arm.

"We have a lot to talk about."

Meryl Lawrence was in her mid-forties, with sandy hair and the trim, sturdy build of a woman who took care of herself. She wet her lips as she stared at the phone, thinking, and finally glanced up.

"What did you tell them?"

"You're out of it, but I told them about Lerner."

She stared at me curiously, as if the words arrived in slow motion, then looked back at the phone.

"Here it is. Jesus."

"I had to tell them, Meryl. The police will question everyone in the neighborhood. They'll find out I asked about Thomas Lerner. Better they heard it from me."

She read a few seconds before glancing up.

"They'll want him to confirm your story."

"Yes. They're suspicious. They don't like it I was at the house. They'll come down on me to pick apart my story."

She went back to reading, touching her lower lip as if making a prayer.

"Unbelievable. A murder. Someone had to murder this guy *last night*?"

"Lerner moved out at least three years ago, so I might be able to find him first. They'll look, but Lerner won't be their top priority. They have plenty to do."

Meryl Lawrence suddenly lowered her phone and held out a plain white envelope.

"Forget Lerner. Don't waste more time with him. Here's the key and alarm code. Her house is probably filled with clues about her boyfriend."

I didn't take the envelope.

"What does Amy Breslyn do for your company?"

"I told you, she's our vice president in charge of production. What does this have to do with anything?"

"I read her file last night. Your company makes fuels, accelerants, and chemical energy systems. Is a chemical energy system another way of saying 'explosives'?"

She frowned as if she were getting angry and the armor plates returned.

"Everything we make is explosive. What does it matter?"

I reached across to scroll her phone. The *Times* posted the original story at 3:20 that morning. I read it at 4:15. The photo illustrating the story showed a Bomb Squad vehicle parked in front of Lerner's house. An update posted at 3:34 described the munitions removed from the house.

"This is Lerner's house. This is the Bomb Squad. When the police went in, they found four rocket-propelled grenades, a dozen forty-millimeter grenade cartridges, and plastic explosives."

I watched Meryl Lawrence stare at the picture.

"Kind of a crazy coincidence, you making explosives and all these munitions and explosives in the house."

Meryl shook her head and lowered the phone.

"I wouldn't know a rocket-propelled grenade if I sat on it and neither would Amy."

"I read the file, Meryl. Her corporate biography makes a big deal out of her experience. Double- and triple-based composite fuels. Slurries, gels, and castable propellants. Plasticized accelerants. I had to Google those things to see what they were."

"We don't make weapons."

"You make what's inside. You make the bang."

"You can't honestly believe Amy has something to do with this nonsense."

"You believe she stole from your company."

She started to say something, but stopped. People often do that when they hire a private investigator. They try to say what they want me to hear, which isn't always the truth.

She waved the phone as if everything I needed to know was in the story.

"I don't know what to say. I don't know anything about rocket-propelled grenades or this dead man or why you had to get involved. I gave you the boy's address because she was close to him. If he moved, her connection moved with him and he doesn't matter anyway if you figure out who she's been seeing. Take the key. Find her damned boyfriend."

She held out the envelope again.

"I want you to find her. You said you would find her."

We were back to the boyfriend, only now she was more desperate than angry. I wondered why she was desperate. I still didn't take the envelope.

"There's something you aren't telling me."

"I told you everything."

"No. Not yet."

"Take the damned key. Find her. I need to make this right."

The envelope trembled.

"How did you make it wrong?"

She took a long deep breath and sighed as she folded the envelope in her lap. She stared at the diner, where normal people with normal lives were going inside to enjoy waffles and omelets. She mumbled so softly I barely heard her.

"I made her do it."

"Do what?"

"I hired her, you know? She was so quiet and shy it took a while, but she was so sweet you couldn't help but like her. Here she was, a single mother raising this boy. Her entire life revolved around Jacob."

"The boy's father around?"

Meryl Lawrence made a derisive snort.

"Abandoned her before Jacob was born. Destroyed her self-esteem. An emotionally abusive piece of shit."

"Is that what she says or what you say?"

She glanced at me hard, frowned, and turned back to the diner.

"Me."

"Okay."

"Well, whatever. She had no one, okay? In all these past fourteen years, I don't think she saw anyone. She didn't have a life outside her job and that boy, and honestly, she seemed fine with it. Loved her job. Loved her son. Then she lost Jacob—"

She fell silent for a time, then slowly looked at me.

"She was just so lonely, you know? It was painful. I told her to try one of those online matchmaking services. I pushed. Women like Amy can be—"

She searched for the right word, but wasn't pleased with the result.

"—persuaded. I talked her into it."

"You think this is your fault."

"Isn't it? I badgered. I nagged. She started swapping emails with someone. This is how I know there's a man. I was thrilled and I wanted to know all about him, but she wouldn't say anything. Don't you find that weird? I think it's weird. She told me he was interesting. She told me she liked him. And now here we are."

"Maybe he's just some guy. Maybe he doesn't have anything to do with why she left or why she took the money."

Meryl Lawrence made a tiny self-loathing snort.

"I'll ask her if you can find her."

I took the envelope.

She watched me put it away but didn't look any less unhappy with herself or relieved.

"Thank you."

"I promised."

She gave me a rueful smile.

"If there's anything else you want to know, now's the time. I'm thinking about killing myself."

"Let me get out of the car first, okay?"

"Ha. Ha."

"All this Top Secret stuff is slowing us down. Last night you told me her office was off-limits. If she swapped emails with someone, her emails might be on her office computer."

"They aren't. I read her account."

"I might find something you didn't. I might find something else in her office."

"You won't. This isn't just me being obstinate. Our email, phones, and computers are open to the security division. Our Internet usage and phone calls are recorded and reviewed. This is why I gave you my personal cell number and not my office. We have no internal privacy, so none of us use our office computers for personal mail."

"If they monitor everything, how were you able to read her mail?"

"I oversee the security division."

"Oh."

She glanced at her watch.

"Her home is a different matter. You can tear out the walls for all I care. I want to make this right, but I don't know how much longer I can cover for her."

I felt bad for her.

"Meryl."

"What?"

"This isn't your fault."

She frowned as if she hated me for saying it and started her car.

"You have her key and alarm code and you have her address. Please get out and do something to earn the money."

I got out of her car. It was twelve minutes before eight. I had been looking for Amy Breslyn for less than twelve hours. Meryl Lawrence drove away. I drove away, too.

The clock was ticking for both of us.

7

AMY BRESLYN lived in a yellow two-story Mediterranean with a red tile roof near the southern edge of Hancock Park. Hers wasn't the wealthiest part of Hancock Park, but the homes were built in the twenties for well-to-do people and still suggested affluence. Bird-of-paradise plants framed her windows and a narrow drive sloped up the lawn to a garage in her backyard. A blue-and-yellow security sign stood beside the drive. Armed response.

I parked at the curb across the street and studied the house. A family once hired me to find a retired surgeon named Harold Jessler. Dr. Jessler had been missing for nine days, during which his brother, two sisters, his daughter, his son, and his ex-wife repeatedly phoned and visited his house. Their calls were not returned and Jessler was never home. They feared he had grown ill and wandered away, but Dr. Jessler answered the door when I knocked. I asked why he opened the door for me but hid from his family. His answer was simple. He didn't want to see them.

Amy's house was beautifully maintained and the lawn was neatly trimmed. Newspapers weren't piled on the drive. She could have been inside counting money or watching TV, but probably not. Most people who embezzle four hundred sixty thousand dollars have a plan and the plan usually includes leaving the country.

I was getting out of my car when Meryl Lawrence called.

"Did you go to her house?"

"Yes. I just got here."

"Did you find anything?"

"I just got here."

I hung up. If Amy was hiding from Meryl Lawrence, I couldn't blame her.

I waited for two women to pass on the sidewalk, then went to the door. No one answered, so I let myself in. The alarm went off but stopped when I entered the code.

"Ms. Breslyn? Is anyone home?"

Nada.

The entry was spacious and warm, with white plaster walls, a Spanish tile floor, and heavy oak trim stained dark as dried blood. A living room opened to the right and a formal dining room opened to the left. A stair facing the door climbed to the second floor. A large framed photograph of a boy faced me from the wall. It was the first thing anyone would see when they entered. The boy looked to be eight or nine years old, with pale skin, chubby cheeks, and a crown of curly dark hair. This would be Jacob.

"Anyone here? Hello?"

I locked the front door, reset the alarm, and took a fast tour to make sure I was alone. Amy's house was neat, clean, and as orderly as an empty hotel. No overturned furniture, splashes of blood, or ransom notes suggested foul play. Dr. Jessler had been hiding under his bed, but Amy Breslyn wasn't. When I was satisfied no one was home, I checked the garage. Her car was gone, but this didn't mean she was on the run or even out of town. For all I knew, she was at Starbucks.

I searched the second floor first and began in her bedroom. The bed was crisply made. Clothes weren't strewn about or dangling from open drawers. The ebony nightstands bracing the bed and their matching dresser were uncluttered and showroom clean, and the dresser was filled with orderly stacks of neatly folded clothes. There were also no travel brochures, love notes, or pictures of men taped to the mirror. So much for easy clues.

The same obsessive neatness and order were evidenced in her closet and bath. Her clothes were organized by type and color, and neatly hung or shelved. Two black Tumi suitcases stood at the rear of the closet. The bathroom contained ample supplies of toothbrushes and toiletries, and no evidence she had packed for a romantic getaway, made a fast getaway, or otherwise abandoned her home. I also found nothing to suggest she or anyone else still lived there. The wastebaskets were empty.

There were three bedrooms on the second floor and the next was used as an office. A long, sleek desk crossed one end of the room, with wall-to-wall filing drawers behind it. Low bookcases lined the remaining walls, jammed with eye-catching titles like *Handbook For Chemical Engineers*, *Reactive Mass Inhibitors*, *Fluid Compressive Dynamics*, and *Advanced Polymer Thermodynamics*. Framed photographs of Jacob or Amy and Jacob together lined the tops of the bookcases. The boy in the entry had grown into a tall, gangly young man who towered over his mother. One picture showed Amy holding a tray of oversized brownies. She was surrounded by Jacob and his friends in what appeared to be their high school newspaper office. Another showed a teenage Jacob and a pretty young girl posed with Amy in front of the house. Jacob and the girl were decked out in tuxedo and gown, and were probably heading off to their senior prom. Jacob was beaming. Amy was smiling, too, but something about her was sad. Maybe she was one of those people who always looked sad even when they were not.

Amy's desk was as neat and uncluttered as her dresser and nightstands. A digital phone, two oversized monitors, and a state-of-the-art wireless keyboard and mouse sat perfectly aligned on a pristine surface. The monitors were off. A dark blue binder titled DEPARTMENT OF NAVY BIDDING REQUIREMENTS sat squared beside the keyboard. My desk was a dump site of paper clips, bills, receipts, Post-it pads, notes, more bills, magazines I kept meaning to toss, invoices, used napkins, take-out menus, and stains. Her desk contained none of those things. It was as if someone had gotten rid of the day-to-day evidence of her life and activities.

Something about the desk bothered me.

I sat and touched the keyboard. The monitors didn't respond. They powered up when I turned them on, but the screens showed only a bright blue field. I looked under and around her desk. I found all the necessary system components except for the brain that tied them together. Amy's computer was missing.

I said, "Hmm."

Detectives said things like this when they were suspicious.

I checked her phone next. The phone had a dial tone, so I tried to bring up the incoming and outgoing call logs. The logs were empty. So was the handset's phone book. Either the phone was brand-new and had never been used or someone had erased the logs.

I took out my phone and called Meryl Lawrence.

"I'm in her home. Can you talk?"

"I can talk. Did you find something?"

Her voice was quiet and guarded. As if she thought the walls were listening. From what she told me about her security division, they probably were.

"Maybe. You were in her house last week, right?"

"Yes. I've been there three times since we got her email. Why?"

"Was her computer here?"

"I was looking for Amy. I didn't look at her computer."

"Her computer is missing. Did you take it?"

Her voice was cool and surprised.

"Excuse me?"

"Did you take her computer?"

"What's wrong with you? I wouldn't take her computer."

"You might if you wanted your security division to get into her email."

"No, I did not take her computer."

"I had to ask. She probably uses a laptop and takes it everywhere."

"So find where she is and you'll find the computer. She's with that damned man."

I didn't want her to get started on the boyfriend.

"One more thing. When you were here, did you use her phone?"

"Why are you asking about phones?"

"Maybe make a call on her phone or hit redial to see who she called or anything like that?"

"No. I'm not that smart. If I'd thought of it, I would have. Did you find the bastard's number?"

"I didn't find numbers. The phone logs were erased."

"Can you get them from the phone company?"

"Depends on which service she uses."

"That damned man probably erased them. He probably told her—"

I hung up and turned to the file drawers. They were low and wide with files hanging left to right instead of front to back. I was hoping for banking and credit card statements, but the drawers were filled with news stories about her son's death and the investigations that followed. She had filed hundreds of articles, news items, and reports she'd found on the Internet, and dozens of letters she'd written to the State Department, asking questions they were unable to answer. The files contained nothing about Amy, her work, or her life. The drawers were filled with Jacob.

I photographed her office for my records and moved to the last bedroom.

The last bedroom was Jacob's. His clothes still hung in the closet and his desk and walls were crowded with the things boys accumulate. His high school graduation portrait hung above his bed. It showed a gawky teenager in cap and gown with a garden of angry zits exploding on his chin. Jacob had probably hated the picture and would not have put it up in his room. His mother hung it.

I found three high school yearbooks on a shelf and an old At-A-Glance address book in Jacob's desk. The address book contained only a few names and numbers, but I checked L for Lerner and T for Thomas. Lerner wasn't listed, but the yearbooks gave me an idea. I went back to Amy's office, took the prom night picture from its frame, and tucked it into the yearbooks. I brought the yearbooks and address book downstairs, left them in the entry, and quickly searched the ground floor.

The living room, dining room, and kitchen proved to be a waste of time. Another phone sat in the kitchen with another empty memory. I was having what we in the trade called an unproductive morning.

The remaining room was an alcove between the living room and the kitchen. A glass breakfast table faced the kitchen with an empty cut-glass vase centered in its middle. An antique secretary's desk with a single drawer sat against the wall. The little secretary was the last place I searched in Amy Breslyn's home, but that's where I found what I needed.

Fifteen or twenty thin files hung in the drawer, labeled with hand-written tabs like *Household*, *Medical*, *Car*, *VISA*, and *AMEX*. I was proud of myself for finding the files, but Meryl Lawrence would be disappointed. None were labeled *Boyfriend*.

I pulled the credit card files first and quickly skimmed her statements. I found no airline tickets to Dubai, no spending sprees at Tiffany's, and no around-the-world cruises. Nothing in Amy's past three statements suggested where she was, what she was doing, or that she had ripped off four hundred sixty thousand dollars.

I put the credit card files aside, skipped files with labels like *Gardener* and *Insurance*, and was fingering through *Cash Receipts* when I sat up and spoke her name.

"Amy."

Three months earlier, Amy Breslyn purchased a nine-millimeter Ruger semi-automatic pistol, a one-year membership at the X-Spot Indoor Pistol Range, handgun instruction, a cleaning kit, two boxes of nine-millimeter ammunition, a nylon pistol case, and ear protection. The receipt was marked 'paid in cash.'

I had seen none of these things, so I searched her bedroom again.

I opened shoe boxes, checked the high shelves, and opened her suitcases and purses. I looked between the mattresses, beneath the clothes in her dresser, and in her nightstands. I searched her office, the garage, the kitchen cabinets, and even her fridge and freezer. I found nothing. No gun, no gun safe, no cleaning supplies or ammunition or accessories.

I wondered why Amy had wanted a gun and if she had taken the gun with her.

I took the files from the secretary, brought them to the entry, and stacked them on the yearbooks.

Eight-year-old Jacob watched from the wall.

"Why did she buy a gun, buddy?"

Jacob didn't answer.

I wondered what kind of man Jacob grew into. I wondered what he was doing when the bomb went off half a world away and if he was laughing when he died.

The house was filled with him. His pictures were everywhere. His room was a shrine.

"You're still here so she's still here. She wouldn't leave you behind."

Eight-year-old Jacob smiled. His teeth were pretty bad.

I smiled back.

"I'll bring back your things. Promise."

I reset the alarm, let myself out, and went to my car. I dumped the yearbooks and files onto the passenger seat, but didn't drive away. I thought about the gun. Amy might have had second thoughts. She might have decided it was too loud or too smelly or just wasn't fun. Maybe having a gun around the house made her feel less safe, so she got rid of it. There were plenty of innocent reasons her gun was missing, but guesses weren't facts.

I thought about asking Meryl Lawrence. She would probably tell me the boyfriend took it and I would have to tell her I found no evidence of a boyfriend, no proof he existed, and nothing to suggest Amy Breslyn had gone away with him or anyone else.

I was still thinking about the boyfriend who might or might not exist when a green Toyota sedan eased to a stop across the street and parked at Amy's curb.

A stocky Latina got out with a large woven bag. She wore loose cotton pants, a USC sweatshirt, and her hair was held back with a headband. She slung the bag over her shoulder, trudged up the drive, and opened Amy's front door with a key. I saw her reach toward the alarm panel with an easy familiarity before the door closed.

I settled back and stared at the house.

The woman was likely Amy's housekeeper. Amy was supposedly on the lam, yet here was her housekeeper, come to clean an already immaculate house. I wondered if she knew about Amy's leave of absence and expected to find Amy at home. Amy might not have told her anything, but the woman had her own key and the alarm code, which meant Amy trusted her. Anyone who had been around long enough to earn her own key might know if a new man was in Amy's life and would certainly know more than me.

Six minutes earlier, she would have walked in on me. Six minutes later, I would've driven away and missed her. Sometimes the Private Detection Gods smiled.

I clocked off five minutes to let her get settled, and walked back to Amy's door.

8

I TOOK OUT THE KEY and the envelope with the alarm code, and rang the bell. I tried to look startled when the woman opened the door.

"Oh, hi. I didn't expect anyone to be home."

"Yes? May I help you?"

She had a slight Spanish accent and soft voice. Late forties, maybe, with gentle eyes.

I glanced past her as if trying to see inside.

"Amy isn't here, is she? They told me she was out of town."

The woman smiled, agreeable.

"No, she gone. She go last week."

This fit with what Meryl told me, but still surprised me.

I flashed the key, holding the envelope so the housekeeper could see the Woodson Energy Solutions logo.

"Okay, right. That's why they gave me a key. Eddie Cole. I work with Amy at Woodson. They sent me to get a report Amy forgot to bring back."

I edged closer, but she didn't move.

"I'm sorry. Miss Amy did not tell me."

I nodded, smiling to tell her no one expected her to know.

"That's okay. She told Meryl where she left it. On her desk up-stairs, she said. A blue binder from the Navy. We need it at work."

I moved closer and flashed the envelope again. I didn't care about the binder. It was an excuse to make conversation.

She took a step back.

"Where you say it is?"

"Upstairs in her office. I'll know it when I see it."

"I can show you."

"That would be great. Thank you so much."

I stepped past her and offered my hand. When I unload both bar-rels of charm, it's an awesome display.

"I work for Meryl. What's your name?"

"Imelda Sanchez."

"Imelda, you're the best. I'll be out of your way in a second."

I held her hand longer than necessary and turned to admire the house.

"What a beautiful home. I've never been here before, did you know? Immaculate. You do a wonderful job."

Imelda beamed.

"It's not so hard. Miss Amy likes it clean."

I was friendly and chatty as I followed her up the stairs and Imelda Sanchez was friendly and chatty back. People give what they get. She was also in no hurry for me to leave. The house was so clean there was nothing for her to do.

"How long have you worked for her, Imelda?"

"Six and a half years this May, two days a week."

"Even when she's away like now?"

"Oh, yes."

She paused outside the office and touched my arm as if letting me in on a secret.

"This house don't need to be cleaned. She let me come so I don't lose the money. She a nice lady."

"Yes, she is. Everyone at the office loves her."

We moved into the office but didn't go farther.

"How long will she be away?"

"She pay me for three weeks, but she might be home sooner."

"She told you she might be home sooner?"

"Oh, yes. She say she come home as soon as she can."

Interesting. Amy had given her housekeeper a time frame. Her leave-of-absence email included no time frame.

"Well, I hope she enjoys her vacation, however long she's away. She deserves it."

Imelda frowned thoughtfully and wedged her hands on her hips.

"She on the business, I think. She not on vacation."

"She told you she was going away on business."

Imelda nodded.

"Yes. She sometimes go for the business."

"No kidding? She say where?"

Imelda's frown deepened and left me worried I had stepped over the line. She would shut down in a second if she grew suspicious.

I made a sly grin and leaned closer.

"It isn't business, Imelda. Rumor is, she went away with a friend."

Imelda stared at me and her smile blossomed more brightly than before.

"She did not say."

I wiggled my eyebrows and grinned.

"A man friend."

Imelda's smile turned into a giggle, so I grinned even wider.

"We think she has a boyfriend. You know anything about it, Imelda? Amy have a man-type friend?"

She blushed, and her blush screamed Meryl Lawrence was right.

Imelda seemed almost shy when she answered.

"I think this maybe could be."

"Have you met him?"

She waved a hand.

"Oh, no!"

"Did she tell you about him?"

She knew something and wanted to gossip so badly she squirmed.

I nudged her again.

"C'mon, Imelda, you're killing me! We're dying to know. Don't hold out on me."

"A man give her roses. I see the card."

I hadn't seen flowers anywhere in the house.

"Was this before she went away?"

"Oh, yes. The week before last. They died. I put them out."

"But you saw the card?"

"Oh, yes."

"What was his name?"

She thought for a moment, then shook her head.

"I don't remember. I just so happy a man give her flowers. I hope he nice. She been so sad since Jacob died."

"I hope he's nice, too, Imelda."

Imelda brightened.

"I save the card for her. Get your report and I show you."

I picked up the blue Navy binder and followed her down to the dinette table at the end of the kitchen.

"She didn't say, but the vase is so pretty she might want to keep it. I put the card with it here so I don't forget."

The card was under the vase. It was a pale blue rectangle with the name of the florist embossed on the edge and a handwritten note from the man who sent the flowers.

Here's to the start of a beautiful friendship, Charles.

Original. A play on the famous Bogart line from *Casablanca*. It wasn't a proclamation of undying love, but it didn't have to be.

The florist was a place called Everett's Natural Creations.

"He gave her roses?"

"Oh, yes. The dark roses. They were so lovely."

"Were you here when they were delivered?"

"Oh, no. I only here the two days."

I studied the card for a moment, then took a picture of it with my phone.

"The ladies at work will need to see this to believe it, Imelda. Everyone is going to be so happy for her."

I pretended to be happy, too, but I wasn't. I felt sad. Meryl Lawrence was right about a man, which meant she might be right about everything else.

I watched Imelda tuck the card beneath the vase, then followed her out with a binder I didn't need. When we reached the door, I looked back at Jacob, watching from the wall.

"Did you know him?"

She stared at the picture.

"Oh, yes. He very nice. Like his mama."

"Good. That's good to hear. You've been very helpful, Imelda. Thank you."

She didn't look happy about it when she turned from his portrait. The smile was gone and now her eyes were troubled.

"Sir? Please do not say I tell you about the gentleman."

I gave her an encouraging smile.

"You didn't. I found the card when I looked for the binder."

She nodded, but didn't look any less worried.

I stepped out into the sunshine and heard the door close.

Everything about Amy Breslyn was Top Secret. Even her flowers.

9

THE ELVIS COLE DETECTIVE AGENCY was on the fourth floor of a four-story building on Santa Monica Boulevard. A man named Joe Pike owned the agency with me, but his name wasn't on the door. His choice, not mine. Pike doesn't do doors.

The office was outfitted with a desk, a couple of leather director's chairs, a small refrigerator, and a balcony with a nice view across West L.A. to the sea. The Pinocchio clock on the wall always looked happy to see me. His eyes swiveled from side to side as he tocked and he never stopped smiling. I thought he might get tired, but he didn't. His faith was admirable.

I put the yearbooks and photographs on my desk, and found a message on my voice mail.

"Mr. Cole, this is Detective Stiles from last night. I'm sure you re-member. We have a few more questions, so would you pretty please call to arrange a time?"

Pretty please.

Stiles had left her message at 7:28 that morning, only a few hours after I signed my witness statement. I expected Carter to make another run at me but not on the first morning after.

I wondered if they had Lerner. Maybe Stiles had spoken with him and Carter knew I was lying. But maybe not. Carter wasn't the type to bother with a courtesy call. He would break down my door.

The Information operator found a Thomas Lerner listed in the 747 area code and two Tom Lerners in the 310. I called the 747 number first and got a man's recorded voice mail. I left a message, asking for a callback even if he was the wrong Lerner. Another voice mail answered for the first 310 Lerner, but I had better luck with the second. I knew by the age in his voice he wasn't the right Lerner, but at least a human being answered.

"Mr. Lerner, I'm calling on behalf of Jacob Breslyn. Jacob was close with a Thomas Lerner. Would that be you?"

"I'm Tom Lerner. I'm not a Thomas."

"Sorry. Would you have a relative named Thomas Lerner? He would be in his late twenties. A writer. He lived in Echo Park a few years ago."

"Well, now, I don't think so. My uncle might have been a Thomas, but he's been dead for years."

So much for calling.

An Internet search showed ninety-seven Tom or Thomas Lerners in the United States, three of whom resided in the Los Angeles area. These were the three I called. Searches for 'Thomas Lerner writer' showed nothing on the Internet Movie Database, the membership of the Writers Guild, or various bookselling websites. If Thomas Lerner was writing, he wasn't having any better luck with it than I was having with detecting.

I opened the material I had about Amy Breslyn and studied her picture again. She didn't look like a person who would embezzle four hundred sixty thousand dollars, but people can fool you. She looked like a sad version of someone's marshmallow aunt: a kindly woman, slightly out-of-date, who wore sensible shoes and minded her own business.

I went out to the balcony and studied the view. Most days, I was lucky to see the water, but the hotels and condominiums at the edge of the earth were vivid with morning light, and the peak of Catalina Island was sharp, twenty-six miles to the south. It took a storm to give the world clarity.

I stepped back inside, opened a bottle of water, and tipped the bottle at Pinocchio.

"Why does it always take a storm?"

His eyes tocked, but he didn't answer.

I returned to my desk and flipped through the yearbooks.

Like most kids, Jacob and his friends had written inscriptions in each other's yearbooks. Since friendships overlap, the people who wrote in Jacob's yearbook probably knew Lerner and a few might have stayed in touch. I started on the inside front cover, read the inscriptions, and noted their names. *School's out FOREVER! We're going different ways, but I hope we don't lose touch!* The senior year sentiment was predictable, but one name appeared in three inscriptions on the first page and instantly screamed for attention. *Good luck with Jennie, bro! Have you and Jennie set the date? Jennie's too HOT for a loser like you!* Jennie was mentioned in four more inscriptions on the next page and nine more times in the rest of the book. Then I turned to the inside back cover and found a large red heart filling most of the page. The heart had been drawn with a red marker and contained an inscription.

My J,

2 Js today

2 Js tomorrow

2 Js forever

i luv u

Your J

Jacob's prom date might not be Jennie, but the odds were good, and she would be the go-to person to ask about Thomas Lerner. None of the inscriptions contained her last name, but I found her on the sixth page of the Seniors section in the yearbook, third row from the bottom, second face from the right. Her name was Jennifer Li.

I said, "Hello, Jennie."

I found her again in the J-K-L section of Jacob's address book. Jennie, with no last name, 310 area code.

Jennie would have a different number by now, but her high school number was probably her family's home.

A recorded male voice asked me to leave my name and number. The voice didn't identify himself by name, so he might have been anyone, but I told him I was trying to reach Jennifer Li about a high school classmate named Jacob Breslyn. I asked for a callback whether or not the man knew Ms. Li, and tried not to sound as if I were begging.

I hung up feeling discouraged. People never answered their phones. Callback was another word for frustration.

Next, I checked Jacob's address book against the list of classmate names, and found seven possible matches. Two were still good. Ricky Stanley now lived in Australia and Carl Lembeck was a policeman in Hawthorne. Rick Stanley's mother promised to email her son and Lembeck's mother told me Carl hadn't spoken to her in years. Neither woman remembered Thomas Lerner, and only Stanley's mother recalled Jacob Breslyn.

I gathered my notes and the yearbooks, and decided to look for Charles.

Everett's Natural Creations was on Melrose in West Hollywood. I made pretty good time in the mid-morning traffic. The local talk radio stations were buzzing about the RPG rounds and grenades found with a body in Echo Park. A high-ranking deputy chief and a city councilman were announced as upcoming guests. They would feel the heat of justifiably concerned callers, and the heat would trickle down to Carter, and maybe to me.

I was thinking about Carter when I slipped through a yellow at La Brea and heard a horn behind me. I glanced in the rearview and saw a light blue two-door Dodge bust the red two cars behind me. The Dodge disappeared into a gas station, but the horn blower stayed on his horn and made a big show of raising his middle finger. Drama.

I turned off the radio and thought about Amy until I hit Fairfax and saw the Dodge again. The Dodge was at a light, waiting to turn. I passed in front of them. The driver was a Latin guy with high and tight hair. An Anglo with long blond hair was in the passenger seat. They looked away when I passed and waited longer to pull out behind me than they needed.

Three blocks later I stopped at a taco shop, bought an egg and chorizo burrito, and ate at a window table. I told myself I was being silly, but I didn't like how the Dodge had waited to turn. He could have easily turned behind me, but he waited until another car was between us. Drivers in Los Angeles never waited. Other drivers ran over you.

I finished the burrito and checked both sides of the street as I got into my car. The blue Dodge was gone. I felt better, but the same blue Dodge was behind a UPS truck in a mini-mall parking lot on the next corner. He was good, hiding behind the bigger truck, but I caught the dusty blue as I changed lanes. The driver was the same Latin male with high and tight hair. They were facing the exit, idling there in the parking lot, but they didn't pull out after me. They let me pass. I watched the exit as long as I could, but they didn't pull out. This meant they were working with at least one other car and as many as three.

Detective Carter had made me a priority.

The surveillance cars would not stop me unless they were ordered to stop me. Their job was surveillance. They would hang back, shadow, and report, after which task force detectives would visit the places I went, and question the people with whom I spoke. I couldn't protect Amy if they knew I was asking about her, so the surveillance team had to go.

Slipping a multi-car rolling surveillance wouldn't be easy, but I had a secret weapon.

I turned away from Everett's and called a friend.

Joe Pike.

10

Scott James

SCOTT WAS DRIFTING in an achy void when a woman's voice woke him. Before therapy, before Maggie entered his life, Stephanie Anders haunted his dreams three or four times each night.

"Officer James?"

Stephanie would come to him, forever trapped in her last moments, bleeding to death as a robbery crew raked them with automatic rifle fire.

"Scott?"

Stephanie would come, begging Scott to save her, to stay with her, even as heavy bullets slammed into their bodies.

I'm here, Steph.

I'm not leaving.

I won't leave you.

"Scott? Wake up."

Scott lurched awake, and saw Glory Stiles standing over him. Her face split into the most beautiful, amazing smile, and she held out a cup of coffee.

"Black, two sugars. Watch out now, it's hot."

Scott had worked with a sketch artist until almost three, and crashed on a couch in one of the conference rooms. He winced as he sat up. First move of the morning was always bad, as if the scars across his ribs grew brittle with sleep. He accepted the coffee, and slowly creaked to his feet.

Stiles said, "Sleeping on these couches is just the worst, now, isn't it? Heaven knows, I've done it too many times."

Carter came in as Scott stood, holding a sheet of paper in his teeth as he tapped out a text on his phone.

Scott sipped the coffee, and said nothing about the true reason for his stiffness. He checked the time, and was shocked to see it was mid-morning. The night before, Budress transported Maggie to the K-9 Platoon's training facility when Scott was ordered to report to the Boat.

"I have to see about my dog. She doesn't like being away from me."

Stiles flashed the smile at Carter.

"Aw, Brad, now isn't that cute? You see how they are with these dogs?"

Carter finished his text and handed Scott the sheet. It was a copy of the artist's finished sketch.

"What do you think? Anything you'd change or adjust?"

Scott was impressed with the quality of the artist's work. The hand-rendered sketch wasn't a photograph, but the likeness was good. It showed a fair-skinned man in his early fifties with high cheekbones, a long nose, and short dark hair. The artist had captured the man's pouty mouth in just the right sneer.

"No, sir. Looks good. It's the man I saw."

Stiles arched her eyebrows.

"Anything you maybe forgot earlier? A scar or a tattoo? A little business in his ear?"

Stiles touched the stud in her earlobe.

"No, ma'am."

Carter's phone buzzed with an incoming text. He read the message quickly, then turned to Scott and sat on the edge of the table.

"So we're good to go with the art?"

"Yes, sir."

"We'll pull mug shots based on your description. You'll have to look at them, but we'll let you get some zees first, okay?"

"Sounds good. Can I go?"

"A couple more questions, and we'll cut you free."

Scott glanced at his watch again, and hoped they would hurry.

Carter said, "You were the first inside, right?"

They had covered this at length the night before.

"Yeah. Myself and Sergeant Budress."

"How'd you gain entry?"

"The back door."

Stiles flashed the big smile.

"He means, how'd you open the door?"

"We kicked it. It was locked."

Scott paused and corrected himself.

"Paulie kicked it. I sent Maggie in when it popped, I went in with her, and then Paulie. We send the K-9 first."

Stiles leaned back against the table and crossed her arms.

"So the door was locked, intact, and undamaged before you entered?"

"Yes, ma'am."

Scott wondered if they had inadvertently committed a policy violation.

"Did we do something wrong?"

"Oh, no, you most certainly did not. This is good."

Stiles glanced at Carter, pleased, and Carter nodded.

"First blush, you think, here's this a-hole trying to escape, he wants to hide, so he breaks into a house. Only Etana didn't break in. He didn't have a key, so someone let him in, which means this person knew him, and you know what I'm thinking?"

Stiles grinned, as if this were a regular routine.

"Tell us, Brad. What are you thinking?"

"I'm thinking the man in the house, your man—"

Carter gestured at the sketch.

"—had dealings with Etana, and maybe expected him. But when he realized Etana brought an army of cops along, he killed the little sonofabitch."

Stiles nodded.

"Yes, sir. This would seem to make sense."

Carter glanced at Stiles.

"Check for gang affils. *La Eme*, in particular. Associates in with the cartels, and priors with arms and munitions. Military-grade stuff like this, it might've been coming from or going to Mexico."

Carter pronouced it Meh-hee-co.

Scott suddenly recalled how his eyes burned when he entered the house, and smelled the sharp odors again as if they clung to his skin.

"The place reeked of chemicals. Were there chemical weapons or toxins, or something that could hurt my dog?"

Carter and Stiles traded an uneasy look, and Carter cleared his throat.

"Bomb Squad and SID are checking. As far as I know, it was soaked with bleach and ammonia. We found jugs of the stuff."

Scott glanced at his watch again, even more worried than before. Budress or one of the other handlers would have texted if Maggie showed symptoms, but Scott wanted to check her himself. He put down the coffee.

"Are we finished? I need to see about my dog."

"Another sec. Wanna be sure I have the timeline straight."

Scott was annoyed. These were things they had gone over at length a few hours earlier.

"I don't know what else I can tell you."

"Before you saw Cole, you were in the backyard with Budress and the others, correct?"

Stiles said, "Evanski and Peters."

"That's right."

Scott glanced at his watch again to drive home his annoyance. Carter pretended not to notice.

"The man in the sport coat—our suspect here—had gone back into the house. You saw Etana on the couch, the blood, and realized the man might duck out the front. That's when you ran to the street."

"Yeah. Like I told you last night."

Stiles crossed her arms, staring at him.

"Did you hear anything from the front, something that maybe made you think he was getting away?"

This was a new question. Scott searched his memory, and shook his head.

"No. It just occurred to me, is all. No one was covering the front."

Carter nodded.

"Okay. So you ran to the front, and saw Mr. Cole."

"Yeah. Couldn't miss him. He was in the middle of the street."

"Did you see him get out of a car?"

"I didn't see where he came from. I looked, and here was this guy in the street with some coppers chasing him."

Stiles arched her eyebrows again.

"Last night, you said you were watching the suspect."

"Cole shouted. It could have been Alvin, but I'm pretty sure it was Cole."

Carter pooched out his lips, thinking.

"Uh-huh."

Stiles said, "So Mr. Cole shouted, you looked, and he was running at you?"

"Not *at* me. I wasn't in the street, but yeah, he was running in my direction."

Carter's phone buzzed again, and he frowned at the incoming message. He turned away to respond, and Stiles cocked her head, curious.

"Why didn't you sic your dog on him?"

Scott smiled. Releasing a police K-9 was an action controlled by the rules and requirements outlined in the LAPD Guidelines, no different than firing a weapon.

"It isn't that simple. Alvin was right behind him."

"Not Cole. The suspect. You were closest. You saw him run off down the street."

"Across the street and between the houses. I called it in."

"That's right. Was he too far away?"

Scott wondered if she was implying a failure on his part, but decided her questions were innocent.

"Etana was still inside. Officers were in pursuit, so I opted to join my partners. Better a dog goes first, than a man."

Stiles nodded, and seemed satisfied.

"I saw you and Mr. Cole talking. What was that about?"

"Last night?"

"In the hall here. When we released him."

Scott was annoyed she asked about Cole, and glanced at his watch again.

"I told him he was stupid for chasing a suspect. I almost shot him."

Stiles laughed.

"Uh-huh. And what did Mr. Cole say to *that*?"

"He thanked me for not shooting him."

"That's it?"

"Yeah, pretty much. He's one of those guys, thinks he's funny."

"Don't they all?"

Carter finished his text, and abruptly offered his hand.

"That's all for now, Scott. Thanks for hanging in. Go give your dog a biscuit."

"We're done?"

"Until we have more questions."

Stiles gestured toward the door.

"And we *always* have more questions. I'll be in touch about the mug shots."

Scott hurried out to the elevator. He was tired, hungry, and wanted to sleep, but his concern for Maggie overshadowed everything else. He phoned Budress on the ride down to ask about her.

"She's fine. I checked her, and Leland checked her, too. They cut you free?"

"Yeah. Listen, the fumes in the house were bleach and ammonia. We won't know about toxins or chemical agents for a couple of days."

"Dude. She's good. Relax."

Budress had been a K-9 handler for sixteen years. He had a lifetime of experience.

"She is?"

"Yeah. She's fine. Come see for yourself."

Scott felt better after talking to Budress. He didn't think about Stiles and her question again until he reached his car, and then it began to bother him.

11

Maggie

USMC Military Working Dog *Maggie T415 finds herself standing on a dusty road in the central provinces of the Islamic Republic of Afghanistan. The mid-morning sun is so harsh the Marines surrounding her hide their eyes with sunglasses. Maggie, who stands with her Marine K-9 handler, Pete, does not know she is a military working dog. She does not know her serial number, T415, is tattooed inside her left ear or that she is in Afghanistan or the men around her are Marines. She is a German shepherd dog. She knows what she needs to know. Her name is Maggie, she and Pete are pack, and Pete is currently pouring water onto her head and back. In her dream, Maggie does not feel the brutal heat or the sand burning her pads or the dust blowing into her eyes or the itchy feel of the cool water Pete scratches into her undercoat. In her dream, she remembers only Pete's strong scent, the joy of Pete's attention, and the happiness she shows by wagging her tail. The other Marines are shadows without scent or substance. Only Pete and those memories* she associates with Pete are real to her. In her dream, Maggie does not remember Pete has only twelve minutes left to live.

Maggie does not dream in sequential images as humans dream. Humans are visual. Maggie dreams first of scents, which trigger emotions and images she associates with those scents.

Pete. The scent of his gear and battle rifle and sweat and soap and the nylon and steel leash that bound them together.

The green tennis ball hidden in Pete's pocket. Felt, rubber, adhesive, and ink. The green ball was her favorite toy and her reward when she found the special scents Pete trained her to find. The scent of the green ball was the scent of a promise. Pete's promise to reward her.

The game they play. Maggie dreams of their game often. They walk together on a long road, far ahead of the shadow-Marines. Maggie is searching for the special scents Pete trained her to find. If she finds a special scent, she will drop to her belly, stare at the source of the scent, and Pete will reward her. He will pet her, squeak his approval, and throw the green ball. Pete happy. Maggie happy. Pack happy. Maggie loved to chase the green ball. Maggie loved to play their game.

Her dreamscape unfolds in bits and pieces, snaps and flashes, sometimes connected, other times not. She dreams of walking with Pete on the long road. She dreams of the sweet diesel scent when they ride in the Hummer. She dreams of petting, strokes, Pete giving her water, and the two of them sharing chow.

She dreams of the wild Afghan dogs that attacked her one desert evening and the hot scent of thunder as Pete rushed to her side, pack against pack, the feral dogs screaming as they died. She dreams of the fierce elation she felt at the taste of their blood, and, after, in dominant victory, the warm joy of grooming, Pete checking her for bites and wounds as Maggie licked the gunsmoke from his face, Pete safe, Maggie safe, pack safe.

As Maggie dreams of this canine combat, her paws twitch, her sleeping eyes roll, and she softly huffs.

In her dream, as was the case in life, Maggie and Pete sit together when they rest, sleep beside each other in the cold desert night, and eat apart from the others. Maggie grows wary when others approach, not for herself but for Pete. Pete is hers. Her instinct is to protect him. Maggie and Pete are pack. The others are not.

Her dreamscape turns again.

Maggie and Pete are playing their game when the stink of goats and men smelling of coriander slams into her. Her paws twitch and flicker. Her scent memory screams a warning, but she cannot escape the terrible scents crashing into her like runaway train cars, the goats, the coriander, the first whiff of the special scent, a scent that promised a reward.

Snap snap snap—her dream memories unfold.

Maggie sources the scent to one of the men.

She alerts, and Pete is beside her.

Pete's fear envelops her as he moves to the man and in the same moment Maggie's world explodes.

Her kaleidoscope nightmare turns faster.

Pete is torn and dying before her.

Maggie whines in her sleep at the bitter scent of his death.

She drags herself to him, compelled by instincts bred into her and her kind for a hundred thousand generations. Guard. Soothe. Heal. Protect.

A hard blow kicks her into the air, rolling her end over end. She snaps at white-hot pain in her hips, rights herself, and returns to him. She stands over him now, guarding him.

A second devastating blow throws her into the air, screaming, spinning, so high into the bright blue desert air—

Maggie's nightmare shape-shifts to a warehouse near the Los Angeles

River, where she stands over Scott. The scent of burnt gunpowder is sharp again. The scent of Scott's dying body is stronger.

Though Maggie has no measure of time, almost two years after she lost Pete in Afghanistan, she finds herself in Los Angeles with Scott.

Scott is now alpha.

Scott and Maggie are pack.

The terrible awful dying scents of Scott and Pete melt together in her scent memory as one, and once more her pack is threatened.

The nightmare shifts again. Maggie races through the building. She powers up the scent cone left by Scott's attacker. This is no longer a game she plays. The man she hunts is prey. A green ball is not the reward she seeks.

The other's scent trail is as clear to Maggie as a path of living fire. She runs harder, powering after him with a hunger passed down from the mountain wolves and wild canids who chased their prey for miles, never stopping, never sated until their fangs sank deep, their prey came down, their muzzles dripped with blood.

Maggie sees her prey ahead, a living furnace of scent.

She smells his fear.

The other turns to face her, raises his hands, an act of challenge that fuels her primal fury.

The scent of Scott's pain and blood spurs her across the distance. Her bone-deep instinct commands: If the pack is threatened, the threat must be driven away or destroyed.

This other will not harm Scott again.

Scott safe.

Pack safe.

Her devotion is absolute.

Maggie growls deep in her heavy chest, bares gleaming fangs, and leaps into the flames . . .

12

Scott James

Scott believed the search had gone well. Budress, Evanski, and Peters had all congratulated him, but he couldn't fault Stiles for her question. Scott had seen the suspect disappear between the houses, he had been closer to the suspect than anyone else, and Maggie could cover forty yards in two-point-eight seconds. But Scott hadn't known whether Carlos Etana was dead or alive, or if other individuals were in the house. Chasing the suspect would have meant letting his partners face the unknown without Maggie's help. Scott chose to back up his teammates. He didn't think twice about it, and no one had mentioned it until Stiles. Scott was still brooding about it when he reached Glendale.

The Platoon's training facility was a low cinder-block building at the edge of a fenced grass field. The building was divided into two small offices and a makeshift kennel, where dogs could be penned between sessions. The Platoon's daily shift didn't begin until mid-afternoon, but several black-and-white K-9 cars already dotted the parking lot. A lone Bomb Detection K-9 truck stood out among them like a rhino among cattle.

Scott parked quickly, and hurried inside. He expected to be greeted by barking, but found only silence. The kennel appeared to be empty until he heard a familiar whimper.

Maggie was asleep in the last run. She whimpered and huffed, and her paws twitched as if she were running. Like Scott, Maggie had nightmares two or three times a week. PTSD. Her nightmares probably weren't much different from his.

Scott eased open the gate, and laid a hand on her shoulder.

"Mags."

Maggie lurched awake, heaved to her feet, and wobbled sideways. A shaky start, like nightmares, was something they had in common.

"I'm here, baby girl. You doin' okay? How's my girl?"

Maggie swirled around him, ears back, happily wagging her tail. The outside door opened, and Budress called out.

"Yo, dude. Leland's here. He wants you and Maggie outside."

Scott creaked to his feet.

"Hang on, Paul. I want to ask you something."

Budress seemed irritated.

"I checked her, man. She's fine."

"Not that. About last night. Maggie could've bagged that guy. Did I make a mistake, not going after him?"

Budress made as if to spit, then realized he was indoors, and stopped.

"Coulda isn't the same as woulda. The guy hops a fence, and she's skunked, over and out."

"Has Leland said anything?"

"Fuck that. You made the right decision, knowing what you knew at the time. Now clip up, and get out here. Leland's gonna test her."

Scott felt a renewed concern.

"You said she's fine."

"We're testing her scent memory. Now c'mon. It'll be fun. We gotta finish before the LT gets here."

Budress waved him toward the door, but Scott didn't move. Their lieutenant didn't roll out early unless he had a problem.

"Why's the LT coming?"

Budress hesitated, and seemed awkward for the first time.

"Something about last night. We probably won't like that part as much."

Budress turned away.

"Paul! What's wrong? Why's he upset?"

"C'mon, Scott. Let's do this."

"Paul!"

Budress kept walking.

Scott's heart was pounding, and his face felt flushed. He took a breath, and gazed at his dog.

"Today is really starting to suck the big one."

Maggie gazed back, and happily wagged her tail.

Scott clipped her lead, and hurried out to the field.

Sergeant Dominick Leland was tall, thin as barbed wire, and peered at the world through a permanent scowl. A rim of steel-colored fuzz circled his mocha pate, and two fingers were missing from his left hand, lost to a monstrous Rottweiler-mastiff attack dog he fought to protect a K-9 partner. With thirty-two years on the job as a K-9 officer, Dominick Leland had served as the Platoon's Chief Trainer longer than anyone in the history of the Los Angeles Police

Department, and was an undisputed, three-fingered legend. The Officer-in-Charge ran the Platoon, but Leland was the final authority and absolute master in all matters regarding dogs, dog handlers, and their place within the Platoon.

When Scott stepped out, he saw Leland with a burly older man who wore faded black utilities sporting a BOMB K-9 patch and sergeant's stripes.

Leland scowled as Scott approached.

"Sergeant Budress believes our Miss Maggie alerted to the explosives you found. Sergeant Johnson here thinks this unlikely. Do you believe her behavior was an alert?"

Straight to business. No greeting; no acknowledgment, comments, or questions about the search.

Scott offered his hand to Johnson.

"Scott James."

The burly sergeant shook.

"Fritz Johnson. Bomb dogs."

LAPD's Bomb Detection K-9 Section was based at Los Angeles International Airport, and worked in conjunction with the TSA and the Bomb Squad. They provided explosives-detection service at high-profile events like the Rose Bowl Parade, the Oscars, and presidential visits.

Scott tried to read through Leland's scowl, but found nothing.

"I don't know, Sergeant. She didn't bark. She laid down, and kept quiet."

The Platoon taught its dogs to bark when they found a sought object. This was because patrol dogs often worked off leash, and out of the handler's sight. Barking told the handler they'd found something.

Budress spit a squirt of tobacco juice.

"She alerted. Guaranteed, and I'll put a hundred on it."

Johnson eyed the rivulets of scars that laced Maggie's hips.

"Military Working Dog?"

"Marines. She was trained up dual-purpose. Explosives and patrol."

Johnson looked over Maggie as if he wanted to buy her, but didn't have enough cash.

"Uh-huh. How long ago?"

"Two years or so. She's been with us for a year."

Johnson shrugged at Leland.

"Two years is a long time. We train up our dogs every day to keep'm sharp. These dogs won't forget a scent, but they forget what they're supposed to do when they smell it."

Budress spit again.

"She dropped, and didn't make a sound. Didn't paw the door, or try to get in. That's a bomb alert. A dog doesn't bark, it's been trained not to bark."

Leland stepped back and crossed his arms.

"Get started, Fritz. The boss is coming, and he's already pissed off."

Scott tried to read Leland again, but Leland turned away.

Johnson pointed out five blue cans lined up in the grass against the kennel. Scott hadn't noticed them earlier, and wasn't interested now. He watched the parking lot for the LT's car.

"Those cans are scent cans. We use'm to train our dogs. Got cat food in one, beef jerky in another, a cotton ball wet with gasoline, and liver treats. The fifth can has a little RDX, the stuff they use to make plastic explosives."

Scott nodded, but paid little attention.

"Which one?"

"Won't say. What you know can affect her hunt, so it's best you don't know."

Scott knew this was true. Handlers unwittingly directed their dogs to finds through subconscious changes in body language, tone, and expressions. Dogs noticed everything, and constantly read their handlers for behavioral cues.

"Work her off leash, and direct her to the cans. Doesn't matter where you start, left to right or right to left. Let's see what she does."

Scott glanced at the parking lot.

"You listening?"

Scott unclipped Maggie's lead and forced himself to stop thinking about Stiles. He slapped his thighs, and spoke in a high, excited voice.

"Let's find something, Maggie-girl! Wanna find it for me?"

Maggie dropped into the play position, and Scott instantly walked toward the building. He pointed at the far left can.

"Find it, baby. Seek. *Seek!*"

Maggie trotted toward the left can, but abruptly veered to the right. Her ears pricked and her speed increased, which told Scott she whiffed a scent much more compelling than liver. She sniffed quickly from can to can, and pulled up short when she reached the far right can.

Behind them, Budress spoke, but Scott ignored him.

"I still have that hundred."

Scott was watching his dog.

Maggie took a careful step closer, lifted her nose, and abruptly circled around the last can to a downspout. She dropped to her belly just as she had in the Echo Park hall, glanced proudly at Scott, and stared at the downspout.

Budress hooted.

"Alert!"

Scott moved closer, and found a small black box hidden behind the spout. He turned to show the others, and that's when he saw the

Platoon's Officer-in-Charge watching from the kennel. The LT's eyes were unusually grim, and Scott quickly looked away. He hurried back to the others, and tossed the box to Johnson.

"You tried to trick her."

"Not her, you. Like I said, best you know nothing. Better, if what you know is wrong."

Johnson smiled at Leland.

"Smart gal, here. She gets too old for patrol, I might be able to use her."

Scott felt a touch, and Leland nodded toward the lieutenant. He was coming toward them.

"He wants to talk about last night. Stay calm, and let's hear the man out."

Scott wanted to go to the bathroom.

As Johnson retrieved the cans, Lieutenant Jim Kemp joined them. Kemp had never been a handler and wasn't a dog man, but he was an excellent commanding officer. He was on the short list for a captaincy, and Scott would be sorry to see him go, but the man's grim expression had him worried.

"Thanks for keeping him here, Dom. I know you all must be tired."

Kemp considered Scott.

"Especially you."

"I'm fine, LT. Is there a problem?"

Kemp glanced at Leland.

"Sergeant, have you found out what in hell happened last night?"

"Haven't spoken with Officer James yet, but I discussed the matter with Sergeant Budress here, and Evanski and Peters. I have a pretty good idea what happened."

"Then please clue me in so I can return all these damned calls."

Leland scowled so hard, Scott thought he looked like he was passing a stone.

"Seems to me, and after careful consideration, Officer James did a damned fine job. Superb, in fact. So I'll be submitting a letter of commendation for your approval."

Leland glared at Scott.

"Well done."

Budress burst out laughing, and Leland couldn't hold the scowl. Kemp flashed an ear-to-ear grin.

Scott stared from one to another, and realized what they had done. The tension drained away with an enormous sense of relief, and Scott found himself smiling. This would be his first commendation letter as a K-9 officer.

"You guys had me worried."

Kemp slapped his shoulder.

"Congratulations, Scott. A good job last night, and important. No telling what those munitions would have been used for. You saved lives."

Scott glanced at Budress.

"We. It was a team effort."

Budress winked, and Kemp slapped Scott's shoulder again.

"Say it on camera. PIO phoned. The press wants an interview. They want video of what we do, so we're making the arrangements."

PIO was the LAPD Public Information Office. Scott had never been interviewed or seen himself on television.

"Sounds good. Kind of exciting."

Kemp nodded.

"A gold star for the Platoon, and an opportunity to show the public what we do. Now go home, and get some sleep. You'll want to look pretty on camera."

Leland scowled again.

"You heard the boss. Go."

Scott shook hands again, and led Maggie out to his car. He fired the engine to start the AC, but he didn't intend to go home. He wanted to share the good news.

Scott had been shot on two different occasions in the space of a year, and both times, his injuries were bad. The first was when Stephanie Anders was murdered. The second, not quite a year later, when he and a Robbery-Homicide detective named Joyce Cowly found the men who killed Stephanie. Cowly visited him at the hospital often, and even more often once he was home.

Cowly answered in her deadpan homicide voice, which told Scott she was at a crime scene.

He said, "It's me, babe. Can you talk?"

"Stand by."

When she returned to the line a few seconds later, her voice was light and cheerful.

"Hey, buddy, what's up? You caught me at a crime scene."

"Maggie and I found a DB and a stash of military munitions in Echo Park."

"Wait. That was you? Oh, baby, that's so great! I heard something on the news. The Bomb Squad rolled out, right? They evacuated the neighborhood?"

Scott loved the delight in her voice, and was pleased she'd heard about the recovery.

"I'll tell you everything. What's your schedule?"

Cowly spoke to someone in the background, then returned.

"I'm in Laurel Canyon. Where are you?"

"Glendale."

"We're clearing the scene in ten. I have to go downtown, but I'll have a few minutes. Want to meet at the top of Runyon Canyon, up on Mulholland?"

"The top gate. Sure."

"Twenty-five minutes. Prepare to be kissed."

Scott tucked away his phone, pulled out of the parking lot, and turned toward Laurel Canyon. He was too excited to sleep, and anxious to see Cowly. Stiles and her depressing question were in the past, and falling farther behind.

Scott grinned at Maggie in the rearview.

"I was wrong. Today doesn't suck."

Maggie licked the partition, and panted hot breath.

Scott didn't see the nondescript white car parked next to a building across from the training field. He didn't see the man in the white car watching.

13

Mr. Rollins

MR. ROLLINS peered through Nikon binoculars at the dump where cops trained their mutts. He was parked alongside a brake shop, pretty well hidden behind a tree, a telephone pole, and a chain-link fence, checking out the cops who arrived. So far that morning, three K-9 cars and a Bomb Detection K-9 truck had arrived. No sign of the clown.

Mr. Rollins had a lousy night. He dreamed that the police had connected him to the house. Between dreams, he raged about the loss of the house, and worried Charles would bail on the deal.

Mr. Rollins finally gave up on bed, popped a couple of Adderall, and hooked up with Eli.

So here they were, watching.

A fourth K-9 car arrived. A cop got out and headed into the building. Rollins focused the Nikons, but only saw the back of the cop's head.

Mr. Rollins popped another Adderall and decided to call Charles.

Keeping Charles in the game could prove difficult, but Rollins wanted the money. Charles wanted the money, too. He didn't know what the woman wanted.

Charles answered with a mumble like his mouth was covered.

"Hullo."

Mr. Rollins launched into his pitch.

"I had a situation after you left. If you haven't seen the news, you will, so I wanted to reach out. Everything's fine. What happened last night, it absolutely will not affect me, or you, or us doing business."

Charles said, "Hang on."

Mr. Rollins readied himself for the battle, but Charles surprised him.

"Did your buyer test the product?"

Just like that, and the deal was on. Mr. Rollins didn't rock the boat by saying Eli had other plans for the sample.

"Absolutely. He was impressed, and wants to proceed."

"Right? I told you, man. There's nothing else like it on the market."

What a turd. A part-time hustler who sounded hungry.

"Then let's make the arrangements."

"How much does he want?"

Charles had offered two hundred kilograms. Two hundred kilos was just shy of four hundred forty-one pounds.

"All of it."

"No shit?"

"I wouldn't shit you, Charles. All two hundred kilos."

"I don't know. I'm not sure my seller wants to sell all of it to a single buyer."

Chiseler.

"Talk to her. We're not looking for a discount. My guy will pay the same amount per pound whether we get forty or four hundred. If she lets him have everything, you'll make your commission faster."

"I hear you. Just remember, she has to meet with the buyer. It's a deal point."

"I understand. Not a problem."

"The buyer's okay with it?"

"I convinced him. It's a deal point."

In fact, Mr. Rollins had not mentioned this point to Eli. Better to lie. Rollins lied to the people he dealt with ninety percent of the time. He was also not going to tell Eli the deal was still on until Eli got rid of the clown.

"Charles, one thing—wait."

A fifth K-9 vehicle pulled in, and parked. A shiny SUV that looked newer than the others. Mr. Rollins scoped the tall man who got out and entered the building. Wrong clown.

"What she said last night, was it true?"

"What did she say?"

"That she can make more. You and I can bank a lot of cash with this material. Know what I'm saying?"

"I hear you."

"Think about it."

"I think about it twenty-four seven."

Charles hung up.

Mr. Rollins scanned the parking lot, and thought about Charles. Charles didn't seem concerned about what happened at the house. Mr. Rollins wondered if Charles was too stupid to understand his exposure, or too greedy to care. Their three prior dealings had gone well, but stupid, greedy people eventually got arrested. Fortunately,

Charles knew nothing about Mr. Rollins except an alias, a disposable phone number, and the dates they met at the Echo Park house. Charles and the false things he knew couldn't hurt Mr. Rollins.

The clown could hurt him.

Fourteen minutes later, Mr. Rollins was stretching his back when a cop with a dog came out of the building. He raised the Nikons.

The dog was a German shepherd, and the cop kinda looked like he could be the one, but Mr. Rollins couldn't see him well enough to be certain. He had to be certain. This was a rule.

The cop and the dog went to the fourth car, which Mr. Rollins remembered. The cop opened the back door, and the dog jumped in. Mr. Rollins squinted through the Nikons, and adjusted the focus, but he still couldn't see the cop's face.

Then the cop went to the driver's door, and turned as he got in. Mr. Rollins saw him clearly, and was certain.

Rollins copied the K-9 car's number and quickly called Eli.

"The guy who just got into the car. You see him?"

"Yes. The K-9 car."

"He just got in, him and the dog. A sedan. Not the SUV."

"The sedan. Yes, we see him get in."

"That's him."

Mr. Rollins lowered the phone, and finally relaxed.

The clown had to go.

Now he was gone.

14

Elvis Cole

PIKE LISTENED QUIETLY as I told him about Amy Breslyn and the surveillance team. Pike was always quiet. The High Sierras are quiet before thunder rocks the sky.

"What do you want me to do with them?"

As in, should he bury the bodies, or leave them?

"I don't want you to do anything with them. They're cops. I need
to lose them."

Losing a trail car was easy, but surveillance teams didn't follow a
target like ducklings. They surrounded their target in a loose and
changing formation like a school of dolphins, tracking their target
from positions ahead, behind, and on parallel streets. The only way to
beat them was to force them into a group.

Pike said, "Kenter Canyon."

I saw the plan the moment he said it.

"I'll need wheels."

"Give me an hour."

Kenter Canyon was in the hills above Brentwood, not far from UCLA. I made two stops on the way, once for gas, and at a discount store known for home entertainment bargains. I bought a disposable phone with texting and voice mail features, and four hundred minutes of anonymous prepaid call time. I activated the minutes in the discount store's restroom, and set my office and cell phones to forward my calls to the burner. I texted the new number to Pike as I walked to my car.

I called Meryl Lawrence next and got her voice mail. If callbacks were my business, business was good.

"This is a new number. Don't use the old number. I'll explain when you call."

The burner rang thirty seconds later with a chirpy ring I didn't like.

"Why do you have a new number?"

"The police are following me. They're upping the heat."

Her voice softened and she sounded afraid.

"Did they see us this morning? Did they follow you to her house?"

"I don't think so. They probably picked me up at my office, after."

"Wonderful. You don't think so."

"This is me protecting you, Meryl. If they grab my phone records, they'll know we spoke when I was in Echo Park, and they'll contact you to find out why. I don't think they saw us, but if they did, they'll find you through your license plate, and ask the same questions."

"I cannot believe my life has come to this."

"Tell them the truth or make up a cover story, but let me know so we tell the same story. Do you understand?"

She took a single breath.

"Here's what I understand. My husband has a gambling problem. I found money missing from our retirement accounts and he gave me a bullshit story about investing the money. I hired you to find out. You followed him to those gambling clubs in Bellflower and that's what we talked about. How's that?"

"One more thing."

"Can this get any better?"

"A man named Charles sent roses to Amy about ten days ago."

Meryl Lawrence made a long I-told-you-so hiss.

"I knew it. I knew someone was using her."

"Flowers don't mean someone is using her. They may not mean anything. Does she work with a Charles?"

"No."

"He could be someone who's thanking her for business or a favor. What about an outside contractor?"

Meryl spoke quickly.

"If I knew who he was I wouldn't need you. Find him."

The line went dead as I checked the mirror. The blue Dodge was back, but didn't stay long. It appeared twice more, never closer than three or four cars, and I never picked out the cars that replaced it. I wouldn't have known the Dodge was following me if they hadn't jumped the red. Jumping the red had cost them.

I passed UCLA and the National Cemetery in Westwood, and reached Brentwood when Pike texted.

HERE

Pike, saying he was ready.

12OUT

Me, saying I was twelve minutes away.

Kenter Canyon was a narrow box canyon in the foothills of Brentwood above Sunset. The canyon was dense with upscale homes, but higher, beyond the houses, the hills were undeveloped, and thick with scrub oak and brush. Unpaved roads and trails had been cut for fire crews, and were open to hikers and runners. Pike and I ran the trails often, and knew the canyon well.

A single, innocuous residential street led into the canyon, and appeared to be the only way to enter or leave. Smaller streets branched and re-branched from this larger street as it wound its way higher, but the smaller streets appeared trapped in the canyon. This wasn't true, but the convoluted route using these smaller back streets wasn't easily found. Pike and I knew this way, and another, but I was betting the tail cops behind me didn't, and wouldn't, until I was already gone.

I didn't use my blinker, and gave them no warning. I turned abruptly, at the last second, onto the sole street into the canyon. The trail car was forced to turn with me, and the flankers had no choice but to fall into line. Just like that, they were bunched together, and behind me.

They'd feel a quick jolt of panic, worried that I could give them the slip, but they'd feel better when they checked their maps. They'd see only one way in or out of the canyon, so the lead car would fall back to give me plenty of room. One car would remain at the bottom to guard the exit, and the rest would follow, confident they had me trapped. I was counting on their confidence. They wouldn't know they were wrong until I was gone.

I wound and twisted to the top of the canyon, where the street ended and the fire road began, at a heavy black gate. Cars belonging to hikers and dog walkers lined both sides of the street. Pike texted again as I parked.

GO

Pike was nearby, watching.

I gathered everything connected to Amy Breslyn, locked my car, and hurried around the gate. There was only one street in or out of the canyon but two ways to leave. I would be gone in fourteen minutes.

I tucked the yearbooks under my arm like a football and fell into an easy jog.

A quarter-mile in, Pike texted.

1W2M

The first car had arrived with two male occupants. I picked up my pace.

At the half-mile mark, a second text arrived.

2W2MW

A second car had arrived, this one with a male and female team.

I slowed at the mile marker to shoot Pike a text. I was almost gone. Half a mile to go.

CALL?

The burner chirped. I hated the chirp.

I said, "What's happening?"

"Two men in a light blue Dodge two-door. White guy with long blond hair. Latin guy driving, high and tight."

"That's them. What about the second car?"

"Gray Sentra. Man and a woman. The woman is driving."

The Sentra meant there would be a third car. They wouldn't leave the exit unguarded.

"What are they doing?"

"The Latin dude walked up past the gate, but he's already back. No way he saw you."

"Tell me if they leave."

I picked up my pace again. I didn't want them to leave. I wanted them to waste time trying to figure out why I came to this place, and whether they should hike in after me, or hang back and wait. The more they talked, the better. Each minute they yakked brought me a minute closer to gone.

The burner chirped again.

"Sentra leaving."

I jogged faster, and saw gated homes ahead. Three minutes to go. Maybe four.

"The Dodge?"

"Still here. The blond is on the phone."

Sooner or later, they would bring up a map and study the area at the mouth of the fire road. They'd eventually expand the map, and trace the fire road to a housing development separate from the canyon to which I led them. And this was when they'd realize I'd lost them.

Pike said, "The Dodge is rolling. They're coming your way."

"Hundred yards."

A bright yellow gate at the top of a cul-de-sac marked the end of the fire road.

Pike said, "Green Lexus. Key behind the left rear. Tank's full."

I squeezed around the gate, and felt for the key. The Lexus was ten years old, but purred in a flash.

Halfway down to the freeway, a gray Sentra blew past going up-hill, but the man and woman inside didn't see me. The light blue Dodge turned in front of me as I reached the bottom, and powered up the hill. The men in the Dodge didn't see me, either.

Slipping their tail was what we in the trade called 'suspicious be-havior.' Carter would react fast, and come down hard, but Amy and Meryl were covered.

I picked up the freeway, and headed for Everett's Natural Cre-ations.

15

EVERETT'S NATURAL CREATIONS was on a hip street in Los Feliz lined with music conservatories, purveyors of artisanal coffees, and taquerías selling 'hand-crafted' tacos for eight bucks a pop. Hipness came with a price.

I parked around the corner but didn't get out of the car. The police would be all over whoever owned Lerner's house, but the current owner might not have been Lerner's landlord. Rental applications were gold mines, and often contained contact information for employers, personal references, and relatives. I called a real estate agent I knew named Laura Freeman.

Laura and I went on one date eleven years ago and had a great time, but the next day she met the man she would marry. Her husband was a real estate agent, too, back when they met, and a struggling developer. He was smart, he worked hard, and together they built his business from single-family spec homes to shopping centers. My loss, her gain. Laura answered on the first ring.

I said, "Do me a favor and you can tell everyone I'm your boyfriend."

"Who is this?"

Humor.

"I need the title history of a property in Echo Park."

"Single family or commercial?"

"Single family."

I gave her the address along with the burner's number.

"We miss you. When are you coming for dinner?"

"When's Donald out of town?"

More humor. Kinda.

She called me a horrible flirt, told me she'd phone when she had the information, and hung up. It wasn't the first time.

I slid out of the car and was halfway to Everett's when the burner chirped. Pike.

"The Dodge came back with a dark blue Ford."

The Ford made three cars.

"Are they watching my car?"

"The Ford is watching. The Dodge crew hiked up the fire road twenty minutes ago. My guess, the Sentra is hiking down. They're looking for you."

"They're going to be disappointed."

Pike was silent for a moment, then simply hung up. To expect more was to be disappointed.

Everett's was a world exploding with color. Arrangements of cut flowers and potted plants were displayed on tables and pedestals and hung from the ceiling. Buckets containing yet more flowers mazed the floor and filled cases lining the walls. The flowers were vibrant with life and color but absent of scent. The little shop smelled like plants, but not like flowers.

A young woman with heavy frame glasses and short dark hair was taking a phone order behind a counter. A second woman and a man in his forties were arranging flowers on a workbench behind her. The second woman wore a white tank top to show an enormous peacock tattooed on her shoulder. The man was bunching violet and pink roses in a heavy glass bowl. The roses were so densely packed they looked like a rose balloon.

I smiled at the girl taking the order. She held up a finger, asking me to wait. She finished scribbling, slapped the order on the workbench, and hurried back.

"Sorry. I hope you don't need anything delivered today. We're crushing to make the last truck."

The man arranging the roses sang out over his shoulder.

"Not crushing, *crushed*! We are crushed! The pressure to create beauty has crushed us!"

The girl rolled her eyes.

"He loves it."

The man sang out again.

"Oh, you wish!"

The girl had a nice smile.

"Okay, so, how can I help you now that you know we can't help you?"

The man glanced from his roses.

"Speak for yourself, honey. Some of us here would love to help him."

The girl giggled again.

I said, "You guys should take it on the road. You're funny."

The man fluffed at the roses.

"Some of us have *many* talents."

The girl rolled her eyes again.

"He's incorrigible. What can I do for you?"

I showed her the picture I took of the card delivered with Amy Breslyn's flowers.

"You delivered flowers to us, but we don't know who sent them."

"It says Charles."

"It says Charles, but there's no last name. We know five Charleses. Could you please look up who sent them? We want to send a thank-you."

The man with the roses made a swooning noise.

"He said please. OhmyGod, you must help this poor man, he said PLEASE!"

Her face grew serious, as if researching the order required great concentration.

"What was the name on the delivery?"

"Amy Breslyn."

I spelled Breslyn.

The man eyed me while the girl went to a computer. His hands didn't stop moving the roses.

"You don't look like an Amy. Are you a Dorothy?"

"My wife."

"Crushed!"

The peacock woman bumped him with her hip.

"Don't you ever stop?"

"Not until everyone's HAPPY!"

The counter girl typed Amy's name into the computer and made a sad face.

"I'm so sorry. They were really nice, but it was a cash sale. There's no purchaser information."

Screwed. If Charles used a credit card I would have been golden, but Charles had paid cash. I stared at her, thinking about the cash, then checked the ceiling, looking for a security camera. The ceiling was bare.

"Do you have a security camera?"

The man hooted.

"Everett's too cheap. If we had sex in here he might spring for a camera, but otherwise, oh please!"

"Maybe whoever helped him remembers what he looked like. I might recognize him if you describe him."

The girl looked exasperated.

"We must get a hundred people in here every day."

The man glanced at her.

"How much was the arrangement?"

"Jared!"

"You said it was nice. I'm trying to help the gentleman."

"Three-sixty plus tax. A dozen Pink Finesse gardens."

Jared smiled broadly.

"Someone wanted to impress. When was the purchase?"

The girl read from the card.

"Nine days ago. One dozen Pink Finesse garden roses. Thirty a stem including the vase. Three-sixty plus tax total."

He thought for a moment.

"I was here, but it wasn't me. I would remember."

The peacock florist spoke as she worked.

"Wasn't me. I did the peach and the yellows."

I smiled at them. Their shop was filled with hundreds of roses in every possible color.

"With all the arrangements you guys make, you'd remember these particular roses?"

Jared said, "Of course! Garden roses have fragrance. Standard roses like these last so much longer, but have no fragrance. A rose without fragrance is like unrequited love, don't you think?"

"I had that very thought this morning."

"We order only a few at a time because they fail so quickly. This is why they're so expensive. Can you imagine anything more tragic? The greater the beauty, the more fleeting the life."

Jared was something.

"Maybe Everett took the order."

Jared hooted again.

"Everett's a lox. Let's see, nine days ago was week before last. Stacey was probably here. Stacey and maybe Ilan."

I wrote my name and the new number on one of their cards.

"Would you ask them? Maybe Stacey or Ilan got his last name. It would mean a lot."

The girl blinked at the card as if she didn't know what to do with it and Jared finally turned from his arrangement. He studied me, thoughtful and curious.

"My. I think we have a story here."

Now the peacock woman and the counter girl stared at me, too.

I said, "What?"

Jared smiled sadly.

"So much trouble to send a simple thank-you?"

I glanced away. I tried to look embarrassed and made my voice hoarse.

"Amy says he's just a friend, but I found the card and I don't know what to believe. I just want someone to tell me the truth."

Jared considered me for a moment and picked up the card.

"I'll check with the others."

The counter girl adjusted her glasses. Nervous.

"I don't think Everett would like this, Jared."

"Everett knows nothing."

He sounded bitter.

Jared tucked the card into his pocket and turned to his arrangement.

I said, "Thank you, Jared."

"Everett's a damned fool."

I wasn't the only one with a story.

The burner chirped as I left. I hoped it was the Lerners or Jennifer Li, but it was the phone letting me know I had a message. Laura Freeman returned my call.

"Check your email. The property is owned by a Juan Medillo. The tax records are attached. Am I not amazing? Any questions, just call. Or just call. Donnie hates it when you flirt with me."

Her laughter sounded like chimes and made me feel better.

Amazing.

I was still smiling when I climbed into the Lexus, but when I saw Amy's purchase receipt from the X-Spot my smile went away.

I started the car and drove north to the Valley, wondering why Amy Breslyn bought a nine-millimeter pistol and what she intended to do with it.

16

THE X-SPOT INDOOR PISTOL RANGE was housed in a white block building not far from Bob Hope Airport in Burbank. The street was lined with similar buildings, each fronted by the same small parking lot, but only the X-Spot lot was ringed by a ten-foot chain-link fence topped by concertina wire. More concertina wire circled their roof. Protection from break-ins.

The X-Spot's lot was full, so I parked on the street. The muffled whoomp-wh-whoomp of overlapping gunfire within the building was audible when I cut the engine.

The entrance opened into a lobby with a long glass counter, where pistols for sale or rent were displayed. A soundproof window behind the counter allowed the clerks to keep an eye on the firing lanes behind the wall. A balding man with a hefty gut and a younger man with lean cheeks and a mustache were behind the counter. The mustache was cleaning pistols at a workbench while the heavy man sat at the counter. Both wore pistols clipped to their waists. Robbing a pistol range was probably a bad idea.

The balding man nodded without much interest.

"Howdy. Can I help you?"

I placed Amy's picture and receipt on the counter and showed him my license.

"Elvis Cole. I'm looking into the disappearance of this woman. I'd like to speak with her shooting instructor and whoever wrote up the sale."

The man stared at the receipt in slow motion.

"Been a while since Amy was here. How's she doing?"

"She's missing. I'm hoping you can tell me why she wanted a gun."

He dripped off his stool like cold molasses.

"I'll get Jeff."

He left to get Jeff through a door at the end of the lobby. Whoever Jeff was.

"Amy's missing, huh?"

The mustache was watching me as he swabbed a slide action with powder solvent.

"Seems to be. Do you know her?"

"Weird lady. Hope she didn't get into trouble."

I moved down the counter, closer.

"What kind of trouble would she get into?"

He shrugged.

"She was kinda pathetic. I felt bad for her."

I was about to ask why he felt bad when the balding man returned. Jeff was in his fifties, clean-cut, and wore jeans and a knit shirt with an X-Spot logo on the left breast. His expression was somewhere between concern and sorrow and he immediately offered his hand.

"Jeff Lombardi. Did something happen to Amy?"

"When I find her I'll tell you. Know of a reason something would happen to her?"

"You said she's missing?"

"Six days. Her gun's missing, too."

He glanced at the mustache.

"We haven't seen her in more than two months. Almost three now."

"She bought a pistol here six months ago and learned how to shoot it. Was she afraid of someone?"

The balding man spoke from his stool.

"She was crazy."

I looked at him as a heavy door at the end of the counter opened. The muffled shooting was suddenly louder, then softer again as the door closed. A man and a woman came out, peeling off ear protection.

Lombardi touched my arm.

"Better in my office."

He led me to a paneled room with a desk, a couch, and a coffee table. Autographed photos of Lombardi with actors and other celebrities hung on the walls. Lombardi offered the couch and sat behind his desk.

I said, "What did he mean, crazy? The other guy said she was weird."

Lombardi shifted, uncomfortable.

"You know about her son, Jacob, how he died?"

"I know."

"She never mentioned him at first, but later, if she found out you were in the Gulf, well, the things she asked made people uncomfortable."

I tried to imagine Amy Breslyn haranguing strangers about Jacob and began to feel queasy. Maybe Lombardi was squirming for the same reason.

I said, "Things about Jacob?"

He stared at me awkwardly, then went to the door.

"Hey, Gordon! Gordo! See you a minute, please."

Lombardi returned to his desk as the clerk with the mustache appeared. Lombardi introduced us. Gordon Hershel had pulled two tours in the Middle East driving armored vehicles for the Army.

"Gordo, tell Mr. Cole what Amy asked you."

Gordon shrugged, as if he were half embarrassed.

"IEDs. Roadside bombs. She had all these questions, like how they made'm, and where they got the components, and it just got really weird. I understand about her son and all, but it was weird."

Lombardi nodded.

"Tell him about the other thing."

Gordon looked even more embarrassed.

"What she told me, or what she told Timmy?"

"You."

I said, "Who's Timmy?"

Lombardi said, "A customer. Gordo?"

"She wanted to talk to them."

"Talk to who?"

"Al-Qaeda. Asked if I knew how to reach them. This other time, she asked if I knew any arms dealers. It got really weird."

Lombardi nodded again.

"Thanks, Gordo. Wanna close the door please?"

Gordon Hershel shut the door as he left. Lombardi tapped his desk, and his eyes were pained.

"Here's this sweet little woman, a really nice person, saying she wanted to meet terrorists, and arms dealers, and all this madness.

Asking young vets about Taliban bomb makers and secret message boards, as if they would know. People complained. I felt terrible, what with her son, but I told her it had to stop. She hasn't been back."

He sighed, as if he didn't know what else to say. I didn't know what to say, either. The queasy feeling became a sharp ache.

"Meet for what reason, she thought they'd know about Jacob?"

"I guess. The things that poor woman had in her head, I don't know."

"Do you have an instructor named Charles?"

"No. Never had a Charles. Why?"

"Amy might be involved with a Charles."

He leaned back.

"She didn't seem like the dating type. Then again, she didn't seem like the crazy type, either. Not at the beginning."

I thanked him, and walked to my car.

The sun was bright in the Valley. The sky was clear and the heat was rising.

Amy Breslyn's interest in al-Qaeda, terrorists, arms dealers, and IEDs had left the men at the X-Spot troubled, and left me troubled, too.

The burner chirped, but this time I didn't mind.

Pike said, "They're leaving."

"Both cars?"

"The Ford left ten seconds ago. The Dodge is leaving now."

"On my way. How about you come up to my place later? I need your help with something."

"Sure. What?"

"Things that blow up."

Amy Breslyn already knew how to make explosives. Maybe now she wanted to make bombs.

The Targets

17

Scott James

Scott saw Cowly's D-ride by the Runyon gate as he rounded a curve. He whooped his siren, waved as he turned in, and parked next to a black BMW. The parking area was usually crowded at peak hiking times, but now only a few cars were present.

Detective-III Joyce Cowly was built small but sturdy, with dark hair cut to her shoulders. Cowly owned a dark gray pants suit, a black pants suit, and a navy pants suit, which she only wore on the job. Today was the gray. She called the suits her murder clothes. The expression made Scott smile. He liked that about her.

Scott got out and clipped Maggie's lead, but dropped the leash as Cowly approached.

Maggie bounced forward to say hello, and Cowly cooed like a little girl.

"I'm glad to see you, too, Maggie. You're such a good girl."

Scott said, "Detective."

Cowly answered formally.

"Officer James."

Then Cowly's face split in a goofy grin, and she whooped.

"You STUD! Congratulations!"

She jumped into him, wrapping him tight with her arms and legs. Scott rocked back, laughing, but Maggie wasn't amused. Her ears pricked, and she tried to nose between them.

Scott kneed Maggie aside, and put Cowly down.

"Here's this guy we were chasing, laid out on the couch with a scrambled head, and a stash of rockets and grenades in the next room. There was so much bleach and ammonia in this place. It was crazy."

"A commendation?"

"Yes!"

"We have to celebrate. Dinner. Something nice."

"Absolutely!"

"But until then—"

She took a white paper bag from her purse, opened it, and revealed an enormous frosted muffin.

"We were by Du-par's, so I picked it up. Cinnamon raisin and cream cheese."

"You're too much. It's perfect."

Cowly hooked her arm through his, and gave him a tug.

"Walk and eat. I don't have much time."

Scott unclipped Maggie as they entered the park. Runyon allowed dogs to run free, but Maggie didn't stray. She occasionally fell behind to sniff a passing dog, but when Scott grew too far ahead, she quickly caught up. Separation anxiety.

Cowly said, "Tell me everything. Don't leave anything out."

Scott loved sharing with Cowly, and he loved having something to share. He'd been sidelined so long by his injuries, he felt as if he'd never get back in the game. Now the words flooded out. He told her about the search, the body, and Cole, and how the house reeked of so much ammonia his eyes had burned, and that he'd wanted to watch the bomb techs clear the munitions, but missed it because he was sent to the Boat.

Cowly said, "Who's working it?"

"Carter and Stiles. You know'm?"

Cowly swallowed some muffin.

"Know the names. No, wait—"

She frowned for a moment, thinking.

"I've met Carter a couple of times, but not Stiles."

Talking about Stiles brought back the doubt he'd felt earlier.

"She's good?"

Cowly pushed a piece of muffin into his mouth, and took one for herself.

"Must be. She wouldn't be with Major Crimes if she wasn't."

Major Crimes was a premier LAPD assignment, as was the Robbery-Homicide Division, where Cowly worked with Homicide Special. The word 'Special' signified that the crimes investigated by this unit transcended the scope of divisional detective bureaus, but the word had come to describe the detectives. Cowly had jumped quickly from a uniform to the Detective Bureau, and climbed even faster to Homicide Special. When Scott considered their differences, he wondered what a fast-track detective like Cowly saw in him.

"Do you think I should've gone after him?"

Cowly seemed surprised. She pushed another piece of muffin into his mouth.

"Who?"

"The guy who got away. The suspect."

"You're talking about before you entered the house? When Paul was in back, and you were in front?"

"If I'd gone after him, Maggie probably could've taken him down."

"What about Paul?"

"I know, I'm just saying. We've got a murder suspect running loose, and I might've been able to stop him."

Cowly ate a piece of muffin.

"I get it. The supercop wants to be in two places at once."

Scott rolled his eyes.

"That isn't what I mean."

"Shut up and eat—"

Cowly pushed more muffin into his mouth.

"—and let's examine the facts. You found the fugitive you were chasing, you're last night's hero, and you're getting—"

She cupped her hands to her mouth like a megaphone and shouted.

"—a commendation."

She sighed and ate another piece of muffin.

"Monday-morning quarterbacks are assholes."

Scott laughed, and felt the doubt vanish.

"Thank you."

"You're welcome."

"For all of it."

She bumped him.

"I knew what you meant."

They reached a bench at the end of the ridge and sat to admire the view, but Scott found himself looking at Cowly. He liked her bent nose and the full curve of her lips, but he liked her eyes best. They were bright with intelligence, and crinkled from smiling, but sometimes he saw the shadows left by the terrible things she saw on the job. He touched her cheek.

"This thing we have, I like it."

"I'm liking it, too."

He leaned toward her, and they were still kissing when her phone rang. Cowly checked the number, sat back, and sighed.

"Bud. I have to go."

Scott wanted to stay, and fall asleep on the bench beside her, but he smiled, and followed her back toward the gate without complaint. They were spending more and more time together, at his place or hers, and leaving her or seeing her go had become more and more difficult.

Their conversation drifted between TV shows they enjoyed and plans for the weekend as they walked back along the fire road. A few lethargic hikers passed them, heading into the park, and two speed-walking men blew past on their way out. Only a few cars remained when they reached the parking lot, so Scott didn't bother to clip Maggie's lead. The speed walkers were stretching by the BMW, and an older woman with a nest of frizzy gray hair was lifting an overweight pug from a Volvo.

The pug lady glared at Maggie, and held her dog like a bloated baby with its feet in the air.

"He won't attack my dog, will he?"

"No, ma'am. She won't hurt your dog."

"He's supposed to be leashed when you leave the park. A police officer should follow the rules."

Cowly said, "She's a she."

Scott was turning away when Maggie pricked her ears and raised her nose. She trotted forward, stopped, and tested the air. Scott saw the change immediately, and so did Cowly.

"What's she doing?"

"Smells something. She's trying to source it."

Maggie stared at Scott's car, then abruptly lowered her head and trotted to the black-and-white.

Scott saw nothing out of the ordinary. The two men were talking, but Maggie ignored them. She sniffed along the underside of their K-9 car to the rear bumper, returned to the fender and wheel, and abruptly dropped to her belly. She glanced over her shoulder at Scott as if she'd found something wonderful, then stared under the car.

Cowly frowned.

"I hope it isn't a cat."

"It isn't a cat. Get behind your car, okay?"

A knot formed in Scott's belly, and grew tighter. Maggie was alerting in exactly the same manner she had alerted for Johnson, and as she had in Echo Park.

Joyce didn't move.

"Why behind my car? What's she doing?"

"Please, Joyce."

"No fucking way."

Scott called Maggie back, told her to stay, and went to his car. He squatted to peer underneath and saw nothing. He lowered himself and edged his way under. Rocks cut into his elbows, but then he saw the box and no longer felt the rocks. A box wrapped with silver tape was attached to his gas tank. The box was clean and showed no sign of road dust or grime, as if it had just been placed on his car.

Scott flashed on the man from the Echo Park house and the room filled with explosives. He scrambled to his feet and away from the car.

"Back away, Joyce! Something's on the car."

"What something?"

"I think it's a bomb. MOVE!"

He jerked out his badge and waved it at the men.

"Police! Get behind the gate. Do it, man, MOVE! This isn't a joke!"

Cowly shouted as she pushed the pug lady away.

"I'm calling it in! Wave off those cars! Keep people away!"

Scott ran to Mulholland and waved a car past. Maggie broke from her stay and joined him, anxious and wary. She smelled his adrenaline and took it as her own.

Scott hunkered low and scanned the surrounding area. If the box was a bomb, whoever planted it might be watching and they might have a detonator. Scott clipped Maggie's lead and held her, expecting his car to erupt in a raging inferno. He pictured the man from Echo Park as clear as a snapshot and wished he had shot him. He pictured the flash.

Maggie's fur bristled.

Scott had seen the man, the man had seen him, and now the man wanted him dead.

Scott waved past two more cars, then hunkered low again, and held Maggie close. She growled so deeply, it might have come from his chest.

"That's right, baby. He tried to kill the wrong people."

Four black-and-white units arrived eleven minutes later, followed by three additional units, all rolling Code Three. Thirty-eight minutes after Joyce Cowly called for assistance, the Bomb Squad arrived.

18

Maggie

MAGGIE WAS NOT THINKING of Pete when the bright green ball dropped from the sky ahead of her and bounced away. The flash of green and familiar bounce triggered a rush of scent memories: Pete, the approval Pete lavished on her when she found a special scent, and her joy when Pete threw the green ball to reward her. Maggie instinctively charged after the ball, but she slowed when the scent memories dimmed, and watched the ball roll away. She sniffed, and knew Pete had not touched this ball. She sniffed, and Pete was gone.

A skinny white dog raced to the ball, but Maggie paid no attention. The green ball was no longer her favorite toy.

Maggie returned to Scott's side.

Wag.

Scott was pack. Her favorite reward was baloney.

Scott and the woman were talking. Maggie knew they weren't talking to her because Scott looked at Maggie when he spoke to her, and now Scott and the woman were looking at each other. Maggie did not understand their words, but their tone was warm, and Scott often laughed. Laughter was play. Maggie felt joy when Scott laughed.

Wag wag.

The woman was not pack. Maggie was comfortable with the woman, but Scott was her world.

Maggie was a German shepherd dog. She was bred to protect what was hers, and selected by the Marine Corps based on the strength of her drives. Maggie stayed close to Scott. She watched passing dogs and people for signs of aggression, and checked the air for unusual or threatening scents. She smelled coyotes and deer, and the rabbits that crossed the trail before dawn, and the dogs and people who had walked the trail earlier, and the dead eggs of a lizard at the base of a yucca. She smelled gophers hidden in tunnels on the slope above them, and the fading scent of a dead owl in the canyon below. None of these scents were unusual or held special meaning. This was good. In Maggie's German shepherd world, the familiar meant safety.

Scott safe.

Maggie safe.

Pack safe.

Wag.

Scott touched her head.

"Good girl."

Wag wag wag.

Maggie loved being near him. This close, Scott's scent enveloped her. Maggie did not know she was smelling the millions of skin cells a person sheds with each step and the bacteria that thrived on those cells and the amino acids and oils produced by Scott's skin. She did not know this snowstorm of cells swirled in the air—falling, climbing, drifting, settling—and left a spreading cone of scent like a boat's invisible wake. Maggie knew nothing of skin cells and amino acids, but she knew what she needed to know.

Maggie knew they were returning to the car. She knew this because their walks always followed the same pattern. Ride in the car, get out, walk, return to the car, get in, ride. Now, as they neared the gate, she smelled the two sweating men and the older female with the little pug dog. The men smelled of sweat, but not the threatening scent of adrenaline. The older woman smelled of bitter flowers, and the little pug dog smelled of fecal matter and a growing infection.

Maggie followed Scott around the gate into the parking lot, and that's when she caught a faint scent. The scent tickled a memory, but was too faint to identify, so she lifted her nose, and tasted again.

Sniff sniff sniff.

Each time she sniffed, scent molecules collected on bony plates in her nasal cavity. These molecules collected a few at a time until enough were gathered for Maggie to recognize. This didn't take many. With more than two hundred million scent receptors in her long shepherd's nose, and almost a fourth of her brain devoted to her sense of smell, Maggie could recognize scents so faint they were measured in parts per trillion.

Sniff sniff sniff.

Sniff.

The memories of Pete and the special scents he trained her to find rushed back, exactly as they had the night before, and joy filled her heart. Finding the special scent led to a reward. Love. Approval. Baloney.

Maggie trotted away, working the edges of the scent cone. She sourced the scent to Scott's car, where the air underneath was hot with the special scent. Pete had taught her never to approach or touch these special scents, so she pegged the hottest point, and dropped to her belly. Maggie glanced proudly at Scott, pleased and giddy with anticipation.

"Maggie, out! Out!"

Scott's alpha voice was commanding.

Maggie bounced to her feet and ran to his side.

Scott squeaked approval, stayed her, and went to his car. Maggie sensed something was wrong by the change in his gait. She desperately wanted to follow, but Scott had stayed her. She obeyed, but whimpered anxiously when he crawled under the car.

Maggie saw him tense, and the frantic way he scrambled to his feet, and heard the strain in his voice when he spoke to the woman. Then the woman shouted, and Scott ran to the street. His smell reached her, and was ripe with the thorny scents of danger and fear.

Maggie trembled and quivered.

Scott's fear poured into her.

Danger.

Threat.

Maggie broke from her stay, and ran to him. His thundering heart filled her with fury.

Protect Scott.

Defend.

Scott pulled her close, but his closeness did not comfort her. His fear screamed they were in danger. She bunched and coiled, and tried to pull free to find the threat, but Scott held her close.

Her huge ears swiveled and tipped, seeking their enemy. She sniffed frantically, searching the air, but found only Scott's fear.

His fear was enough.

Scott was hers.

Maggie growled, low and deep in her massive chest, a primal warning to whatever might hear.

This pack was hers.

The fur on her back and shoulders bristled like wire, and her nails raked the asphalt like claws. A danger she couldn't see or smell or hear was coming, but a fire passed down from a hundred thousand past generations prepared her. Maggie knew what she needed to know.

Hunt.

Attack.

Pull the threat down with her fangs, and destroy it.

Maggie didn't need to know anything else.

Nothing else mattered.

19

Scott James

AFTER THE AREA surrounding the gate was cleared, the Bomb Squad's senior bomb technician, Jack Libby, asked Scott to describe the box and its location on Scott's vehicle. Libby was short and dark, with calm eyes and a spiky flattop. Scott and Cowly wanted to watch Libby de-arm the bomb, but were moved to a protected location on the far side of the curve.

Two Criminal Conspiracy Section detectives named Mantz and Nagle were waiting. CCS handled investigations involving explosives and explosive devices for the Major Crimes Division. Mantz identified himself, and asked Scott to join him in the command vehicle.

"My dog has to come."

"Sure. Bring him."

Scott followed until Nagle told Cowly to remain outside.

Scott said, "What the hell? You don't have to separate us."

Joyce said, "It's okay, babe. Go. It's how we do it."

The command vehicle was a motor-home-size bus packed with communication equipment, computers, and video monitors. Mantz steered Scott to a narrow table, and told him to sit. Maggie settled at Scott's feet, filling the aisle like a black-and-tan island.

"Okay, let's assume this box is an explosive device. Why do you think the Echo suspect is involved?"

"I saw his face. I can identify him."

Mantz was a slight man in his forties with wire-frame glasses. He listened to Scott recap the events in Echo Park, and seemed dubious.

"This was what, twelve hours ago? The guy found you, followed you, and hung a bomb on your car in all of twelve hours?"

"I'm K-9. He probably staked out our training site. It doesn't take a genius to hang out and wait."

Mantz took out a notebook.

"This is in Glendale, right?"

"I was there this morning after I left the Boat."

"You think he put it on your car in Glendale?"

"No, *here*. My dog alerted when we got back to the car. If it was on the car in Glendale, she would have alerted *there*."

Scott realized his voice was rising. He was tired, and angry, and told himself to slow down.

"Sorry. I didn't get much sleep."

"No worries."

Mantz studied Maggie. She was lying on her belly with her chin on her paws. Her ears were tipped and her brow was bunched. Listening.

"Bomb dog?"

"Used to be. She still remembers. She alerted to the stuff we found last night."

Mantz scribbled a note, and asked Scott a series of questions about his movements that morning, including the names of anyone who knew where Scott was going, any stops Scott made between the Boat and the park, his routes, and the times of his arrivals and departures. When they finished, Mantz shouted for Nagle, and spit out instructions.

"Where's Carter?"

"Inbound."

"We need the suspect likeness for the door-knocks. Have someone email it. We'll print'm here."

"Did it."

"Ask Cowly if anyone knew she was meeting him up here. Get her times in and out. I'm showing a window of forty minutes."

"She says forty-three minutes, start to stop. She got here first."

Scott said, "Can she come in now please?"

"No. We aren't even close to finished."

Mantz adjusted his glasses, and went on with Nagle.

"Scott didn't see anyone following him. Ask if she remembers a vehicle pulling in behind him, or off the street, or slowing down, or whatever."

"Already asked. She doesn't."

"Check these houses for security cams, here to the east for half a mile. Street views. We see the K-9 car, we'll see who was behind him."

"Got it."

"Ask the hikers and the dog lady if they took any pictures."

"I know. I'm on it."

"How's Jackie doing?"

"Playing with his robot."

"Go."

The door slammed when Nagle left, and Mantz peered at Maggie.

"I heard something about a German shepherd. Was he blown up in Afghanistan?"

Maggie's brow beetled again.

"She. She was shot. Twice. She wasn't blown up."

Mantz leaned closer to study her scars. Maggie gave a low gutter, and Mantz leaned away.

"You need the bathroom? You want some water?"

"I want to finish."

"Describe the box. I know you told Jackie, but describe it to me."

Scott was describing the box when a uniformed lieutenant came in, and introduced himself as the incident commander. The lieutenant asked how Scott was doing, and whether he needed anything. Five minutes after the lieutenant left, a uniformed captain from Holly-wood Station interrupted them, and Scott could tell Mantz was get-ting irritated. They had just returned to work when Kemp and Leland arrived. Scott wasn't expecting them, but was pleased.

Kemp was furious. His face glowed like a boil, and his jaw flexed with anger.

"We'll get the bastard, Scott. This sonofabitch, he's working on borrowed time."

"Thanks, LT. Thanks for coming."

"We're here for the duration. You need anything?"

Mantz offered his own answer.

"He needs to be left alone so we can finish."

Kemp wheeled toward Mantz.

"This man is in my command. I'll pitch a goddamned tent in here, if I want."

Mantz showed his palms, taking himself out of the fight, as Le-land eased forward, taking Kemp's place.

"They say she alerted."

"Like today and last night. If she hadn't—"

Scott shook his head.

"I can put her in my car, if you like. Until you finish up here."

Scott saw Maggie's eyes shift between them.

"She's fine where she is."

Leland managed a smile.

"As it should be."

When Kemp and Leland left, Mantz went to the door.

"Nagle? Nagle, you know how to lock this damned thing?"

Carter and Stiles arrived six minutes later. Stiles entered first, and made with the wide Betty Boop eyes.

"Oh my Lord, this must have been scary, finding a bomb on your car! I would've just died!"

Scott was getting tired of the wide-eyed act.

"My dog found it."

"Well, I guess Mr. Dog earned an extra biscuit tonight, now didn't he?"

Mantz said, "She's a she."

Carter came in holding a phone.

"Get the art? We sent it."

"Nagle. Did you ID the suspect?"

Carter waved his phone at Scott.

"Glory just sent him a mug file. Give me a break."

Mantz took off his glasses.

"I guess that means no."

Carter's phone buzzed. He checked the incoming number, and turned away as he answered. Mantz asked Stiles about Echo Park, so Scott took the opportunity to text Cowly.

I'M STUCK. SORRY.

A few seconds later, Cowly responded.

BUD HERE. GOTTA GO. CALL LATR.

Scott replied.

KISS.

A few seconds later, Cowly answered.

KISS MORE.

Scott was putting away his phone when Jack Libby entered. Carter acknowledged Libby, but stayed on his call. Libby held up a plastic evidence bag and tossed it to Scott. The bag held a metal wafer the size of a postage stamp.

"This is why he didn't wait. Assisted-GPS chip like we have in our phones. It reads your location change. If you'd driven away, we'd be at the morgue."

Scott stared at the little chip.

"This was in the box?"

"That, an initiator, and a quarter pound of plastic explosive."

Libby grinned.

"Blew the sucker apart with a water cannon. Rolled a robot under your car. Blamo. Disrupts the device."

Carter moved closer to examine the chip.

"Same plastic as Echo?"

"Same white-white color, but that's up to the lab. I'll put it together when we get back, and toss it to SID."

Libby would reconstruct the device at the Bomb Squad office, looking for details of design and materials that might match with the techniques of known bomb builders.

Mantz took the bag, and studied the chip.

"A quarter pound isn't much bang."

"It is if you know what you're doing. Whoever built this isn't a wannabe. It's a smart device. Excellent workmanship."

Libby looked at Scott.

"He put it on your gas tank."

Scott flashed on Stephanie Anders, her blood glistening on the street, her red hands reaching, and was trapped in the memory until Libby spoke again.

"A flatbed's coming for your vehicle. We're trucking it in for the criminalists."

Mantz gave back the bag.

"Good work, Jackie. Email the serial number off the chip, and I'll start the trace."

Scott thought about the device as Libby left—the work that had gone into building it, and the risk someone took to put the device on a police car in a public space in broad daylight.

"It would've been easier to shoot me."

Mantz checked his watch, and stood.

"Shooting you didn't occur to him. The person who built this gets off by the power inherent in an explosion, like a pyromaniac setting fires."

Stiles made a big deal out of shivering.

"You are creeping me out."

Mantz stared at her for a moment, and Scott sensed Mantz didn't buy the wide-eyed bit, either.

"So, as of now, we assume the Echo Park suspect or an associate has targeted Officer James?"

Carter and Stiles answered at the same time.

"Yes."

"I'll start the canvass. Maybe we'll get lucky."

Carter waved his phone toward Scott.

"We need him. You get anything, copy me."

Mantz stepped over Maggie to leave, but turned back.

"This person is dangerous. He's organized and capable. Work under the assumption you are not safe."

Scott wasn't sure what to say.

"What am I supposed to do?"

"Stay alive."

Scott touched Maggie's head. She stood, shook herself, and the two of them watched Mantz walk away.

20

CARTER DROPPED into the seat Mantz had been using.

"Bet you're sorry you let this asshole get away last night."

Scott told himself to let it go but a tight knot clenched in his belly.

"Are you getting in my face, Carter?"

Carter raised his hands.

"It was a joke. Hey, I'm the guy trying to find this asshole."

Stiles said, "Brad didn't mean anything."

Maggie shifted and whimpered. Scott realized they had been on the bus for almost two hours, and stood.

"We need a bathroom break."

Carter frowned with irritation.

"Let her wait. We have a couple more questions about last night."

"Brad, between you and this dog, don't hold your breath."

Scott picked up Maggie's lead, and snagged a bottle of water on the way out. He felt better once they were outside, but he was angry at Carter's stupid comment, and also embarrassed.

Mulholland had become an LAPD parking lot behind the CV, with black-and-white vehicles and unmarked sedans extending around the curve. A circle of command officers and detectives had gathered by the CV. Scott saw Kemp and Mantz, and realized most of the officers were focused on a tall uniformed woman in her fifties. She was a deputy chief. Targeting a police officer was an aggressive move, and almost never occurred. Even stone-cold gang killers knew better than to green-light a cop, so the department had rolled out in force.

Scott led Maggie to a gnarled oak overlooking the Valley and thought about what Mantz told him. *This person is dangerous.*

When Maggie finished her business, Scott poured water into his hand, letting her slurp from his palm. Maggie drank until she didn't want more, and Scott finished the bottle.

"James!"

Carter. Carter and Stiles had followed him out. Carter called again as they approached.

"I apologize, okay? Get past it. Let's catch this guy."

Scott waited until they arrived.

"What, Carter? Ask."

"Last night, when you saw Cole—"

Scott interrupted, cutting him off.

"What's the obsession with Cole? Talk to the people who live on that street. Maybe they know what happened. And what about Carlos Etana? His asshole buddies might know."

Carter showed his palms, trying to make peace.

"We're doing those things."

Carter's phone buzzed. He checked the incoming number and glanced at Stiles.

"It's them."

Carter answered as he turned away, and went to the edge of the slope.

Stiles picked up where Carter left off.

"We're doing those things, Scott. Detectives are talking to the neighbors right now. We have people naming Etana's family and associates, and we'll talk to them."

"I told you what happened with Cole, and so did Alvin. He was trying to help. He seemed like a good guy."

"Have you known him for long?"

"Have you ever been bitten by a German shepherd?"

Stiles glanced at Maggie.

Scott said, "Don't be cute with me, I won't be cute with you. Deal?"

Stiles made a slow nod.

"Cole's been arrested four times, including felony pops for burglary and interfering with an investigation. Doesn't sound like such a good guy now, does he?"

Scott found this sobering, but something didn't add up. The State of California didn't license convicted felons.

"Wait. I thought he was a PI."

"The burg was dropped. The interference cost his ticket on a plea deal, but the plea was later reversed. You know the name Frank Garcia?"

"No."

"Monsterito tortillas and chips?"

"Yeah, sure. I love 'm."

Carter finished his call and rejoined them with his phone clenched in his fist. Scott thought he looked furious.

"Frank Garcia was a dipshit banger who made a billion dollars."

Carter and Stiles looked at each other, something in Carter's eyes giving her bad news about the call. Stiles took in the news, and calmly continued her explanation.

"Cole is a known associate of Mr. Garcia, and Mr. Garcia has known gang ties."

"Etana's gang?"

Carter took over again.

"We're checking, but if Cole has dealings with one gangster, why not two? Maybe he was there to pick up Etana. Maybe Cole killed him, and got trapped by the blockade before he could leave."

Stiles smiled as if she didn't believe this for a second, but knew better than to dismiss it.

"Point being, we're not wasting your time or ours when we ask about Mr. Cole. Okay?"

Scott didn't argue, but this business about Cole seemed like a stretch.

Stiles said, "Okay, this is important, so let me refresh. You ran to the front of the house hoping to contain the suspect. Reaching the front, you saw the suspect cross the street four or five houses to your right. This was when Mr. Cole drew your attention to the left."

"Yeah. That's correct."

"How far away was Cole when you saw him?"

"Couple of houses. Not far. I ordered him to stop. He stopped. Like I told you last night."

"How did Mr. Cole attract your attention?"

"He waved his arms. He was shouting. He shouted a man ran from the house, and pointed down the street."

"Did you look to see what he was pointing at?"

"I had my gun on Cole. I didn't look anywhere else until Alvin waved me off."

Carter jiggled his phone. Scott couldn't tell if he was excited or nervous.

"What if Cole wasn't trying to catch the suspect? Maybe he was distracting you, or warning the suspect about you."

"It wasn't like that. He told Alvin he saw the guy, way before he reached me."

"Same difference. He created a distraction to help the suspect escape."

A phone buzzed, but this time it belonged to Stiles. She glanced at the message, and nodded to Carter.

"Federales. It's a go."

"Tell'm we're on our way. Meet me at the car."

Carter walked quickly to the brass circle. He huddled with Mantz and the deputy chief, and Kemp joined their group.

Stiles said, "Look through the photos. The hair and skin tone will vary, but we'll tweak the parameters. Tomorrow or the next day, I want you to come in."

"You weren't there, Stiles. Cole wasn't trying to distract me."

Kemp left the group, and came toward them. Carter pointed at Stiles, pointed at the line of parked cars, and hurried toward the cars.

Stiles made a small smile, not one of her oversized, flashy smiles. This smile felt real.

"Mr. Cole knows more than he's telling. So do me the courtesy. Think about what he did last night in this new context. We'll talk again."

Stiles hurried after Carter, and passed Kemp as he arrived.

"Sergeant Leland is getting his car. He'll transport you and Maggie home."

"Thanks, LT. I'll be in as soon as I shower."

"Not today. Stay home. You're off the roster until this is resolved."

Scott hoped he misunderstood.

"Home as in I get today off, or home until further notice?"

"Further notice. And PIO canceled the interview we discussed. They don't think it's wise to put you on TV."

"I just got back. I don't want to be off the roster."

"This is serious, Scott. We'll have a patrol car at your house around the clock."

"I don't want guards. What could be safer than being on the job surrounded by policemen?"

"This comes from the top. You're home until further notice."

Kemp returned to the brass circle. Scott led Maggie along the line of cars to find Leland. He was angry, and frustrated, and wondered what Cole knew.

Mr. Cole knows more than he's telling.

Leland's K-9 car appeared, and Leland gestured for Scott to get in. Scott opened the back door for Maggie, but she wouldn't jump into Leland's car.

"Get in. C'mon, Maggie. In."

Scott finally lifted her. He climbed into the passenger seat, and Leland immediately pulled away. His three-fingered hand was draped on the wheel.

"I'm off the roster."

"So I was told."

Leland drove the oldest and rattiest of the K-9 vehicles. An ancient Crown Vic with almost a million miles, but it was immaculate.

"This is bullshit."

Leland didn't respond. The crackle of the radio was soft noise. They drove without speaking for almost fifteen minutes before Leland broke the silence.

"You and Miss Maggie are welcome to stay with me."

Scott couldn't bring himself to look at the man.

"Thank you, Sergeant, but no. We have a crate. We're not going to leave."

This was the last time they spoke until Scott was home.

21

In Scott's nightmare, the man in the sport coat stepped from the house as a helicopter thrummed overhead, so crazy low the trees shivered and whipped. Blood and brain spattered the man's face, and he held out the box from beneath Scott's car in the palm of his hand.

He said, "Boom."

Scott turned to escape, and found himself on a downtown street, facing Stephanie's killer, a large, masked man clad in head-to-toe black. The man raised an AK-47 and said, "You're next."

The muzzle exploded with a bright yellow flash, and Scott lurched awake, diving out of the line of fire to find himself on the couch. He woke the same way each time. Damp with cold sweat, trembling.

Maggie's big face was only inches away, her ears folded and eyes sad. Just as he went to her when she had a nightmare, she came to him.

"Sorry, baby girl. This one's on me."

Maggie circled away, sniffed a good spot, and lowered herself.

Scott checked the time. He had fallen asleep after dinner, and now it was only a few minutes after nine. Scott had refused Cowly's offer to let them stay at her place, and now he was doubly glad. She knew about his nightmares, but hadn't yet seen him wake up as a thrashing, sweat-soaked mess. The thought of it embarrassed him.

Scott got up and went into the bathroom. Maggie shoved to her feet and followed.

He peeled off the T-shirt and washed his face and neck. He still felt slimy, so he stripped and took a shower. Maggie was in the doorway when he got out, waiting.

His medicine chest was lined with a row of brown bottles. Antidepressants. Anti-anxiety meds. Painkillers and anti-inflammatories. Lined up and waiting. He opened the mirror, looked at the row, then closed the mirror, and looked down at Maggie.

"We're in it together, Maggie Marine. If you're not taking, I'm not taking."

Maggie's tail thumped the floor when it wagged.

Thump thump thump.

Scott talked to his dog. This used to bother him until he learned the other handlers all talked to their dogs. Leland told him, so long as Maggie doesn't talk back, you're fine.

"How about a walk?"

Maggie scrambled to her feet and raced to the door. She didn't talk, but she knew the word 'walk.'

Scott dressed, and found Maggie waiting in the living room. Scott rented a one-bedroom, one-bath guest house from an elderly woman named MaryTru Earle near the Studio City Park. It was small, private, and tucked behind a wooden gate in Mrs. Earle's backyard. Scott liked the quiet. Mrs. Earle liked having a black-and-white police car parked in her front yard. She gave him a break on the rent.

Scott said, "Treat."

Maggie scrambled into the kitchen, and sat at rigid attention. She knew the word 'treat,' too.

Scott took a baloney log from the fridge, carved two hefty chunks, and tossed the pieces to her one at a time. She snapped them out of the air.

"If they made baseballs out of baloney, you could play for the Dodgers. Let's hit it."

He saw his laptop on the dining table, and remembered he still needed to answer Stiles's email. He had looked at the photo file she sent when he got home. She had sent almost two hundred mug shots, and most looked nothing like the man in the sport coat. Scott had grown angry as he worked his way through the pictures, feeling as if Stiles had ignored his description.

Scott opened the laptop and tapped out a smart-ass reply, then thought better of it and simply told her none of these were the man. He hit Send as Maggie pawed at the door.

"Hang on, I'm coming. I wanna get outta here, too."

Scott grabbed two bottles of water from the fridge, clipped Maggie, and walked her past Mrs. Earle's house to the patrol car parked on the street. Henders and Martinez were from Devonshire Station in the northwest part of the Valley. Scott felt guilty they were stuck playing babysitter and vaguely ashamed he was the baby.

"Thought you guys might like some water."

Henders took the bottles and passed one to Martinez.

"Thanks, man. Appreciate it."

"This wasn't my idea. I'm sorry you're stuck out here."

Martinez leaned forward to see past Henders.

"Dude, please. You doin' okay?"

"We're taking a walk. You need the facilities, the door's unlocked."

Martinez checked the time.

"Next car comes at twenty-two hundred."

Cars were being posted for two-hour shifts with the duty being shared between the North Hollywood, Van Nuys, Foothill, and Devonshire Police Areas. The next car would relieve Martinez and Henders in thirty minutes. They were probably bored silly and couldn't wait to get gone.

"No problem. We won't be long."

Scott turned toward the park at the end of his street, and let Maggie set the pace. He wanted to call Cowly, but knew he would end up complaining, and didn't want to come off as a whiner.

He thought about Mantz.

Work under the assumption you are not safe. This person is dangerous.

Great.

Someone had tried to kill him. Someone built an explosive device with the intent to incinerate him.

Scott tried to get his head around it but couldn't. He had spent seven years as a patrol officer. Drunks, assholes, and people with chemical brains had taken swings at him, thrown bricks and bottles at him, and tried to brain him with baseball bats. He had been shot and almost died two separate times, but the violence had been spontaneous, random, or grew from the moment. This was different. A certifiable killer had planned, stalked, and attempted to murder him.

This person is dangerous.

Scott turned to gaze at the patrol car. They were halfway to the park, and the car seemed far away. Scott suddenly felt vulnerable and angry. This would be his life until the man in the sport coat was caught.

"What are we supposed to do, sit around like a couple of ducks?"

Maggie wagged her tail, and found something more interesting in a bush.

Carter and Stiles were supposed to be top cops, but their theories about Cole left him doubtful.

Cole knows more than he's telling.

The business about Cole having a record bothered him, but Cole had seemed okay when they spoke, and even last night on the street.

Scott followed Maggie toward the park. He tried to reframe Cole the way Stiles had asked, as if Cole created a distraction so the sport coat man could escape. It felt like a stretch. Cole had seemed for real, but maybe he knew more than he was telling.

Scott clicked his tongue. Maggie pricked her ears, and looked at him.

"We're not going to wait for the sonofabitch to kill us."

Maggie squared herself, ready for his command.

Scott glanced at the patrol car again, and made up his mind.

Scott was off the duty roster, but he wasn't out of the hunt.

22

Elvis Cole

THE FREEWAY MOVED like a dying pulse. The air tasted of burning oil as I worked my way out of the Valley, or maybe I imagined these things because I didn't like what I learned about Amy Breslyn.

Amy might be crazy and weird, but she was a Ph.D. engineer who knew how to solve problems. If the people at the X-Spot were unwilling or unable to answer her questions, she would've found others to ask, and maybe Thomas Lerner had helped.

The more I considered it, the more it made sense. Writers were researchers. If Amy asked Lerner for help, maybe Lerner found people who knew what Amy wanted to know. Lerner had been Jacob's best friend. Amy and Lerner remained close after Jacob's death. Lerner once lived in the Echo Park house. The roads came back to Lerner. Meryl Lawrence believed Lerner might know who Amy was seeing, and maybe Thomas Lerner was the person who introduced them.

Pike called as I reached the Sepulveda Pass.

"They went to your house."

"Who?"

"Blue Dodge. There's a black-and-white, what looks like a D-ride, two white sedans, and the Dodge."

Carter was hitting back fast.

"Are they in my house?"

"Yes. I count five, but there could be more. Keep the loaner as long as you want."

"No need. I'll pick up my car, and come home. Where are you?"

"Top of the ridge, across from your house."

"Stay put."

The climb up Kenter took forever. I parked the Lexus behind my car, left the key on the tire, and drove home to meet the policemen.

Home was a redwood A-frame perched on a narrow road off Woodrow Wilson Drive near the top of Laurel Canyon. I stashed the burner, the yearbooks, and Amy's file behind a century plant off Woodrow. My street was too narrow for the line of police vehicles parked outside my house. The D-ride, the blue Dodge, and the black-and-white were tattered and dinged, but the two white sedans were sparkly-new. Federal money. They bore Department of Homeland Security emblems.

A man and a woman sat in one of the white sedans, blocking my carport.

I parked behind them, and went to the driver's window. The male agent.

"You're blocking my carport."

They were in their mid-thirties, fit, and wore sunglasses like the Men in Black.

"Inside."

"How about you move the car so I can park?"

The woman peered over the top of her shades.

"Go inside, Mr. Cole. Don't be boring."

Carter, Stiles, and a man in a dark blue suit were in the living room. Carter was going through the hutch by the dining table. Glory Stiles and the blue suit sat at the table. Two uniformed officers were outside on my deck with the blond from the Dodge. One of the uni's was pointing at something down in the canyon, and the other was bent over the rail to see. The blond leaned with his back to the rail, staring at me.

I said, "If my lock is broken, I'm suing the city."

Carter turned from the hutch.

"Ditching my guys was stupid."

"Did I ditch someone? Wait, Carter, are you following me?"

Stiles was all business, and ignored the suit.

"Where did you go, Mr. Cole?"

"When?"

"You know when."

"Today? I slept in, went to my office, grabbed a burrito, and went for a hike. I came home, and now I want a shower and something to eat. How about you get the hell out of my house?"

Carter snorted.

"You didn't hike for four hours. Where did you go?"

"Kenter to Mandeville, then up along Sullivan to the old missile base on Mulholland. They have a park up there with a bathroom and fountains. I took a break, then circled back along Mulholland to Kenter again. It's almost twelve miles, Carter. Let's see how fast you make the loop."

Stiles looked embarrassed. Carter had nothing, and all of us knew it.

The suit finally stood and came around the table. He was in his late forties, with webs around his eyes and a deep tan.

"Russ Mitchell. I'm a Special Agent with Homeland Security."

He gave me plenty of time to read his credentials. Russell D. Mitchell. Department of Homeland Security. Investigations.

"Nice picture. Makes you look tough."

He shrugged as he folded the creds.

"Not tough. I'm concerned. You were seen at a home containing stolen military munitions."

"I saw your badge. I didn't see a warrant."

He returned to his seat, and laced his fingers across his knee. Casual.

"I'm not required to show it. I pulled a no-knock federal warrant earlier this afternoon. As for how we got in, we had the legal authority to use any means necessary, up to and including forcible entry. I didn't see the point. Detective Stiles offered to pick the locks."

I glanced at Stiles.

"A woman of many talents."

Mitchell loosened his tie, telling me he was prepared to stay.

"Did you know military munitions were in the house?"

"No. I know now, but not then."

"If I dig deep enough—and I will—will I find a connection between you and Carlos Etana, or associates of Etana?"

"No. Dig all you like."

"Do you know who killed him?"

"No."

"Did you kill him?"

"No."

"Will you agree to take a polygraph?"

"Only on the advice of my lawyer. Those things are wrong all the time. Unreliable."

Mitchell made a soft smile.

"Don't blame you. We have to take them as part of the job. All the times I've been wired up, I still get nervous."

Mitchell was being my pal. Good guy, bad guy. He settled back.

"Why were you in Echo Park?"

I told him exactly what I told Carter and Stiles. I told him why I was there, and what I saw, and who I spoke with, and what I did. The true answers didn't change, and neither did the lies.

Mitchell nodded when I finished.

"So you saw only the one individual exit the home."

"The man I chased. Yes, sir."

"You didn't see anyone else, male or female, enter or leave?"

"No."

Mitchell studied me for a moment, then went to the glass doors that led to my deck. The uniforms and the blond guy thought he wanted them, but he didn't.

"I like it up here. Quiet. Woodsy. Woodsy is good."

He turned back to Carter.

"We're done."

Carter crossed his arms like he didn't like being done. Like he wanted to rake me over the coals for eight or nine more hours.

"He's full of it. He knows something."

Mitchell tightened his tie, smoothed his sleeves, and ignored him.

"You know what we found in the house?"

"I know what I heard on the news."

"The grenade cartridges were stolen from Camp Pendleton, likely by a civilian employee. The RPGs were manufactured in Czechoslovakia twenty-two years ago. They were probably smuggled into the country by a collector, and later stolen. Being illegal, collectors won't report the theft, so weapons like this end up wherever. These found their way to Echo Park—the RPGs, the grenades, and two pounds of plastic explosive in a Tupperware. That kills me, a Tupperware."

Mitchell stared, and seemed to be watching me.

"You know what these things can do. I've read your record. Army Ranger. Combat. Damned fine combat record, by the way."

"They made me sound better than I was."

Carter made an angry flip with his hand.

"Big fucking deal. This guy and his nutcase partner have dropped bodies all over town. Turds like Cole don't give a shit."

I didn't say anything. I could have said plenty, but didn't.

Mitchell still ignored him. He searched my eyes like he was trying to see into my head.

"These are weapons of war. Weapons someone could use to bring down an airliner, or blow up a building filled with innocent people. Why do you think they were in that house?"

"I don't know."

"I don't, either. But I'm going to find out."

Mitchell walked out, and didn't look back.

Stiles called the uniforms in from the deck and followed them out after Mitchell. The blond guy tipped his head as he passed.

"Nice play."

He meant it, but I didn't react.

Carter stayed the longest. He stood in my living room as if all his suspicions had been confirmed.

"You're hiding something. I can smell it on you like rotten meat. You're hiding something."

Carter was a good cop. I didn't like him, but he wanted to find whoever put the munitions in Thomas Lerner's house for all the right reasons. I wanted him to find them, too.

"Carter, I'd help if I could. If I can, I will."

"Save it. You're a suspect. I'm on you like a suspect. If I find evidence that ties you to that house, or Etana, or those fucking explosives, I'm going to arrest you like a suspect."

He walked out, and left the door open.

I didn't move. Five engines started. Five cars drove away. I waited to make sure they were gone, and waited some more.

After a while, I took my car to pick up the burner and books, drove home, and let myself in through the kitchen.

Joe Pike stood by the sink, as still as a statue, waiting.

I said, "I have a problem."

23

A BLACK CAT pushed through the cat door. His fine flat head was striped with scars, his eyes were angry yellow coals, and his ears were tattered from too many fights. One ear was cocked sideways from the time someone shot him. He circled Pike's legs, and flopped on his side. Purring. Pike picked him up and held him, the cat dripping off his arm as limp as liquid fur. Anyone else would lose a hand.

Pike stood six-one and weighed one ninety-five, all ropy muscles and crimson arrows inked on his delts. He wore a sleeveless gray sweatshirt, sun-faded jeans, and running shoes. Dark glasses masked his eyes.

No fashion sense.

I told him about Amy and Jacob Breslyn, and Echo Park, and why the police and Special Agent Mitchell were on me. Pike was so still he might have been sleeping, even when I described the stories I'd heard in the X-Spot and the munitions that were found in the Echo Park house. When I finished, Pike's head tipped to the side. Not much. Just a hair.

"Why is Ms. Breslyn mixed up with people like this?"

"Jacob."

We went to my computer, where I Googled news accounts about Jacob and the Nigerian bombing. Pages of links appeared. Pike read over my shoulder. The stories repeated, and drew the same terrible portrait: Fourteen people enjoying dinner and drinks at an outdoor café were murdered by an Islamist fanatic with a bomb strapped to her body. Another thirty-two people were wounded. Authorities believed a fringe al-Qaeda affiliate in northwest Africa was responsible, though no group or individual had claimed responsibility. Each story ended the same way. The investigation was continuing.

I said, "Amy printed hundreds of articles like these. Maybe thousands. She has files filled with correspondence she's had with the State Department. No one has answered her questions."

"She wants to know who killed her son."

"That's what I'm thinking. The government hasn't been able to tell her, so maybe she decided to find out for herself."

Pike's head tipped again.

"She'd need access to people who move in those circles, and access is guarded."

I told him about the missing four hundred sixty thousand dollars and Amy Breslyn's specialized skill set.

"She has money to spend, and a calling card not many can offer. She's a Ph.D. chemical engineer, and she makes explosives for the United States government."

Pike said, "Oh."

"Uh-huh. If you're looking to contact people like this, you don't put an ad on Craigslist. She would've put out the word and word always spreads."

Pike stroked the cat.

"There are people who listen for the word."

"Who?"

Pike squatted, and poured the cat from his arms. The cat hissed, spit, and raced through the cat door. Clack-clack.

"Jon Stone. Jon knows people who listen."

Jon Stone was more Joe's friend than mine, though 'friend' probably wasn't the right word. Jon was a private military contractor, which meant he was a mercenary. He was also a Princeton graduate and a former Delta Force operator. His primary client was the Department of Defense. Same boss, different pay grade.

Pike stood.

"I'll ask him."

Pike slipped out, and I went back to my computer.

I opened Laura's email, and studied the attachments she sent about Juan Medillo and the Echo Park house.

Juan Adolfo Medillo, a resident of Los Angeles, had owned the Echo Park house for the past seven years, having taken possession from a Walter Jacobi, a resident of Stockton. The Tax Board records showed a Boyle Heights address for Medillo the year title was transferred. The property tax was up to date, with the most recent payment having been made three months earlier.

I did a quick Internet search to see if Medillo still lived at the Boyle Heights address, only the link that appeared wasn't the link I expected to find.

JUAN ADOLFO MEDILLO—HOLY REMEMBRANCE

It was an obituary.

Juan Adolfo Medillo, beloved brother and son, was tragically murdered yesterday at the California State Prison, Solano, where he was incarcerated. His heart was pure and his soul was good. Preceded in death by his beloved mother, Mildred, and survived by his loving sisters, Nola and Marisol, and his father, Roberto. The family requests prayers for Juan's eternal soul.

I read the date of his death, checked the tax records, and leaned back.

I said, "Wow."

Murdered.

Juan Medillo acquired the house while he was in prison, and he was murdered not long after. He'd been dead for seven years, yet the tax record showed that he had paid the tax on his home only three months ago.

Survived by his loving sisters, Nola and Marisol, and his father, Roberto.

During the seven years since Medillo took title, the property taxes were paid, the house was maintained, and renters like Thomas Lerner had lived there. Only Juan Medillo was dead. I wondered if Medillo's father or sisters had been Lerner's landlord, and if they knew how to reach him.

It was late. I was tired and hungry, but I called a reporter named Eddie Ditko. Eddie had walked the crime beat for every dead paper in Los Angeles. He was old and sour, but he still reported for Internet outlets.

First words out of his mouth, "Did I tell ya about my tumor?"

He coughed into the phone.

"You doing anything with the murder in Echo Park?"

He hacked up a big one and spit.

"I couldn't give two loose shits about a banger with scrambled brains. I want the bombs, but those pricks at the Boat are keeping it tight. Why?"

"The house where they found the bombs is owned by a Juan Adolfo Medillo."

"Everybody knows that."

"Medillo was murdered up at Solano seven years ago."

"The prison?"

"He was inside when he took title. How many people buy a house while they're in prison?"

"This is kinda interesting. I could maybe do something with this."

"Call Solano. What happened up there might be connected to what happened down here."

"I'm seein' potential."

"The Boat knows what I know. Move fast before the door closes."

"I do everything fast. Old as I am, I could drop dead takin' a shit."

"Thanks, Eddie."

I lowered the phone and stared at the obituary. The house had a criminal past to go with its criminal present. It was like finding another piece for a puzzle, only I didn't know if the pieces were part of the same puzzle.

Dinner was leftover chicken and hummus on pita bread. The chicken was rich with cilantro and lime and pepper and smoke from my grill. I took the food and a beer outside and sat on the edge of my deck, wondering if someone was watching.

The cat sat beside me. I tore bits of the chicken and let him lick them from my fingers. I poured a small puddle of beer and watched him drink. We ate together and watched the sky deepen from blue to purple to black.

Amy Breslyn might be watching the same sky, but I doubted it.

The Amy described by Meryl Lawrence and her housekeeper was much different from the Amy described by the men at the X-Spot. Almost as if there had been a secret Amy, one hidden within the other, a secret Amy doing secret things, a world apart from the other.

"What are you doing, Amy?"

The cat bumped me with his head.

We went inside when we finished. I stretched out on the couch and closed my eyes. After a while I slept and found myself alone in a dark jungle half a world away. Sparse moonlight penetrated the triple-canopy growth overhead, casting a glow too faint to light the trail I followed. The heat was brutal, sweat soaked my clothes, and clouds of insects relished my blood.

Something large and unseen moved in the darkness, just out of view, a terrible beast that crept along the trails as I crept, sharing my world.

Somewhere else in my dark dream, I knew Amy Breslyn was feeling her way along a similar trail, calling for Jacob. She looked as she did in her picture—a sad, round woman with uncertain eyes. She was alone and afraid, but the secret Amy within her did not let her stop. She moved through the darkness, calling for Jacob, lost in a nightmare she never imagined in a world not her own.

But I was not Amy Breslyn and this world was mine. I asked to be there. I volunteered, and fierce men in black shirts trained me to thrive.

Something dark slipped through the shadows, just out of view, enormous and hungry, seeking Amy Breslyn as it also sought me.

I did not fear it.

I wanted to find it.

I whispered quietly, so quietly only Amy and I could hear.

"I'm coming."

I pushed through the night, trying to find her, trying to stop the monster.

24

Jon Stone

JON STONE WAS HOME. Second night back after eighteen abroad, most of them spent on the Anatolian Plateau north of the Syrian border. Except for the nights he trucked south. Home was above the Sunset Strip, a sleek contemporary offering privacy, steel and black finishes, and an enormous Italian platform bed that cost as much as a Porsche. Sprawled naked on the vast plain of the bed, Jon roused. The night air kissed his chest with a pleasant chill. Nothing like the Plateau.

A low voice in the dark woke him.

"Jon."

Jon Stone did not move nor fully open his eyes. A southern moon filled his bedroom with blue shadows, but the person who spoke was invisible. Jon wondered if he was dreaming.

"Your eyes are open, Jon. It's me."

Not dreaming. Pike.

Jon still couldn't see him.

"Don't wake them. Come out."

Deep purple moved through the blue as Pike left. Pike was creepy good at this stuff, but Pike had taken a serious risk by entering Jon's home. A cocked-and-locked Kimber .45 was only inches away, not that it had done Jon any good.

Embarrassing.

Jon wondered if Pike needed money. If Pike needed money, Jon could make money. And Jon loved making money.

The woman on the far side of the bed snored. The woman beside him stirred. Her voice was cloudy with three-hundred-dollar Scotch.

"Qui est-il?"

"Rendors-toi."

Backpacking French hippie chicks Jon met when he came through Customs.

The girl made a hazy smile as her eyes closed.

"Il est soldat comme toi?"

"Personne n'est comme moi, chérie. Dors."

The girl asking if Pike was a soldier like Jon, Jon telling her to go back to sleep. This was the French girl, being a smart-ass.

Point of fact, the French chicks didn't believe he was a soldier. Jon never told people what he did for a living, but here they were, Jon and these girls, queued up with three hundred people, inch-worming their way through Customs at LAX. Jon told them he was a mercenary as a goof, wanting to see what they'd say. They giggled and called him a liar, Jon being a trim guy in his thirties with spiky blond hair and a stud in his ear. They asked what he really did, the one girl guessing he played in a band, the other insisting he worked in the movies, the two girls flirting him up. Jon flashed his surfer's grin, told them he was a spy, which led to more giggles, a soldier of fortune, a professional warrior, a scholar, a historian and assassin, the one girl finally touching his arm, and that was it, baby, over and out. Welcome home, Jon.

Jon Stone spoke thirteen languages and was fluent in six, French being one. He spoke it so well the girls thought he was a native Parisian pretending to be an American. This ability to blend with the natives was a valuable tool when Jon plied his trade.

Jon eased from the bed.

Floor-to-ceiling sliding glass doors lined the back of his house, ten-foot-tall, custom-designed monsters so Jon could Zen on the view. Golden lights glittered to the horizon, ruby flashes marked ghetto-bird prowlers, jets descending toward LAX were strung like pearls across a tuxedo black sky. The doors were heavy as trucks, but silent as silk when they slid open. Jon stepped out and went to the pool.

Pike was a silhouette cutout, backlit by the city as Jon swaggered close.

"What do you think of the next Mrs. Stone?"

"Which one?"

"Doesn't matter. They all end up the same."

Jon had been married six times. Six was six more than enough.

"What the fuck are you doing in my house? I could've shot your ass."

"Is someone in Los Angeles selling military munitions?"

Talk about non sequitur.

Jon glanced at his bedroom, irritated.

"Waitaminute. I'm standing here naked, it's three in the morning, and I would know this why?"

"The people you work for listen."

"I'm home two days, bro. What are you talking about?"

"Stolen ordnance in Echo Park. RPGs and forty-millimeter grenades. Cole's trying to find a woman. He thinks she's with the dealer."

Now Jon was pissed. After thirteen years in the Army, the last six with Delta, Jon Stone had jumped the shark to become a private military contractor. He sold his services and the services of others to various clients, one said other being this very Joe Pike, who, by the way, commanded top dollar, which meant a top commission if Pike let Jon set a contract, which he wouldn't, because Pike wasted his time with Elvis Cole, a low-rent peeper without two twenties to wipe his butt.

"What the hell, Pike? I don't care about Cole and his problems. Tell me you didn't pull me away from those women without serious cash on the table."

"If the woman's with him, he probably sells to al-Qaeda."

Stopped Jon cold. Jon Stone's primary client was the United States of America, with most of his work being directed against various terrorist factions and the governments, corporations, and individuals who supported them. Off the books, and deep in the black. When Jon Stone told the French chicks he was a professional warrior, he wasn't lying.

Jon glanced at his bedroom again. Nothing moved within the black rectangle framed by the doors.

"Al-Qaeda."

Pike nodded.

"Listen, so you know, just because some idiot sells this crap doesn't mean it's going to terrorists. All-American morons turn grenades into paperweights, and RPGs into lamps."

"The woman doesn't care about morons. She's been trying to contact an FTO."

FTO. Foreign terrorist organization.

Jon was totally disgusted.

"This is why I hate you wasting your time with Cole, bullshit like this. What are we talking about here, a crazy person, or some kind of anti-American lunatic?"

"They killed her son."

Jon Stone studied his friend. Pike's face was an empty mask, unknown and unknowable. The reflection of the city in his dark glasses was the only sign of life.

Pike said, "Suicide bomb in Nigeria. No suspects or arrests. She wants answers, Jon. I guess she figures she has to go to the source."

"Terrorists."

"Or someone with access and connections."

"In Los Angeles?"

"Echo Park."

Jon went to the edge of the deck. He watched the helicopters prowl, and the big jets slide down the night.

"Here."

Pike said nothing.

"Dude, listen, Homeland Security should be on this."

"They're on it. FBI and LAPD, on it. Elvis and I, on it."

Jon sighed.

"And you want me on it, too."

"The people you work for listen. If someone here was talking, they might know who."

"I'm on it."

After Pike left, Jon returned to his bedroom but not to his bed. Phones were all over the house, but Jon's private cell was in his pants. The French girl woke while he was digging through his clothes at the foot of the bed. She rolled over, sleepy and sexy, stretching to offer her body.

"Ton ami, il va se retrouver avec nous?"

"Vas á dormir."

"Mon guerrier."

"Tais-toi."

The girl asking if Pike was going to join them, Jon telling her to go back to sleep. The girl thinking she was funny, calling him her warrior, Jon telling her to shut up.

Idiot.

Jon found the phone and took it outside. This particular phone, the phone Jon used for business, scrambled its signal into garbage only a phone with a similar chip could unscramble.

Deep in the black, the people Jon worked for did more than listen. They collected. Phone calls, email, text messages, video feeds, the sum total digital flow of everything pouring through the Internet was collected and stored. Supercomputers built of bubbles and light, running algorithms written by smart nerdy geeks, as deadly in their way as Joe Pike and Jon Stone, analyzed all of it, searching for patterns and keywords. Little escaped their attention.

Jon made the call from the edge of his deck. A voice with a special phone answered. A little while after, Jon phoned for a limo, woke the two French chicks, and told them to leave.

He was on it.

25

Mr. Rollins

MR. ROLLINS owned a great house in Encino, up in the hills with a killer view of the Valley. Not under his true name or Rollins, natch, but he owned it free and clear along with a condo in Manhattan Beach, a West Hollywood bungalow, a loft downtown in the Arts District, and a 1923 Spanish classic beneath the Hollywood Sign. The Encino home was his favorite. Big pool in the backyard, outdoor kitchen. Mr. Rollins liked to sit by the pool at night, smoke weed, and watch losers fighting their way home on the 405, nothing but red to wherever workaday assholes lived.

That night, Mr. Rollins was on the chaise lounge, smoking, watching assholes, feeling a little better about losing the Echo Park house, when Eli called and ruined his evening.

The clown was alive, and the police had recovered the package.

"Eli, wait. Stop talking. Can your device hurt us?"

"The components will lead nowhere. No one saw us place it. This I can swear to you."

Bullshit. A fingerprint, a part number, or DNA on the device could lead to Eli, or someone in Eli's crew.

Violent fantasies crept into his thoughts. Mr. Rollins saw himself shoot the clown, midday, downtown, walking up close from behind, pushing the gun into his back, popping off four fast ones, turn the bastard inside out, the body still falling as he walked away; he saw himself swing for the fences, a Louisville slugger, catching the side of Eli's skull; Charles and the woman were on their knees, blindfolded and bound, one shot each in their heads, pop, pop; problem solved, over and out, and he could move on.

Mr. Rollins realized this was his fear talking, and reminded himself of another rule: Control your fear, or your fear will make you stupid.

Mr. Rollins put Eli on hold, and took a few seconds to organize his thoughts. Eli had screwed up the hit, and now Mr. Rollins wondered if he was screwing up anything else.

"The boy you sent, I saw he died."

"Carlos."

"He didn't look banged up so bad when I saw him. The police must've tried to make him talk."

"He would have said nothing."

"I have to ask. Can they put him with you?"

Eli fell silent.

"This was your guy, Eli. You understand I have to ask."

"Carlos cannot be put with me."

"Okay. Good. That's very good."

"Yes."

"The officer. He still has to go."

"It is more difficult now, but we will do this."

"He won't be as easy to find. They probably won't let him go back to work."

"We know his name. I have people who will find where he lives."

"You know his name?"

"I have people. There are not so many dog officers. It was easy."

Mr. Rollins did not doubt Eli had people who could help. Eli's career was based on information no one was supposed to know.

Eli said, "I will do this thing. Even now, it is happening. Do not let this slow our business."

"It isn't, and won't."

Rollins put down the phone. He told himself Eli would come through, but he had a major case of the doubts. One day might roll into two, two days could roll into three, and with each passing hour, the clown would grind through more mug shots. Sooner or later, he'd see Mr. Rollins.

This was one of the most important rules: If the police have your number, walk away. Friends, family, wives, lovers, houses, money, children, goldfish, whatever. You didn't stop to explain or say good-bye, or pick up a stash of cash. Wherever you were and whatever you were doing, you dropped everything, walked away, and never looked back.

Mr. Rollins accepted this fact, and was prepared. He had plenty of money in secret accounts under various names. He had DLs, credit cards, and passports. He could walk away without looking back, but he cautioned himself not to be hasty. Haste smacked of panic.

Eli was a professional and a cold-blooded killer, but Mr. Rollins wasn't up to leaving his fate in Eli's hands.

He picked up the phone and hit the callback button.

"One more thing, Eli. What's his name?"

"His name is Officer Scott James."

"When you find out where Officer James lives, call me before you kill him."

Mr. Rollins hung up. He watched the line of red lights trapped on the freeway, inching through hell toward nothing, each light a loser too stupid to know what he was.

Mr. Rollins didn't want to get back into the murder business, but he had been good at it. He had been excellent. And sometimes he missed it.

The Predators

The African lion makes a kill only twice out of every ten hunts. Leopards do better, catching their prey twenty-five percent of the time, and cheetahs do best of all the big cats, with a kill ratio of nearly fifty percent. The deadliest four-legged African predator is not a big cat. It cannot be outrun or outdistanced, its pursuit is relentless, and it capturer its prey nine out of every ten hunts. The most dangerous predator in Africa is the wild dog.

26

Elvis Cole

THE SUN WAS IN FULL BLOOM above the eastern ridge, and the air was blush with warmth as I spun through a tae kwon do kata before an audience of hidden police officers. Joe Pike and Jon Stone stepped onto my deck a few minutes before seven that morning.

Jon Stone went to the rail.

"Bro. You showing off for the cops?"

An hour of fighting myself, and my shorts were soaked and the deck spattered with sweat. The cat was under my grill, safe from the spray. His tail flicked when he saw Jon, and he made a low growl. Not the friendliest animal.

"Thanks for coming, Jon. I owe you."

"At your rates, I'll be in the red forever."

He pointed across the canyon.

"Got yourself a spotter. Far ridge at ten o'clock, left of the blue house. Another on the way in, watching the turn."

"I know. They've been here all night."

Jon made a big show of waving at whoever was across the canyon.

"Seeing as how you showed them up yesterday, they might've bugged up your car. I'll give it a sweep."

Jon's work often required him to search buildings and vehicles for hidden devices. His life usually hung in the balance.

Pike said, "Check the house, too."

Jon gave Pike a sour look.

"Keep in mind, I get the big bucks for things like this. Just saying."

I wiped my face, and pulled on a T-shirt.

"Do your people know anything about Echo Park?"

Jon shifted the sour from Pike to me.

"Me first. The woman whose son was killed, Breslyn, who is she to you and what do you know about her?"

I went inside for Amy's file, and opened the Woodson brochure to Amy's corporate portrait.

"You gotta be kidding. She looks like my aunt."

"She embezzled four hundred sixty thousand dollars. She bought a nine-millimeter Ruger and learned how to shoot, and she's spent months trying to make contact with radical Islamist jihadists."

Jon looked dubious.

"What took her so long? Al-Qaeda and ISIS have media centers. Hezbollah has a TV station. These assholes use Twitter and Facebook for recruitment and fund-raising. All she had to do was drop'm a note."

"She's smart. She'd know the people you work for watch those sites."

Jon grinned, but it was nasty and mean.

"The people I work for watch everything."

Jon skimmed the file as I told him about Meryl Lawrence, Amy, and the things I'd learned at the X-Spot. When I finished, he handed back the file, and his manner was different. He wore his Delta face. The Delta face made me uneasy.

"You wanted me to ask a question. I asked. This conversation is not something we can discuss on the phone or in email. Not today, or whenever. We clear?"

"Yes."

"This isn't bullshit."

"I understand."

"Fourteen weeks ago, posts began to appear on certain private message boards that drew attention."

Pike said, "Pro-jihadist sites."

"Did these posts originate in Los Angeles?"

"Eleven weeks ago, the source was narrowed to the Los Angeles area. Note the word 'area.' NSA believed they should be investigated, and tossed the ball to Homeland Security."

Maybe Special Agent Mitchell was remembering the posts when he told me about terrorist nightmares.

I felt a stir of hope. Computers and smartphones left a number trail as distinct as tracks in the snow each time they touched the Internet. One of these numbers was assigned by providers but one was hardwired into the device. From the instant a person signed on, their computer's numerical path was logged and recorded by Internet service providers, networks, wireless hotspots, servers, and routers, forever linking the time, location, and path of service to your specific machine. Surf the Net, check your email, chat with a friend—each new router and service provider recorded and stored your numbers. The geolocation of a computer could be found by back-tracing this trail of numbers. Finding an approximate location was relatively easy. The spooks Jon knew could probably back-trace to a specific sign-on address, identify a specific machine, and pull the name of the person who bought it from the manufacturer.

I said, "Was it Amy?"

"If it was, she was too smart for them, which is what drew their attention."

Pike said, "They couldn't ID the source."

"Meaning what?"

Jon smirked.

"Meaning the crap on these boards is usually posted by a crank in a garage, or a thirteen-year-old idiot, toked up on the big sister's weed. Thirteen-year-old idiots are easy to find. This computer was hidden behind anonymous proxies, virtual networks, and spoofed identity numbers. One post looked like it came from Paris, the next from Birmingham, another from Baton Rouge. Each post appeared to be written on a different computer, only none of the computers actually existed."

I glanced at Pike.

"She's smart."

"There were sixteen posts in all. They weren't filled with threats to blow up the White House or hate for the West, but they were clear appeals to engage with extremist factions."

Jon described the posts. The first was a respectful request to correspond with principals of the Islamist jihadist movement in northwest Africa. As soon as I heard this, I knew.

"Amy. Her son was killed in Nigeria."

Jon held up a finger and continued. The author reached out to al-Qaeda members in northern Africa twice more and expressed willingness to meet reasonable security requirements. Later posts used phrases like 'willing to share my technical expertise' and 'able to offer insights into regulated materials and their availability.'

I interrupted again.

"It's Amy. She's talking about explosives."

Jon seemed to consider me for a moment, but maybe it wasn't me he considered.

"Then the posts stopped. The sixteenth and last post was made seven weeks ago. Since then, nothing."

"Were there responses?"

"Plenty. They were checked and dismissed. Cranks."

"Is Homeland still investigating?"

"Negative. When the posts stopped, they kicked it back to D.C."

"What's your friend think?"

"Only two ways to go. Contact was made, and the conversation was taken off-line, or no contact resulted, and the poster quit posting."

"Quit."

"Yeah. Like a kid making crank calls. They start off really into it, make stupid calls for a couple of months, get it out of their system, and move on. If contact was made, they got past D.C."

"She was reached."

I told him about Charles.

Jon sighed.

"She's gonna get herself killed."

"Not if we find her."

Jon turned to the canyon again, and leaned into space.

"Pike said it was a suicide bomb."

"Fourteen dead, thirty-eight wounded. He was a journalist."

Jon leaned farther out over the rail.

"War is a bitch, isn't she?"

Jon pushed away from the rail.

"I'll get my gear, and see if they bugged you."

Pike touched my arm, and nodded to the street.

"Not yet."

A dark blue Trans Am pulled off the street by the side of my house. A policeman was behind the wheel, and a German shepherd stood next to him in the front seat. The shepherd was huge, and filled most of the car.

Jon Stone smiled broadly.

"Groovy. A dog."

27

Scott James

Scott bought a 1981 Trans Am two-door sport coupe as a project car, but the project languished once he was shot. The interior was tattered, the right rear fender was dented, and rust pimpled the paint, but it ran well enough, and he didn't worry about Maggie ruining the seats. They were already split.

With his K-9 vehicle in the hands of SID, Scott drove the Trans Am to see Cole. Maggie rode in front, straddling the console and blocking his view. The Platoon required their K-9 service dogs to be transported in a secured crate, but Maggie had perched on the console since their first day together. Scott had tried to make her ride in the back, but she seemed happier in front. Scott reasoned she had ridden this way with the Marines, so he gave in and let her. He had to push her out of the way to see and to shift, but Scott didn't mind. When he pushed, she pushed back. He liked that about her.

Scott didn't need to check the address when he reached Elvis

Cole's home high in the canyon. Cole and two men watched him pull up from a deck off the back of the house. Scott didn't expect Cole to have company.

"Could our luck be any worse?"

Maggie panted hot breath on his neck.

A red Jeep Cherokee and a black Range Rover were parked in front of Cole's house. Scott's first impulse was to keep driving, but racing away probably wouldn't inspire Cole to cooperate.

Scott parked in plain view by a gnarled podocarpus tree, nose to nose with the Jeep. He tucked the suspect sketch into his pocket, got out, and went to the edge of the slope. Cole and his buddies were watching him like three crows on a fence. A rumpled black cat with a crooked ear was watching him, too. The cat's eyes were hateful.

Cole raised his hands.

"If this is a raid I give up."

"Scott James, Mr. Cole. Remember me?"

"I do. Thanks again for not shooting."

Cole looked as if he had been exercising, but his friends were neatly dressed. The taller man wore sunglasses and a sleeveless gray sweatshirt, exposing red arrows tattooed on his arms. The shorter was a gel-spiked blond about Cole's size, wearing desert utility pants and a black knit shirt tight across his chest and biceps.

"I'd like to talk to you about the other night. Could I have a minute, just you and me? Without your friends."

The blond made a smirky grin.

"Who said we're friends?"

Cole ignored the man's comment.

"Carter and Stiles talked to me yesterday, Officer. I'm a suspect. You shouldn't be here."

Cole was clear-eyed and direct, same as the first time they met.

"I know what Carter thinks, and I don't agree. Can we talk? Carter doesn't know I'm here."

The blond man laughed.

"And on that point, you would be wrong."

The blond had an edge Scott didn't like.

"On that point, this is between me and Mr. Cole."

Cole pointed at the hills behind his home.

"Carter has a surveillance team watching me. They can see you."

Scott fought the urge to look. He suspected Cole was jerking his chain, but still tried to make himself smaller so the podocarpus would hide him. The man with the arrows read his mind.

"They have a clean sight line. The tree won't help."

Scott felt a flush of guilt and anger, but if he'd screwed himself, he might as well keep going.

"I still need to talk. The man you chased is trying to kill me. He put a bomb on my car."

Cole darkened, and the blond stopped smiling. The change in their body language was obvious. Scott felt a rush of hope, and pushed forward.

"The device was made with a plastic explosive, similar to what we found in Echo Park. It was sophisticated. The person who built it knew what he was doing."

The blond glanced at Cole, and Cole moved to the rail.

"I'd invite you in, but it wouldn't look good. We'll come out."

Cole and his friends disappeared into the house.

Scott let Maggie out, and clipped her lead. She parked herself by his left foot, happy to be out of the car, but her ears spiked when Cole and his friends came out the front door.

"Settle, girl. Easy."

Then Cole's cat growled, and drew Scott's attention. It was creeping sideways along the edge of the deck, glaring at Maggie. Its back was arched, its fur stood on end, and its eyes were nasty slits. Maggie fidgeted but held her stay.

Cole shouted, as if this kind of thing happened every day.

"Stop it!"

The cat leaped from the deck, charged toward Maggie, then jammed on the brakes and spun sideways again, howling as if it had rabies. Scott tightened Maggie's lead.

Cole clapped his hands, and shouted even louder.

"Get out of here! Go!"

The cat spit, jumped sideways, and scrambled up the podocarpus. The howling continued high in the leaves. Maggie swiveled her head, trying to see.

"What's wrong with your cat?"

"Forget the cat. Who's the man I chased?"

Cole's interest was a tell. He wasn't expressing casual curiosity. He was all business, and carried himself like a man with a need to know. Scott didn't like the way Cole's friends were staring, like a couple of lions waiting to pounce.

"I'd rather speak alone."

"We're good."

Cole tipped his head toward the man with the arrows and the blond.

"Joe Pike. Jon Stone. Who is he?"

"I'm hoping you know."

Scott unfolded the sketch and gave it to Cole. Pike and the blond leaned close, bracketing Cole like a couple of bookends. Cole studied the sketch, and offered it back, but Scott didn't take it.

"Sorry. Don't have a clue."

"I don't believe you. I think you know more than you're telling."

The blond took the sketch and studied it.

"This the arms dealer?"

"I don't know what he is. He was in the house. I spoke to him."

"Have an accent?"

Scott found this an odd question, and wondered why the blond asked.

"No. But we spoke, and the next day the bomb's on my car. If it wasn't for my dog, I'd be dead."

The blond glanced at Maggie.

"No shit? This dog?"

"Yes."

"She's a bomb dog?"

"She was with the Marines before we got her. Explosives and patrol."

Pike came to life, and circled to the side. The blond smiled, still staring at Maggie.

"War dog! Man, these dogs saved my ass too many times to count."

Pike moved closer, and studied her scars.

"IED?"

"She was shot."

Pike offered the back of his hand. Maggie sniffed, and wagged her tail.

"Welcome home, Marine."

The blond laughed.

"Semper jarheads."

Something passed between the two men, but Scott didn't care. Cole had come out to talk, but hadn't said anything useful. Scott pointed at the sketch.

"I was as close to him as I am to you, and now he's trying to kill me. If you know anything that can help find him, I need to know."

Cole seemed uncomfortable.

"Hasn't Carter come up with anything?"

"Carter's wasting time on you. I don't have time to waste."

Cole concentrated on the sketch and seemed to be thinking. Scott thought he was going to open up, but he turned to the ridge.

"They'll take your picture. They'll use a long lens, and they'll get clean shots. What you do is, call Carter. Call him before he calls you. Tell him you were here. Say you thought you could get me to cooperate. He'll be angry, but he might cut you some slack."

Scott felt like Wile E. Coyote, as if he had run off a cliff into the air, in that terrible moment when he realized nothing was holding him up.

"That's all you have to say?"

Cole stared at the ridge as if trying to see something too far away. Scott was about to tell him to go to hell when Cole turned.

"If I helped you, I'd need your help in return."

The blond burst out laughing, but Pike stood like a statue.

"What are you talking about?"

"You came here for help, didn't you?"

"You're not hearing me. You've been arrested four times, Carter suspects you, and I think you know something. You seem like a good guy, so talk to me. Tell me what you know."

Cole held up the sketch.

"I'm a detective. I can probably find him."

"I didn't come here to hire you."

"I'm not offering to be hired. I'm offering to help, but you're going to have to help me help you."

The blond flashed a grin filled with predator teeth.

"What could it hurt? He's the World's Greatest Detective."

Scott tried to read Cole's face. The man seemed guarded, but something about him felt true, and authentic.

"Think about it. Got a pen? I'll give you my number."

Scott felt uneasy, but he took out an LAPD business card and copied Cole's number.

Cole said, "Don't forget to call Carter. Calling him before he calls you is important. It'll look like you weren't going behind his back."

Scott glanced at the ridge.

"Are you sure they're watching?"

The blond laughed again.

"They're always watching."

Cole went back into his house, and his friends went with him. Scott watched them, wondering what to do. Cole's crazy cat howled somewhere up in the tree. It was a terrible, savage sound.

Scott opened the Trans Am, let Maggie in, and drove slowly away. He tried to decide if Cole was for real, and if he could help. When Scott finally remembered Cole's advice to call Carter, he was too late. Carter called first.

28

CARTER STOOD when the Special Operations Bureau commander entered the room. Scott was already on his feet, and Maggie was standing beside him. Carter's face was blotchy with anger.

"Commander."

Commander Mike Ignacio had small eyes, a thin nose, and a wide mouth. Though K-9 Platoon was part of Metro Division and Carter was in Major Crimes Division, both fell under the command and control of the CTSOB, the Counter-Terrorism and Special Operations Bureau. As one of the Bureau's assistant commanding officers, Ignacio oversaw these two divisions and three others. He spoke fast, and moved like a man with too many balls in the air. Scott had added another.

"Why is the K-9 here?"

"She's mine, sir. SID has my K-9 vehicle. My personal car isn't equipped to—"

Ignacio cut him off.

"You could have left her with the Platoon."

"Didn't have time, sir. Detective Carter wanted to see me right away."

"Got it. Fine."

Ignacio glanced at Carter and leaned against the wall. They were back in the conference room, which Carter now used as the task force headquarters. The table was spread with papers, binders, and two computers. Carter's tie was loose, and his skin had the dull sheen of a man who needed a shower.

Ignacio smiled at Scott.

"You trying to ruin my day, Officer?"

"I didn't know Cole was being watched, and no one told me to stay away. I was trying to help."

Ignacio glanced at Carter again.

"So what do you want, Brad? You filing a personnel complaint?"

"I want to make sure nothing like this happens again."

"I can guarantee it won't happen again. Here's what I want. I'd like to get this squared away so I don't have to ring up Metro, and drop a shit bomb on this officer. Sound good?"

Ignacio didn't wait for an answer.

"Russ? Concerns?"

Scott hadn't been introduced when Mitchell arrived, but Scott knew who he was from listening. Russ Mitchell was a Homeland Security agent working with Carter and Stiles.

"I have a few questions. Maybe some good comes from his little adventure."

Carter said, "Wouldn't that be a nice change?"

Carter rubbed Scott the wrong way with every word out of his mouth.

"I wasn't trying to screw up your investigation."

Stiles went to the door. A hard-looking detective with a computer tablet came in. Stiles introduced him as Warren Hollis, one of the task force detectives.

Carter flicked his hand toward Scott.

"Show him."

Hollis held the tablet so Scott could see a photograph of Cole, Pike, and Jon Stone on Cole's deck. Scott saw himself in the background, at the top of the slope.

Cole had been right. The surveillance team had been watching, and texted his picture to the task force.

Carter said, "You want to help, help. Besides yourself, you recognize the men in this picture?"

"Yes."

Hollis said, "We know Cole and Pike. Who's the blond?"

"Jon Stone. That's all I know about him."

Hollis glanced at Carter, and referred to a note page.

"I can't confirm the name. Drives a black Range Rover. Registered and titled to a limited liability corporation called Three Sides LLC, address of record being a P.O. box in West Hollywood. No wants, warrants, or citations. He and Pike arrived at the same time, Pike in the Jeep, the blond in the Rover."

Carter shifted his gaze to Scott.

"Who is he to Cole?"

"Friends, I guess. He cracked a few jokes, but didn't say much. Pike said even less. Cole and I did most of the talking."

Carter showed his impatience.

"You were up there with these people, and you don't know who they are?"

"I didn't know Cole would have company."

Hollis asked if Stone had scars or tattoos, or characteristics they could use in an identity search.

"Six feet, one ninety, brown eyes. The hair isn't natural. It's bleached."

Another thought occurred to him.

"I'm pretty sure he's ex-military. An Army guy."

"He mentioned the service?"

"He said dogs like Maggie saved him. Stone made a crack about Pike and Maggie being jarheads. It was the kind of thing soldiers and Marines say to each other."

Stiles nodded at Hollis.

"Check it. Jon Stone. Veteran. Army. See what you get."

Hollis left with the tablet, and Carter turned back to Scott.

"So what did you and your friends talk about?"

Scott gave an accurate but incomplete account of their conversation, including Cole's admission he was a suspect and his warning about the surveillance team. He left out the parts where Cole advised him to call Carter and offered to help. He didn't mention the cat.

"I told him about the bomb on my car, and made a pitch for his help. He was sympathetic, but that's as far as it went. He said he'd help if he could, but he didn't offer any information."

"Do you believe him?"

"I believe he knows more than he's telling. I don't think he had anything to do with Echo Park."

Carter arched his eyebrows.

"How so? Are you a swami?"

Stiles tipped forward, serious.

"Why, Scott?"

"He asked if we ID'd the suspect."

Carter glanced at Ignacio.

"They're probably partners."

Scott shook his head, trying to explain.

"It wasn't like that. The way he asked. His manner and tone. He was hoping I'd give him a name. I think he was disappointed."

Carter scowled, even more irritated.

"What did you tell him?"

"I told him the truth. We don't have an ID."

Carter threw up his hands, making a show for Ignacio.

"Jesus, man, this is a suspect."

He spread his arms, making an even bigger show.

"This is what I'm talking about. He doesn't need to know what we know, or anything else."

Scott grew angry, and embarrassed.

"I didn't go up there because I'm stupid. Cole and I had a moment the night you questioned him, joking about how close I came to shooting him. He brought it up again today. I thought I could kick something loose if he knew the man he chased was trying to kill me."

Mitchell seemed interested.

"How did Mr. Cole and his friends react when you told them about the bomb?"

"Everything changed. It was like flipping a switch. They went from being smart-asses to asking questions."

Mitchell leaned forward.

"Were they knowledgeable about explosives?"

Scott replayed those parts of the conversation.

"No, they mostly asked about the suspect. The blond—Jon Stone—asked if he was the arms dealer."

Stiles cocked her head.

"Meaning, the man we believe tried to kill you?"

"Yeah. But I think he was asking because of the munitions we found. 'Is this the arms dealer?' Meaning, was this the guy selling the munitions. And this is kinda weird. He asked if the man had an accent."

Stiles scribbled a note.

"Now that is a curious question. An accent. Mr. Stone asked this?"

"Yes."

Carter glanced at Stiles as if he resented her question.

"What else? End of the conversation?"

Scott thought back again.

"He asked how we're doing, and if we've made progress. That was about it. Since I don't know what we're doing or if we've made progress, I had nothing to tell him."

Carter caught the dig and started to say something, but Ignacio cut him off.

"Russ? You okay with this?"

"No problem here. Sounds like much ado about nothing."

Mitchell glanced at Carter, and made a tight smile.

"Oughta wire up this guy and send him back, Carter. No telling what we might learn."

Ignacio stepped away from the wall to shake Mitchell's hand.

"Thanks, Russ. Sorry for the inconvenience."

"No harm, no foul. Could've been worse."

The room was silent until Mitchell was gone, and Ignacio turned to Scott.

"What do you suppose he's thinking, that we're a bunch of half-assed cowboys? I'm embarrassed. Are you embarrassed, Officer James?"

"Yes, sir. I'm sorry if—"

"You're not as embarrassed as you could be, but I see no great harm done to Detective Carter's investigation, do you, Detective Carter?"

"Not unless Cole gets away with it."

"Agreed. So, unless Mr. Cole hops the next boat to China, you won't file a personnel complaint, will you, Brad?"

"No, sir."

Ignacio turned back to Scott.

"Stay away from Cole. That's an order. Your involvement with this investigation comes only with Detective Carter's approval. Are we on the same page?"

"I'd like to be kept informed. I don't know if they're making progress, or what they're doing. With respect, sir, it's my blue ass on the line."

Ignacio shot his response to Carter.

"Keep him informed."

Ignacio turned to leave, but stopped when he reached the door.

"We'll get him. Every officer in this building, every officer in this city, we're in it together. We'll get him."

After Ignacio left, Carter pulled on his jacket, and spoke to Stiles. He ignored Scott.

"Inform him while he looks at mug shots."

Carter left without looking back.

Stiles rubbed her forehead, and Scott thought she looked even more tired than Carter.

"Most cases, you got wits, prints on the weapon, you're done. This one isn't like that. All that bleach and ammonia, my Lord, there isn't one print. Those neighbors, not one knows who's been taking care of that house."

She pushed a blue binder toward him.

"Mug shots."

Scott touched the binder but didn't open it.

"I don't think I was out of line."

"You were. I know it's frustrating, but you should apologize."

"I'm not frustrated. I'm angry this asshole is trying to kill me. I want to get him."

"We want him, too. Believe it or not, we want to get him even way more than you. That make sense?"

"No."

"If he gets you, we have to live with it."

Scott opened the binder. The first mug shot looked no different than the two hundred he'd already seen.

"You're wrong about Cole."

"Been wrong before."

"We could get him to help."

"Look through the pictures. When you finish, we have plenty more."

Scott turned the page. The face staring up at him looked nothing like the man in the sport coat.

29

Elvis Cole

PIKE AND I worked out an exit plan while Jon Stone checked my house and car. He used a dull black wand a little larger than a TV remote to search for infrared heat points, electromagnetic fields, and the frequencies used by audio/video devices and GPS trackers. Officially, Jon's equipment didn't exist. It was provided by the National Security Agency for Jon's government contract work. Like Amy Breslyn, much about Jon Stone was secret.

Jon shrugged when he finished.

"Nada. Guess you aren't worth the cost of a bug."

Pike went to the door.

"We'll get set up. Call when you roll."

I went back to my deck, and thought about Officer James. The sun was higher, and prickled my skin with a distant heat. I didn't like surveillance teams watching me, or federal agents entering my home.

I didn't like that the woman I sought was probably connected to a man who was trying to murder a police officer. Keeping faith with my client left me resentful.

The cat leaped onto the deck. He looked surprised to see me and shook himself.

"That dog had you by seventy-five pounds. You have a death wish."

He plopped onto his side and licked his anus.

I went inside, showered, and found three messages from Meryl Lawrence. Two were left yesterday, and the third while I was with Officer James.

"Are you ducking my calls? I'll be on your side of town this morning. Call me. I want to know if you're earning your money."

One message was enough.

Jennifer Li and the Lerners hadn't returned my calls. Eddie Ditko hadn't called, but I'd only spoken to him the night before. Jared promised to get back to me about Ilan and Stacey, but hadn't. If Ilan or Stacey remembered Charles, I wanted to show them the sketch, so I phoned Everett's even though it was before business hours. The inevitable voice mail answered. Karma.

Meryl was a pain, but maybe no one returned my calls because I didn't return hers. Maybe bad karma was piling up like flies on a corpse, and my calls wouldn't be returned until the causality books were balanced. I dialed Meryl Lawrence, and was surprised when she answered. Magic.

She spoke in a fast rush.

"Can't talk. Meet me in forty minutes. Say where."

Forty minutes. Not half an hour or an hour. Forty. Like we were Ukrainian spies.

We agreed on a parking lot at Sunset and La Cienega. Forty minutes gave me plenty of time, so I tested my karmic balance with Jennifer Li. A woman answered, making me two for two.

"Sorry to bother you, but I'm trying to reach Jennifer Li. This was her number in high school."

"This is Jennie's mother. Who is this, please?"

"I'm a friend of Jacob Breslyn's. Jacob and Jennie went to school together."

Her voice took a sad note.

"Oh, that was so awful, what happened. Are you the gentleman who called yesterday?"

"Yes, ma'am. Sorry to call again, but I'm only in town a few days, and got to thinking about Jacob."

"Jennie doesn't live here, you know. She married Dave Tillman. She's a physician."

"A doctor. You must be proud."

"A pediatric surgeon. She does surgery on little babies."

"If you don't mind, I'd really like to talk to her."

She hesitated, and her voice grew awkward.

"I gave her your message. She's so busy, you know. Residents work these terrible hours. She's always exhausted."

It was obvious she didn't want to give Jennie's number, so I didn't press her.

"I understand, Ms. Li. No problem. I'll catch her next time. Did Jennie and Dave stay in L.A.?"

Ms. Li's voice relaxed, now that I wasn't pressing.

"Yes, thank goodness. We were so lucky she found a position."

"You've been kind, Ms. Li. Sorry I bothered you."

Three for three.

I tucked the sketch in my pocket, and called Joe as I went to my car.

"Leaving."

"Ready."

They were set up at pre-arranged locations along a convoluted route down through the canyon, with Pike down low and Jon above, where he could keep an eye on the surveillance teams. When a tail car moved to follow me, Jon would alert Pike, who would position himself between us, and block their route.

I was three minutes from my house when Jon came on the line.

"They're not moving."

Two minutes later, I was farther down in the canyon when he came on the line again.

"Still no movement."

Pike said, "Check the area."

"These guys haven't moved, and I don't see anyone moving to track you."

I said, "Nobody's following me?"

"Makes you feel less special, doesn't it?"

We kept watch as I worked down the canyon and into the flats near Hollywood Boulevard.

"Still nothing?"

Pike said, "Nothing."

"They're still on my house?"

Jon said, "A-firm."

"Maybe they're dummy units. Is anyone in the cars?"

"Might be dummies, but I see real, live people."

Strange.

Pike said, "You're clear. What do you want to do?"

I cut them free, and turned toward Meryl Lawrence. She arrived first, and was already parked.

The two-story strip mall was home to a vegan cheese shop, a

comic book store, and a mom-and-pop donut shop. I parked on the street a block away, walked back, and got into her car. Meryl was sipping a coffee, but it hadn't helped her mood.

"You're late."

"I was working."

"Next time, work on picking a better parking lot. This crappy lot sucks."

"No more crappy lots. Check."

She wore a black pants suit with a string of white pearls, but her jacket was rumpled and smudges hollowed her eyes. The strain was starting to show, and it was about to get worse.

I said, "I have a lot to tell you, but you should know the police came to see me again yesterday. An agent from Homeland Security was with them."

She closed her eyes.

"Shit. Shitshitshitshit."

She opened her door and poured out the coffee.

"I can't sleep. I can't keep anything down."

"Maybe it's time to tell your boss. You don't have to tell him you tried an end-around with me. I won't give you up."

She stared into the cup as if she didn't remember why it was empty.

"If you have something to report, please just tell me."

I showed her the sketch art, but I did not tell her about Scott James or that the man in the sketch had tried to kill him. Meryl Lawrence was a pain, but my guilts were mine to bear.

"Do you know this man?"

"No. Who is he?"

"This is the man I chased from Thomas Lerner's house. The police believe the munitions were his."

She shrugged as if she didn't see the importance.

"Okay. So?"

"Did Amy express a consuming interest about the people behind the bombing that killed her son?"

"Consuming how?"

"Obsessive. Rage, anger, venting about why they hadn't been caught."

"Not at all. She never talked about it. Or them."

"Did you know she bought a gun?"

Meryl Lawrence stared as if I were testing her.

"I don't know anything about a gun."

I showed her the receipt, and repeated what I'd heard at the X-Spot. Meryl stopped me with an aggressive wave at the sketch.

"What does this man have to do with Amy?"

"She wanted to contact al-Qaeda, or people who deal with al-Qaeda. You believe Charles convinced her to embezzle almost half a million dollars. This man had stolen military munitions in Thomas Lerner's house, and that stuff ain't cheap. You see how it fits? Maybe this is Charles."

She eyed the sketch doubtfully.

"You think this is Charles?"

"I'll know if he's Charles by the end of the day."

I told her I had a line on the florist who sold Charles the flowers, and Jennifer Li gave us a good shot at finding Lerner. Her eyes brightened when I told her about the florist, but she was less enthusiastic about Jennifer.

"Don't waste time with Lerner, but the florist could pan out. Maybe they have a security camera."

"Lerner isn't a waste of time. Lerner ties Amy to the house where the explosives were found. Amy might have asked Lerner for help, and Lerner knew the house could be used for a drop. These things don't come together unless Lerner is part of it."

She squinted doubtfully, and shook her head.

"You're confusing yourself. And even if you're right, the police will be all over Lerner. If they find out you're searching for Lerner, too, I'm screwed. Stay with the florist. They might have a video."

"I asked. They don't."

The burner vibrated in my pocket. I checked the caller and saw it was EVERETT'S.

"It's them. I have to go."

"Ask if he used a credit card."

"I asked. He paid cash."

I opened the door to leave, but she caught my sleeve.

"The florist might have seen his car. Ask. We might get a make and model. See if the businesses next door have cameras. We could luck into a walk-by."

The instructions rattled out as if she were giving orders. I opened the door wider.

"I have to talk to the man, Meryl."

"Good. Go. This is much more productive than chasing the kid. We might be finally getting somewhere."

I pulled my shirt free, and got out. She leaned across the seat.

"Don't duck me like before. Call."

I shoved the door closed, and escaped to my car.

30

"GOOD MORNING, ELLLLVIS! Saying those words is a fantasy in SO many ways! Ilan recalls the so-called gentleman in question. We're here . . . for *anything* your heart desires."

Jared did an excellent Big Bopper.

I touched the callback icon, and tried to sound calm.

"Hey, Jared, thanks for getting back to me."

"Why hello, Mr. Man! I'm moving to Everett's office so we can put you on speaker. Everett, of course, is elsewhere, doing God alone knows what."

Jared put me on hold but picked up again two minutes later.

"We're he-re! Elvis, Ilan. Ilan, this is my dear friend, Elvis. Don't you love his name? Say it. Doesn't Elll-viss feel simply wonderful in your mouth?"

A second voice spoke, young and uncertain.

"This is Ilan. Can you hear me?"

Their voices had the hollow, faraway quality that came with being on speaker.

"I hear you fine, Ilan. Did Jared explain who this is about?"

"The Pink Finesse gardens."

"A dozen Pink Finesse garden roses were delivered to a woman named Amy Breslyn. You wrote the order. This was ten or eleven days ago."

"Uh-huh."

"The man paid cash, and signed the card Charles. Do you remember him?"

"Uh-huh."

Jared sighed dramatically.

"Please do not mumble. Use your adult voice."

Ilan spoke louder, and sounded annoyed.

"Yes, I remember him. I didn't remember his name, but Jared reminded me."

"Okay, great. Do you recall his last name?"

"He paid cash. Why would I know his last name?"

Ilan sounded even more annoyed, and Jared didn't like it. His voice was quick and sharp.

"Don't be short. The poor man asked a simple question."

Ilan didn't respond. He was sulking.

I said, "Don't sweat it, Ilan. No reason you should know. I just thought he might have mentioned it."

"He didn't."

Now he sounded pouty.

"Did he mention why he was buying the flowers, or say anything about the woman he was sending them to?"

Ilan said something, but his voice was so low I didn't understand him. Then I realized he was talking to Jared. Jared answered in his normal tone.

"Vaguery is no friend to a delicate heart. Tell him, not me. Healing comes with clarity."

Ilan cleared his throat.

"He told me he wanted to impress the lady."

Jared's voice was gentle.

"When a gentleman says he wants to impress a lady, he isn't talking about his mother. Would you like a moment?"

I unfolded the sketch art. I wanted Ilan to describe Charles before he saw the sketch. Memories could be distorted by after-the-fact influences.

"I'd like to keep going. Ilan? Can you tell me what the man looked like?"

"I wouldn't know what to say."

Jared's voice cracked like a whip.

"Did he have three arms? A goiter? Don't be a twit!"

Now Ilan's voice rose and he sounded scared.

"Why are you getting up?"

"Look at me! I am five feet nine inches of blue steel love. Was he bigger than me? Smaller? A burly Adonis, or a spindly pear? *Speak!*"

Damn. Jared was good.

Ilan made a humming sound, as if he were trying to picture the man.

"Taller. He wasn't skinny, but he wasn't overweight, either. He was fit, and he was totally suburban."

I said, "Suburban means what?"

Jared jumped in.

"Boring. A straight, white, conservative, middle-aged male."

Ilan was suddenly into it.

"Yes! He looked like my dad. The combed brown hair going to gray, the tennis tan, the whole impatient businessman thing. Ohmy-God, his collar was open. That is *totally* my dad. End of the day, the tie comes off, the Johnnie Walker goes down."

"He was wearing a sport coat?"

Ilan made the humming sound again.

"Mmmm. I'm not sure if he was in a suit or a sport coat, but he was wearing a jacket."

The man in the sketch was a middle-aged Anglo with short brown hair. The sketch showed him wearing a sport coat with an open collar. Maybe the man I chased was Ilan's father.

I said, "Anything else? Scars or tattoos? A big flashy watch?"

Ilan hummed again, straining his memory.

"Jeez. I'm sorry. I didn't spend that much time with him."

Jared was gentle.

"You did well."

"It was madness. The Eastside truck was almost ready to leave. Then the gentleman walks in, and wants the arrangement delivered that day. He was adamant. We had to drop everything."

Something confused me.

"What's the Eastside truck?"

Jared explained. Their deliveries were divided geographically, with one truck delivering to locations east of their shop, and a second truck handling deliveries to the west.

"The flowers went out on the Eastside truck?"

"Yeah. That's why I had to rush."

"Hancock Park is to the west."

Jared made a sad, dramatic sigh.

"Oh my Lord, the betrayal. A love nest."

"They weren't delivered to Hancock Park?"

Jared recited an address in Silver Lake. Silver Lake was east of their store. I copied it, wondering why Amy's flowers were delivered to Silver Lake when I had found them in Hancock Park.

"One more thing. Ilan? If you saw Charles again, would you recognize him?"

"After all this? I'll never forget him!"

I told Jared I wanted to email a picture, and asked for Everett's email address. Jared gave me his personal email.

"Discretion," he said.

I smoothed the sketch, took a picture, and sent it. Jared opened the email a few seconds later.

"A likeness of the gentleman in question?"

"Provided by a friend."

Ilan's response was immediate.

"This isn't him."

Jared said, "Be certain."

"His face was thinner. His nose was smaller, and different. The whole forehead thing is wrong, and his jaw. This isn't Charles. I'm sure."

I should have been relieved, but my head was filled with Silver Lake. Amy had walked away from one life to another, but maybe she only walked across town. Maybe Charles lived in Silver Lake and Amy had joined him.

"Jared? If Charles comes back, will you let me know?"

"Immediately."

"Don't tell him I asked about him, okay?"

"As if I could be so indiscreet. Your secrets are mine."

I thanked them, and lowered the phone.

Charles might or might not live in Silver Lake and Amy might or might not be with him, but someone in Silver Lake received Amy's flowers, and likely knew Charles. Charles might even have sent the flowers to himself, and taken them to Amy in person.

Joe Pike answered on the first ring.

"I think I found her."

"What about Charles and the man in the sketch?"

"Find one, find all."

Joe Pike and Jon Stone met me in Silver Lake.

31

Jon Stone

WHEN COLE CUT HIM FREE, Jon amscrayed back to West Hollywood. He hadn't been home long enough to heat his pool, but Jon stripped as he walked through his house, and hit the water like a naked lawn dart.

The cold water slapped him; lit up his skin with a thousand stingers, but was clear, and clean, and cleansing. Jon loved it. First thing he did when he got home from a job: into the pool, out; it was like being reborn.

Jon thought about the woman as he swam, the lady in the brochure. Her eyes were kinda vacant, like holes in her soul, but damned if she wasn't familiar. Jon felt as if he'd seen her before, and may even have met her, but he couldn't place her. Pissed Jon off, a man with his memory.

Jon pushed up out of the water, passed under the outdoor shower (the French chicks loved it: sized for three, six wall-mounted black titanium spray heads with matching overhead rain heads—the award-winning heads unavailable in the U.S., so Jon had carried them from Europe aboard an Air Force MC-130), and went inside to eat.

The lady's eyes followed him.

Jon nuked a couple of frozen tamales. He took the tamales, a carton of nonfat milk, and his laptop to the couch. Sat there naked, eating while he read about Jacob Breslyn. Articles from the *New York Times* and *Washington Post* confirmed the facts he learned from Cole: A suicide bombing at an outdoor café in Abuja, Nigeria, left fourteen dead and thirty-eight wounded, one of the dead being a young journalist named Jacob Breslyn. Jon Googled the original CNN and BBC video broadcasts. Jon was a practiced expert in bomb damage assessment, and wanted to see if his own assessment would agree with the published accounts.

A female correspondent with a British accent was first on the scene. She broadcast while efforts to secure the area unfolded behind her. For the first minute or so, the reporter filled the frame, but she finally stepped aside, revealing Nigerian emergency vehicles crowded into a small square. The cafés and shops lining the square were lit red and white by the flashers topping the vehicles. Policemen and soldiers ran through haze, shouting in British-accented English and Hausa.

Jon muted the sound and studied the carnage. The windows and glass storefronts lining the square were blown out, and the café's striped awning was partially collapsed. Vehicle-born IEDs typically blew out walls and left behind the smoldering hulks of obliterated cars and trucks, but Jon saw no significant wall or structural damage. When the camera moved closer, Jon noted the café's signage and walls were pocked. Tables and chairs in the outdoor area were pushed to the side and upended, but appeared otherwise undamaged. Jon decided shrapnel had caused the pocking, and patrons and first responders had most likely upended the tables. He concluded that the damage and casualties were caused by forty to sixty pounds of high-explosive material packed with lug nuts and nails to create shrapnel. The device had been designed to kill and maim as many as possible. A terror weapon.

Jon Stone said, "Animals."

The news reports described the suicide bomber as an unidentified female, approximately twenty to twenty-five years old, whose blood showed traces of methamphetamine, cocaine, and LSD. She carried the explosives in an Australian-made backpack beneath her robes, strapped to her belly. Anyone who saw her would think she was pregnant.

Jon ate the second tamale. He drank a little milk, put his laptop aside, and went outside.

Beautiful day. Sunny and bright.

Jon had spent most of his career gathering intelligence, providing security, rescuing hostages, and, one way or another, in direct, boots-on-the-ground combat with individuals identified as terrorists by the United Nations, the United States government, and the civilized world. This being Nigeria, Jon knew the people responsible for the bombing would be members of Boko Haram, an Islamist militant group with ties to al-Qaeda, or a Boko Haram splinter group known as Ansaru. Both were big on suicide bombings, and often employed women and children as their designated suicides. Neither group had claimed responsibility, but Jon knew this meant little. So many dip-shits with ties to al-Qaeda were running around that part of the world, you couldn't keep track with a scorecard. The shot caller who ordered the bombing would probably never be known, and was likely already dead.

More's the pity for Ms. Breslyn and the other families.

Jon went back inside, and Googled pictures of Jacob Breslyn. He found a tall young man with a thin face, relaxed smile, and high forehead. Geeky, but growing into himself. An everyday, normal civilian.

Jon suddenly realized why Amy looked familiar, and felt his eyes well.

"Suck it up."

D-boys sucked it up.

Jon shut his laptop and tossed it aside. He thought of the men who died when he was with Delta, and the eyes of their wives and mothers. Jacob Breslyn had been a civilian. Amy Breslyn was a civilian's mother. She went to bed one night in a rational world, and woke as collateral damage.

No group or individual has claimed responsibility, and no suspect has been named.

Well, what the fuck?! The poor woman wants to know who killed her son, and she thinks all she has to do is ask a terrorist, hook up with a lunatic here, who somehow—magically—can hook her up with fanatics on the other side of the world, and these people will actually KNOW, and they would actually TELL HER??

Jon said, "I know. It hurts."

He said it out loud. She wanted the pain to stop, but sometimes it didn't. When the hurt held tight, a troop had only one choice. Suck it up, or the hurt would kill you.

Jon's phone chimed, like a bell at the start of a prize fight.

The Caller ID showed E BOWEN, E for Ethan, who ran a Professional Military Corporation in London. Jon had worked for Bowen many times.

"'Ey, Jonny lad, you all back an' rested? Pakistan, don't you know? A significant bonus."

Jon had drinks with Ethan in Paris. He had a cush gig coming up, and Jon had been all over it.

Jon said, "Sorry, Ethan. I took something. I'm booked."

"Wait now? Eight days, in an' out, as we discussed. You were keen on it."

"Sorry, man. This one's personal."

Jon hung up.

Amy wanted answers, for sure, and someone to blame, but, most of all, she wanted to stop hurting.

Jon's phone chimed again. This time, it was Pike.

"Cole has a line on the woman. Silver Lake. Here's the address."

Jon threw on his clothes and ran to the Rover.

A troop had to suck it up, but another troop could help.

32

Elvis Cole

SILVER LAKE was an older neighborhood between Los Feliz and Echo Park, grown in the hills surrounding a concrete-lined reservoir that gave the area its name. Jon and I parked at the south end of the lake, and drove up with Pike, me riding shotgun and Jon in back. Pike's GPS led us along the west side of the reservoir past joggers, bicyclists, and people with dogs. After we started away, none of us spoke.

Behind me, Jon clipped a .45 pistol to his waist, pulled on an over-sized short-sleeve shirt to cover it, and quietly gazed at the water.

"Pretty today. Look how blue."

I glanced at the water, but wondered what we'd find at the house.

"Yes. Pretty."

The water was a deep, rich blue ringed by an emerald green line. The green was light reflecting off concrete beneath the water. The embankment above the water had cracked and been patched so many times, it looked like wrinkled lips. The reservoir once provided water to six hundred thousand homes, but now only offered a beautiful view. The lovely blue water teemed with cancer-causing ions induced by the sun.

Pike said, "Two minutes."

We climbed away from the lake on a narrow street lined with Spanish-style houses trimmed in colorful shades of turquoise, lime green, or yellow. The homes were lovely, but were cut into the hillside and built to the curb. Most had no driveways, so the street was lined with parked cars belonging to residents and workers from a construction site.

The Jeep felt stifling and close, like a troop transport on dangerous ground. I told myself Amy would be at this place, but I did not believe it. Whoever lived here was probably at work, most likely a woman, and would know nothing of Charles or Amy's obsession. Like Meryl Lawrence, everything she believed true about Amy Breslyn would prove false. Amy kept secrets.

Pike said, "Left side. The gray."

I leaned forward to see.

"Slow down."

The address belonged to a small stucco house set atop a two-car garage on the uphill side of the street. Two large windows overlooked the street from the room above the garage, and concrete steps with a wrought-iron rail climbed from the curb to a covered porch. The garage door and the front door were pink. I wondered if rocket-propelled grenades and plastic explosives were hidden behind the pretty pink doors.

Jon said, "What does she drive?"

"Volvo. A beige four-door sedan."

We passed the construction site, turned around at the first cross street, and drove back. No beige Volvos were seen, no guards were posted, and no one peered from the windows.

I said, "Stop. I'm going up."

We parked in front of the garage. Pike tried to lift the door, but it didn't move. The mailbox was empty. Jon went to the far side of the garage, and disappeared up the slope.

Talking wasn't necessary.

I climbed the steps, and went to the door. Pike flanked to the side, pistol along his leg.

Drapes covered the porch windows, but the drapes were sheer. Glass-door shapes of light were visible, but nothing moved inside, and the house was silent. I pushed the buzzer and knocked. I took out my pick gun to flip the locks, but Jon Stone opened the door. Those D-boys moved fast.

"Clear. Nobody's home."

I stepped in past him, discouraged and irritated.

"How'd you get in?"

"Side door off the kitchen."

The living room opened to a dining room, where French doors revealed a tiled courtyard. Pike peered through the doors, checking the rear.

"Alarm?"

"No. Kitchen's off the dining room, two bedrooms and a bath are off the hall."

Pike moved to the kitchen. Jon stayed at the front windows to watch the street, and I hurried to the bedrooms. A hunger to press the chase grew in my belly. I told myself to slow down, but didn't.

A small bedroom at the back of the house faced the courtyard. The master bedroom was larger and above the garage. I took a quick peek in the back bedroom and hurried back to the master.

A neatly made double bed faced the windows overlooking the street. A dresser hugged the adjoining wall, and a table was set up as a desk by the windows. Eight or nine women's outfits hung on a rail in the closet. Five pairs of women's shoes and three purses huddled beneath the clothes. The clothes looked like things Amy would wear and appeared to be the right size. Eight or nine outfits weren't many. Her walk-in closet in Hancock Park was crowded with so many clothes I couldn't tell if any were missing.

I checked the dresser and went to the desk. More clothes were stashed in two dresser drawers, but another two drawers were empty. An inexpensive monitor, a cheapo printer, and a few pads and pens were on the table, but not a phone or computer. Nothing on the desk or in the bedroom identified the person who lived here.

Maybe no one lived here.

Maybe they had, but were gone.

I went back to the living room. Jon was still by the windows.

He said, "What do you think?"

"I don't know."

A taupe couch faced matching taupe chairs across a blocky coffee table. Matching end tables that were too large for the space bracketed the couch, and a generic mass-produced painting hung on the wall. The furnishings appeared new, but looked like furnishings found in a discount motel chain.

Pike returned from the kitchen.

"A few plates and staples, leftover takeout, some things in the trash. Looks to be two or three days old. One person, no more."

"Phone or TV?"

"No."

I stared at the set-dressing furniture. The woman who lived here was almost certainly Amy, but she hadn't been crashing with Charles or a friend or even Thomas Lerner. I wondered where she was, and whether she would return. Except for a few clothes, nothing of Amy was here, and nothing of Jacob. Maybe she wouldn't return. Maybe she had hooked up with the people she'd been trying to find, and now she was dead, or fleeing the country.

I felt tired. I wanted to sit on the cheap taupe couch, but I went to the door.

"It was her. She was here, but she's gone."

Jon hooked his thumbs in his pockets.

"She went to a lot of trouble to set up this place. She might come back."

"Maybe."

"I can rig something to let us know."

I didn't understand.

"Let us know what?"

"She has Wi-Fi. There's a hotspot receiver under her desk."

Jon tugged at the drapes and tapped the wall.

"Put up a motion sensor, we'll know if someone comes in. AV transmitters here and in the bedroom, we'll have eyes and ears."

He shrugged like it was the easiest thing in the world.

"Won't even charge you, not that you can afford me."

Pike said, "Got something to open the garage?"

"Got the tricks in my car."

Jon Stone was something.

Pike drove us down, and Jon drove back to the house in his Rover. I got into my car, and stared at the misleading blue water. Amy Breslyn was proving herself to be smart, thorough, and well prepared. Bugging the house made sense, but Amy could have similar houses all over town, ready to be used as needed, and abandoned in place. If she didn't return, the Silver Lake house meant nothing. I needed a new trail, and was thinking about it when Eddie Ditko called.

"I was right about the potential. This sucker's gonna have legs."

"Tell me."

"First, you should know we aren't the only horses in the race. A dick from L.A. already called Solano."

"Carter?"

"Stinnis. Know him?"

Doug Stinnis was in Hollywood Homicide when I knew him, before he jumped to the show.

"He's good. Is this your way of telling me they wouldn't talk to you?"

Eddie cackled like a man gargling broken glass.

"It's my way of telling you the cops are ahead. You're losing."

Sometimes you had to ignore him.

"Help lessen my shame. What did you find out about the house?"

"Nothing. The prison didn't know squat about his house until Stinnis told them. You know what else he told them?"

"That he was way ahead of me, and I'm a loser?"

"In so many words. Medillo bought the house from his cellmate, and his cellmate died up at Solano, too."

I knew the name from the tax records.

"Walter Jacobi?"

"Maybe you aren't as far behind as I thought. Yeah, Jacobi. Three weeks after the title changed hands, Jacobi died of a drug overdose. Eleven days later, Medillo was murdered."

"Who killed him?"

"Don't know. There was a gang fight, a black and brown thing. Medillo was supposedly a bystander, but someone stabbed him sixteen times."

"The case is still open?"

"Yeah. You know how it works. Two dozen suspects, but the cameras were covered and nobody talked."

"Do they think the deaths are connected?"

"Never had reason, but they didn't know about the house. Both these guys were addicts, so someone might've blamed Medillo for the old man's death, but that's just talk. I asked for their sheets."

"Did Jacobi have any relatives?"

"Not that they know at Solano, but Medillo had a father and two sisters."

I remembered them from the obituary.

"Roberto, Nola, and Marisol."

"See? You're not as stupid as people say. You want to know about the house, ask his family. They probably helped with the buy."

"Thanks, Eddie. Send the sheets."

I lowered the phone, and stared at the lake. The sale or purchase of property by a competent inmate was legal, but the presence of notaries, loan officers, attorneys, and the other people needed to witness and finalize a legal document required the prison's permission. If the Solano prison officials didn't know about the transaction, then Medillo and Jacobi hadn't wanted them to know, which meant something about the transaction was rotten. I wondered if Medillo's father or sisters were present. Stinnis was probably wondering the same, and might even be with them. I needed a different trail, and the best place to find a trail was at the beginning.

The beginning was Thomas Lerner, and Jennifer Li was still my best and only way to reach him. Her mother hadn't given me Jennie's number, but she gave me enough.

I went to find Jennie.

33

Practicing physicians were easier to find than DUI attorneys. Professional medical associations, hospitals, and medical schools posted licensing and staff information on their websites, as did networking sites, complain-about-your-doctor sites, and scores of pay-to-see-your-doctor's-dirt sites. Thirty seconds after I tapped my phone, I knew where to find Jennifer Li.

Cedars-Sinai Medical Center was the largest nonprofit hospital in the western United States. With a thousand beds and a staff of twelve thousand, the hospital's campus spanned several square blocks. I could leave a message easy enough, but this didn't guarantee she would respond. I called an attorney named Ansel Rivera.

Civil and criminal firms often hired investigators to check the facts of a case, and sometimes for more personal reasons. Ansel was a labor lawyer who represented non-union workers in cases involving unsafe working conditions. A few years ago, Ansel's fifteen-year-old daughter was abducted from a parking lot after a tennis lesson. Ansel called the police and the FBI, and also called me. Three days later, Joe Pike and I found his daughter and the two men hired to kidnap her in an abandoned house in Mandeville Canyon. Since then, Ansel has offered much more work than I want or accept.

I texted his personal phone, and didn't use the burner. I wanted his Caller ID to recognize my number.

911ELVIS

Ansel called back four minutes later.

First thing he said was "We're paid up, right? I swear to God, if they didn't send your check I'll double whatever I owe you."

"We're paid. I need help with something."

"Hang on—I can't hear."

He was in a room with other people.

"Okay, this is better. What?"

"Cedars-Sinai."

"Did Margie tell you about the colonoscopy? It's set up. I'm going."

"This isn't about you. I need to see one of their surgical residents, and I need to see her fast."

"What's wrong? Are you okay?"

"I'm fine. This doctor, she's busy. She doesn't know me, and I don't have a direct way to reach her. I need someone up the food chain to tell her to see me."

"What's she do?"

"Pediatric surgery. What I'm asking is, do you or someone at your firm have juice at Cedars?"

Ansel Rivera wasn't only a labor lawyer. He was a founding partner in a firm employing over one hundred attorneys covering a dozen practice areas. Ansel was rich and connected.

"Hang on, lemme see. I'll have Barry check—"

Ansel was with me again two minutes later.

"We handled a divorce last year, a big-shot surgeon at Cedars. A vice chair, whatever that means. In surgery, right? Barry, in surgery? Yeah, okay, the guy loves us, Barry says. We saved him a fortune."

"I don't want to get her in trouble."

"What trouble? Is she doing something illegal?"

"It's nothing like that. I need to see her about someone she knew in high school. Five minutes is all I need."

"Don't sweat it. She'll be doing a personal favor for her boss, who'll be doing a personal favor for me. When do you want to see her?"

"Now."

"Give me her name. Go. We'll take care of it."

Barry called me with instructions before I reached the hospital. He gave me a phone number, told me to go to the admissions lobby of the South Tower, and text the number when I arrived. That's what I did. Forty minutes later, Jennifer Li Tillman stepped off the elevator. She was small, slender, and prettier than she had been in high school. She wore dull blue surgical scrubs, and carried a cup of coffee. Her shoulder-length black hair was pulled into a ponytail.

I introduced myself.

"Dr. Li? Elvis Cole. Thanks for seeing me."

She looked harried and tired.

"I don't know you and I don't appreciate you involving the vice chair. This is my career."

"The vice chair is doing a favor for a very close friend. You're helping him help his friend. There's no downside."

She sipped the coffee. A wisp of steam touched her nose, but she didn't seem any less upset.

"Did you speak with my mother?"

"Yes. I'm working with Jacob's mom, Amy Breslyn."

The stern tension melted. Dr. Tillman vanished, but Jennie remained.

2 Js today

2 Js tomorrow

2 Js forever

"I haven't seen her since the memorial. I should've called. Is she doing okay? I should've called."

I sidestepped her question.

"She still has the prom picture of you and Jacob."

She smiled. It was sweet and fond, and sad.

"We went together for almost three years. He was such a great guy, and Ms. B couldn't have been any sweeter. It's so awful, what happened. Crazy. Is there anything I can do for her?"

"Amy's trying to find Thomas Lerner. Do you know how to reach him?"

She shook her head, and sipped the coffee.

"Sorry. I don't know him."

Her answer caught me off guard.

"Jacob's best friend. Thomas Lerner."

Jennie shrugged, her eyes oblivious.

"Maybe from college. Dave and Jake were besties in high school. Jacob was the Best Man at our wedding."

"This was before college. Maybe Lerner went to a different school. Amy loves him like a second son."

Jennie seemed more awkward than confused.

"I'm not saying he wasn't. It's just kinda weird, not remembering. Maybe Dave knew him."

She fished a cell phone from her scrubs, and called her husband.

"Hey, babe. I'm here with a friend of Amy Breslyn's. Yeah, Jake's mom. Do you know Thomas Lerner? He was a friend of Jake's."

She looked at me while she listened.

"Jake's mom says they were best friends."

She listened some more, then offered the phone.

"Here. This is Dave."

Dave Tillman sounded like a nice guy. I identified myself, and told him I was trying to find Thomas Lerner for Jacob's mother, who described Lerner as Jacob's best friend.

"Ms. B must be talking about someone Jake met at college."

"This was before college. Jacob went away to school, but Lerner stayed here. Amy stayed in touch with him. A writer."

"I'm drawing a blank. Jake was my boy since junior high, but I don't remember a Lerner. I'll call Ms. B."

I began to feel uncertain, as if the rules were changing.

"Is there someone else I could call? Another friend from those days?"

David Tillman gave me two names and numbers, but I returned to my car with little faith they would help. I got in behind the wheel and dutifully made the calls. One friend had known Jake since pre-school, and the other since fourth grade, but, like Jennie and Dave, neither one knew Thomas Lerner, or had heard of him.

I sat in my car like an astronaut trapped in a capsule, directed by forces I could not see and did not control.

Everything I knew about Meryl Lawrence and Amy Breslyn, and why Meryl Lawrence wanted to find Amy Breslyn, came from Meryl Lawrence. Here's some money, please find my friend. Here's the story, but don't ask, don't tell. No one must know. Promise you won't tell. Promise.

Woodson Energy Solutions was listed with Information. A young woman's voice answered when I called.

"Meryl Lawrence, please."

"I'll connect you to her office."

A young male voice answered the ring.

"Meryl Lawrence's office."

"Hey, Ed Sikes for Meryl. She back yet?"

"She isn't available. May I take a message?"

"Tell you what, when would be a good time for me to call back?"

"She's unavailable, Mr. Sikes. Would you like to leave a message?"

I hung up, and called a friend at the DMV named Ruth Jordan. Ruth found four Meryl Lawrences in California, but only one showed an address near Los Angeles. Meryl Denise Lawrence lived on Belle-fontaine Street in Pasadena. Two vehicles were registered in her name, a Cadillac Sport Wagon and a Porsche Carrera.

"Does the same address show on the vehicles?"

"Same. Bellefontaine."

I copied the tag numbers and drove to Pasadena. I took my time. I stopped for a kalbi burger in K-Town. It was delicious. Traffic was terrible, but the urgency I felt earlier was gone.

The night was cool when I found her address. I timed it that way. I wanted the darkness.

Her street was quiet and lovely. The houses were set back on deep lots with generous driveways, secure in their permanence amid long-standing oaks and elms and magnolias. Towering palms stood peaceful sentry along the sidewalks, and porch lights glowed with warmth, not to defend but to welcome. I parked at the curb, shut the engine, and rolled down the window. The scent of jasmine was strong.

Meryl Lawrence lived in a very nice brick home with latticed win-dows and redwood trim. Her drapes were closed, but the rooms behind them were lit. The Cadillac wagon was parked in the drive. Its tag matched the number Ruth gave me.

I walked up the drive, and circled the Caddie. A sticker on the driver's side of the windshield showed a reserved parking space at Woodson Energy Solutions.

I photographed the parking sticker and the license plate, and walked down the drive to her backyard.

The drapes in back were open. A woman and a man who was probably her husband were in a family room, watching college football on a large flat-screen TV. The man was balding, thin, and enjoying a glass of wine from the comfort of a recliner. The woman sat in the crook of an L-shaped couch with her legs crossed, and a small, raggedy dog in her lap. She shook her fist at the TV as if the game upset her.

This Meryl Lawrence was not my Meryl Lawrence.

This Meryl Lawrence was older, had upswept gray hair, and was thirty pounds heavier than my Meryl Lawrence. This Meryl Lawrence was the real Meryl Lawrence, and my Meryl Lawrence wasn't.

I took a picture of the people inside the house, and walked back to my car.

The woman I knew as Meryl Lawrence answered my call, exactly as I expected she would.

"Did you find her? Tell me you found her."

"I can't talk now, but I need to see you. Can we meet in the morning?"

The woman who wasn't Meryl Lawrence agreed.

34

Jon Stone

JON SET THE MOTION DETECTOR to ping through his phone and laptop. He checked the audio/video link, confirmed the system was golden, and went to his Rover. He could now keep an eye on the house from anywhere on the planet.

Overkill.

Jon found a good place to park uphill from the woman's house, and across from the construction site. Nice little eyes-forward view, couple of upscale cars nearby so the Rover wasn't out of place. Jon booted his rig, locked on a satellite, and re-checked the links. Bedroom. Living room. Empty.

He considered running downhill to grab some chow, but decided against it. Going home didn't occur to him.

Staying close felt right, even though the house was empty.

The sky over the lake deepened. Twilight glowed with orange flame, and slowly purpled to black. Stars appeared one by one, then by twos and threes. Jon cracked the windows. Otherwise, he rarely moved.

One hour and forty-two minutes after sunset, lights coming up-hill flashed across Ms. Breslyn's house. They grew brighter, and the garage door began to rise.

A Volvo sedan appeared, and stopped with its turn signal blinking. When the garage was open, the Volvo maneuvered inside. The lights went off. A few seconds later Amy Breslyn came out, and waited as the door rattled down. She wore a fringed leather jacket and carried a white paper bag. Jon couldn't tell if the jacket was black or dark brown. When the garage was secure, she climbed the steps to the house. Jon's laptop and phone simultaneously chimed when she opened the door.

The cam's high angle and fish-eye lens made her shorter and rounder, but the woman was Amy Breslyn. She locked the door, and crossed the frame to the kitchen with the white paper bag. The inside lighting was better. The fringed leather jacket was brown.

Jon called Elvis Cole.

"Mom's home. What do you want to do?"

Jon felt better, being so close.

35

Elvis Cole

MY A-FRAME WAS QUIET. I locked myself in, and walked through the house, turning on lights. Amy and Jacob Breslyn were real. I had searched Amy's home, touched their belongings, and read news reports about Jacob's death. This was called evidence. Since the faux Meryl had lied about herself and Thomas Lerner, everything else was suspect.

An email from Eddie Ditko was waiting, along with rap sheets for Juan Medillo and Walter Jacobi. I read them, printed them, and tucked them into the file. Jacobi had been in his sixties, with a lifelong history of drug and fraud convictions. Medillo was half his age, with a similar history of drug busts, capped by auto theft, residential burglary, and other nonviolent crimes. The Solano officials were probably right—he wasn't a banger, and wasn't the type for a gang fight.

I showered, put on fresh clothes, and returned to the kitchen. The cat was by his bowl.

"We're having lamb. Sound good?"

He licked his lips. Lamb was one of his favorites.

A seven-rib rack of lamb was waiting in the fridge. I turned on the oven to heat, and rubbed the lamb with olive oil, salt, pepper, Iranian sumac, and a spice I liked called *za'atar*. It was possible the fake Meryl worked for Amy's company. She had pressed me to find Amy before her company found out, but maybe her company knew. Security would be an issue for their contracts with the government, so they might be trying to hide Amy's embezzlement and attempts to contact anti-American extremists. This would explain why the fake Meryl hadn't gone to the police, but not why she was pretending to be someone else.

I seared the rack in a skillet until it had a nice crust, and put the skillet into the oven.

I said, "Twelve minutes, tops."

The cat sat, and stared at his bowl. Hinting.

The hard sell about Thomas Lerner was telling, especially since Lerner didn't exist. The make-believe Meryl had created a make-believe clue, and used it to send me to Echo Park. She couldn't have known I would go to the house on that particular night, but she had known or suspected something, and sent me. I wondered what she knew, and how she had known it. I thought I might ask her, eventually.

I mixed two chopped tomatoes, some cilantro, and half a jalapeño with a box of couscous, and tossed the mix with lemon juice and a little olive oil. I threw caution to the wind, and added a handful of raisins. Daring. I checked the lamb, decided it was perfect, and took it out of the oven.

"Five minutes. It has to rest."

Jon Stone called while we were waiting.

"Mom's home. What do you want to do?"

"Amy?"

"She's here. What do you want me to do?"

I didn't know what to do. Learning Meryl Lawrence wasn't Meryl Lawrence left me short on trust, and uncertain.

"Cole?"

"What's she doing?"

"Eating. Looks like noodles. She got back maybe two minutes ago."

I pictured Amy, eating her noodles. A woman I had been searching for, but not seen. The hour was early. Amy might leave. Charles might drop by.

"I'm coming."

I carved the rack into seven equal chops, and put one aside. I carved the meat off the singleton, chopped it, and put it in a bowl for the cat. I split the remaining chops and the couscous into two plastic containers, and bagged them with napkins, plastic forks, and four bottles of water. I threw a fresh shirt and a razor into a second bag, and drove back to Silver Lake. No one followed me down off the hill, and no one watched my house. The surveillance units had vanished. Interesting.

Jon's Rover sat across from the construction site, facing downhill. I parked two houses above him, walked down, and climbed in the passenger's side. The interior lights didn't come on when I opened the door. Jon's seat was back and a laptop was balanced on the console.

I gave him the bag of food.

"What did I miss?"

He opened the bag as he answered.

"Nada. She ate, hit the potty, and now she's reading. No calls in or out. No visitors."

He popped off a lid.

"Dude, what is this, lamb? I'm starving."

He dived on a rib, and sucked the meat from the bone.

I angled the laptop for a better view. Amy Breslyn was seated on the living room couch, almost dead-center at the top of the frame. The wide-angle lens gave the image a fish-eye bend, but the distortion wasn't bad. Her feet were bare, and flat on the floor. A computer sat on her lap, and a smartphone lay by her leg, handy in case someone called. She seemed smaller and heavier than the woman in the brochure, but she was Amy.

I said, "We have a problem."

"I'm not gonna bill you. Don't sweat it."

"The woman who hired me isn't who she claims. She lied when she hired me, and she's still lying. I don't know who she is, or why she wants Amy, or what she intends. Nothing she's told me is real."

Jon took a second rib.

"You should look into that."

I nodded.

Jon pointed the chop at Amy.

"She's Amy Breslyn. Her boy is still dead. We're gonna do what we do."

I nodded again.

"You want my chops, you can have them."

"Groovy."

The way Amy sat, upright with her feet on the floor, didn't look comfortable. She had eaten and now she was reading, but she didn't look relaxed.

"Her car in the garage?"

"Yeah. The Volvo."

"Can you put something on it?"

"The door's a screamer. I can open it, but she'll hear. It's under the bedroom."

We finished the food in silence, then bagged our trash and put it aside. The occasional car passed, but we were low in the seats, and motionless. A man in a light jacket walked by with a boxer dog on a leash. They stopped at the Rover's front end. The boxer dog peed on the tire, but Jon made no comment. We didn't tell war stories, or jokes, or make conversation. We sat without moving, watching a motionless woman.

Amy's phone rang at seven minutes after ten. It was abrupt, and surprisingly loud.

Jon turned up the audio.

I said, "You recording this?"

"Yeah. Shh."

Amy didn't jump on the call. She watched the phone ring five times before she answered. Her voice was calm and crisp.

"Hello."

We heard only Amy's side of the conversation.

"All right. Good. Yes, the day after tomorrow is fine. Will Mr. Rollins be there?"

Rollins. A new player entered the game.

"I don't care if he comes, so long as I meet the principals. Tell him—"

The caller must have interrupted. She listened for almost two minutes, and her face grew pinched with irritation.

"No, *you* listen, Charles—"

Charles. The man with the flowers, who Meryl pressed me to find. I wondered what Meryl knew about Charles.

"The funds have to be deposited prior to delivery. We're not taking cash, credit cards, or a personal check. When I confirm the transfer, and *only* when the transfer is confirmed, I'll take you to pick up the material, or we can meet them, whatever—"

She listened again.

"Plastic containers, like the sample. Two hundred kilograms less the weight of the sample."

She listened some more, nodding along with whatever was being said.

"You do that. Call me."

Amy hung up, and sat holding the phone. She swayed, so slightly she barely moved. Then she gathered the paper plate and take-out carton, and carried the trash to the kitchen.

I stared at Jon.

"Did you hear what I heard?"

Jon grinned. He seemed delighted.

"Yeah. She's selling two hundred kilos of plastic explosives."

"That's what it sounded like."

"Think she really has it?"

I remembered what Scott James told us. The plastic explosive found in the bomb on his car was the same material found in the house.

"Yes."

The imitation Meryl had made a big deal out of embezzled money, but she'd said nothing about missing explosives. Losing two hundred kilograms of military explosives would jeopardize their position with the government far more than embezzled money.

I watched the screen, waiting for Amy to return.

Jon said, "It's not here, and you searched the other place, right? Maybe it's in her car."

I shook my head, thinking.

Jon said, "Two hundred kilograms is four hundred forty pounds. That much C-4 takes up about eight cubic feet, which is your basic cardboard box."

Amy returned from the kitchen. She made sure the front door was locked, gathered her phone and computer, and turned off the living room lamp.

Jon brought up the bedroom camera. The high-angle view looked across the bed through the length of the room. The desk, the closet, and the bath were on the right of the frame. Amy put her phone and laptop on the bed, and pulled off her top. She was fleshy and white, with folds in her skin. I felt bad for invading her privacy. When she took off her bra, I looked away.

A brown fringed jacket lay on her bed. She hung the jacket and her slacks in the closet, took pajamas from the chest of drawers, and went into the bathroom. We heard the toilet and running water. A few minutes later, Amy turned off the bathroom light, and climbed into bed.

At ten forty-two, Amy got out of bed, and touched a framed photograph that stood on the chest.

I said, "The picture. It wasn't there earlier."

"It was in her purse. She put it there when she got home."

Jacob.

Her touch was loving, but did not linger.

She went back to bed, and turned off the lamp. The video image went dark. Her house went dark.

Seven minutes later, we heard a soft rasp. Sleep.

I said, "You've been here a long time. Take off. I got it."

"I'm good."

I lowered the seat, and settled back.

Jon and I sat in the Rover all night. I stayed until the next morn-ing, when I left to meet the fake Meryl. I left, but Jon stayed. Jon didn't leave, and he never complained.

36

Scott James

SCOTT KENNELED MAGGIE in Glendale, returned to the Boat, and spent the rest of the day at Major Crimes. He phoned Cowly to tell her what happened, but she'd already heard. She was annoyed, but not as angry as Scott expected. Cowly called him a knucklehead, and they made plans for dinner. Scott was relieved.

Stiles brought him up to speed on the investigation, introduced him to several detectives, and tried to answer his questions. She didn't have much to report, but Scott found himself liking her.

The size of the task force was impressive, but they were in the third day of the investigation and didn't have a line on the man in the sport coat, how Carlos Etana was involved, or who had been using the Echo Park house in the name of a dead man.

Scott told himself to be patient, but wondered what Cole knew. Cole's offer to help was like a worrisome terrier that wouldn't let go of his ankle. Cole might be one of those people who colored outside the lines, but people who hung it over the edge weren't always wrong. Cole might be able to use his secret knowledge and shady connections to break the case faster than Carter.

Scott took out the card with Cole's number, but didn't show it to Stiles. He flexed the card under the table, thinking.

"Why do you think Cole was there?"

"Up to no good, most likely."

Stiles was on her computer in the conference room. Scott was at the far end of the table, flipping through reports.

Scott said, "He told me he was looking for someone named Thomas Lerner."

Stiles glanced up, frowning at his interest.

"It's true a resident confirmed that Mr. Cole asked about Lerner, but neither that resident, nor any other neighbor, including the old-timers, remembers a Lerner having lived on their street. And we haven't been able to find any evidence—none—that the Lerner Mr. Cole described even exists."

"You think he's lying?"

She stared at Scott as if she were trying to figure out why he was asking.

"Yes. I believe he is lying."

Stiles returned to her computer, but Scott didn't want to let it go.

"Maybe he can't tell us. Maybe he isn't so much lying as withholding."

Stiles didn't look up this time.

"You're thinking about Mr. Cole too much."

Scott flexed Cole's card again, and put it away.

"Yeah, you're right. He seemed legit, is all. I can't help thinking he might be able to help."

Stiles pushed back from her computer, and crossed her arms.

"Do yourself a favor, stop thinking."

Carter returned a half hour later, and continued to ignore him. Scott felt uncomfortable, and finally left. He picked up Maggie from Glendale, and bought a case of bottled water and two giant bags of chocolate chip cookies on his way home. Guilt snacks for the officers stuck pulling guard duty.

They reached home early in the evening. Scott introduced himself to the latest set of officers, gave them some water and cookies, then changed into shorts, and took Maggie to the park. They jogged for thirty minutes, which was exercise more for Scott than Maggie. Scott jogged with a gimpy lurch. Maggie kept up by walking quickly. They played with a tug toy after the run. The heavy rubber toy was made for large dogs, but dogs selected as police patrol K-9s went through them quickly. Maggie's jaws and neck were so strong, and her drive to hold so fierce, Scott could swing her in circles once she clamped onto the toy. Despite her high drive, Maggie wouldn't chase balls. Scott had tried dozens of times. He could catch her off guard with the sudden motion sometimes, and Maggie would take off, but once she realized she was chasing a ball, she'd break off the chase. No one knew why, not even Leland, but Scott had discovered a substitute.

Scott had brought along three large chunks of baloney, each about the size of a golf ball. He dug the treat bag out of his pack.

"Treat."

Maggie jumped to a full alert, her eyes locked on the greasy cube.

Scott threw it hard, and Maggie sprinted after it.

The chunk bounced and skipped through the grass thirty yards away. Scott didn't know if she could see it, but canine eyes were far more sensitive to motion than human eyes, and her nose would do the rest.

Maggie's momentum carried her past. She clawed up divots of

He glanced at Cowly to indicate his surprise, but Cowly was staring at Stiles.

Stiles bent from the hips and beamed at Maggie.

"Hi, pretty girl! What's all that barking about?"

Stiles stepped inside, and thrust out her hand to Cowly.

"Sorry to interrupt. Glory Stiles. Detective-Three at Major Crimes."

Cowly took the hand, and offered a perfunctory smile.

"Joyce Cowly. Detective-Three, Homicide Special."

Stiles nodded, and took back her hand.

"Well, it's a pleasure to meet you. Maybe we'll cross on a case one day."

"Maybe we will."

Stiles gave Scott the binder.

"More mug shots. I changed the parameters based on your comments. Hopefully, these will look more like our suspect."

Cowly said, "How thoughtful. I usually email a photo-file."

Stiles considered Scott for a moment.

"Truth is, I felt bad about how certain people carried on today. I don't think it was so bad, you going to see Mr. Cole. We learned something useful."

Scott glanced at Cowly. Surprised and pleased.

"Great. I'm glad I could help."

"The man you named, the one you thought was a veteran."

"Jon Stone."

"Turns out, he is, only the government won't tell us about him. Our request for information was denied."

"I don't understand, denied? We're the police."

Cowly moved closer, and now she seemed interested.

"The Department of Defense sealed his records?"

"Locked'm up tight, and threw away the key."

Stiles seemed thoughtful.

"You know what the gentleman told me? He was very nice, by the way. Latin, of all things. '*Si Ego Certiorem Faciam*'—I don't recall the rest."

Stiles focused on Scott. Her voice didn't change, but her gaze was pointed.

"'I could tell you, but I'd have to kill you.'"

Stiles cocked her head, and stared even harder.

"Your Mr. Cole has interesting friends."

Stiles took a quick step back, once again warm.

"I apologize again. I'll let y'all get back to what you were doing. Maggie, you're such a sweetie."

She touched the binder Scott held.

"Look through, and let me know. Y'all have a good night."

Stiles opened the door, and disappeared into darkness. A few seconds later, Scott heard the gate.

Cowly said, "Bitch."

Three minutes later, Maggie charged to the window, and filled the guest house with thunder.

37

Maggie

MAGGIE PACED THROUGH their crate with her head down. She paused in the bathroom, whined, and rounded Scott's bed to the window. The window was closed, but outside air seeped in through hairline gaps in the window's frame. The tiny drafts were too small to be noticed by Scott, but were as obvious to Maggie as plumes of colored smoke. She pushed her nose under the drapes, found nothing alarming, and returned to the living room. Maggie whined at Scott, but Scott ignored her. She pawed the floor, turned in a circle, and lowered herself.

Scott's scent was rich with the rancid oils of tension. Their crate was alive with unexpected sounds and unfamiliar scents. Each time Maggie heard the gate, she barked and charged to the door.

"Maggie, shut up! They're friends!"

Scott's manner with the uniformed strangers told Maggie they weren't a threat, but Maggie remained alert. Each time a visitor left, her ears swiveled, tipped, and followed their footsteps through the gate.

Scott safe.

Pack safe.

Most dogs could hear four times better than a person, but Maggie's enormous, upright ears evolved to detect quiet predators and distant prey. She could control each ear independently of the other. Eighteen muscles articulated each ear, shaping and sculpting her sail-like pinna to gather and concentrate sounds at frequencies far beyond any a human could hear. This allowed Maggie to hear seven times better than Scott. She could hear the whine of a jet at thirty thousand feet, termites chewing through wood, the crystal in Scott's watch hum, and thousands of sounds as invisible to Scott as the scents he could not smell.

When sounds and scents were normal, Maggie lay on her belly with her head between her paws.

She listened.

She sniffed.

She watched Scott.

Not long after they returned from the park, Maggie heard an approaching intruder and raced to the door, but this time the intruder was Joyce. Maggie wagged her tail.

Scott happy.

Maggie happy.

Maggie went to the kitchen, drank, roamed through Scott's bedroom, and returned to the living room. Scott and Joyce were talking. Maggie lowered herself, sighed, and closed her eyes, but did not sleep. She listened to Scott and Joyce, and the world beyond their crate, and heard the gate open as loud as a gunshot.

Maggie scrambled to the door, barking.

"Maggie, down! Quiet!"

Maggie recognized the intruder's scent, and remembered the tall, human woman as friendly and nonthreatening.

"Hi, pretty girl! What's all that barking about?"

Scott allowed the woman to enter.

Maggie picked a new spot on the floor, settled, and listened. The tall woman left a few minutes later.

Scott and Joyce ate their chow. Joyce sometimes stayed, and slept with Scott in the bed, but this didn't happen tonight. They sat on the couch, and talked. Maggie heard strange sounds. The first time, she rushed to the door. The second, she raged into the bedroom. Joyce soon left, and Scott took Maggie to do her business.

When they returned to the crate, Maggie followed Scott to the bathroom where he urinated, showered, and made the blue foam in his mouth. Maggie stayed close.

She followed him through the crate as he turned off the lights and stretched on the couch. Maggie knew patterns. This was their time for sleep. She sniffed a spot near the couch, turned in a circle, and lay.

"Night, dog."

Thump thump.

Maggie's nose crinkled as she tested the air.

Her ears swiveled to listen.

She heard cheeps and chirps from the police car on the street and the mumble of the old woman's television. She heard Scott's heartbeat slow as he fell asleep.

Maggie sniffed.

She listened, and raised her head.

The high-pitched squeak of branches rubbing together was unusual. A board in the fence behind their crate popped. Leaves rustled, and rustled again, closer.

Maggie charged to the door, raging and fierce.

"Maggie, please. I'm begging you."

Her bark was deep-chested, and furious. She ran to the bedroom, reared up, and hit the windowsill with her paws.

"SHUT UP!"

Maggie listened.

The pops and rustle had stopped. Nothing was approaching, but she heard nothing move away.

Maggie sniffed the plumes of outside air—sniff sniff sniff, sniff sniff sniff. She smelled nothing out of the ordinary, but she growled low and deep in her chest.

The air was still. Scent would spread slowly. She sniffed again, and waited.

38

Mr. Rollins

MR. ROLLINS was surprised when Eli called, but the call made his night. That crazy fuck, Eli, had really come through.

Now, later that night, Mr. Rollins stood in deep shadow next to a motor home, across the street and two houses away. He had a clear view of the Trans Am in the old lady's front yard, the patrol car parked by their drive, and the two cops in the car.

Eli, on the phone, whispered in his ear.

"You hear the dog?"

Mr. Rollins, whispering back.

"Where's your man?"

"The house to the west. In the backyard."

Eli was on a roof behind the old lady's property, up on the next street. One of his men, Hari, had a car over by Eli. A second, some guy with a name Mr. Rollins couldn't pronounce, was parked at the mouth of the clown's dead-end street. Eli had called to discuss the dog, and Mr. Rollins had brought the solution. Also, he wanted to share in the kill. Some things never get old.

Eli sent a man so Mr. Rollins could hear the dog. When the dog fired up, a cop got out of the car, and walked up the drive.

Mr. Rollins whispered.

"Move your man. Cop."

The officer stopped at the gate. She waited until the barking tailed away, then went back to the car. Her partner got out to meet her, and the two of them stayed in the drive.

"Clear. They're out here, bullshitting."

"You see what I say, this crazy barking?"

"Yeah. Loud."

"Whichever way we approach, the dog does this. The officers always come look."

All these little yards were fenced, and the fences were overgrown with vines and hedges.

"You know where I am, right?"

"The motor home. Across the street, and two driveways east."

"Right. The package is behind the front right tire."

Mr. Rollins had dealt with dogs before.

"We throw it over the fence?"

"Them. There's four. Toss'm over the fence. The dog will take care of the rest."

"I will send Hari."

"Don't wait. No telling when he'll let the dog out."

"We will not wait."

"Hari has to wash his hands, okay?"

"Wash?"

"You get this in your mouth, it'll kill you. Hari's gotta wash his hands or wear gloves."

"Of course."

"I'm serious, Eli."

"I tell Hari. Wash."

Eli was laughing.

Mr. Rollins peeled off his vinyl gloves, backed away from the motor home, and eased over a fence. Eli didn't take him seriously, or didn't give a shit. People from that part of the world cared nothing for human life.

Hari would probably be dead by morning, just like the stupid dog.

Alpha Dogs

39

Scott James

THE LAST PURPLE was fading from the gray dawn sky when Scott eased open the door. Maggie pushed her snout through the crack, and tried to shoulder her way out, but Scott blocked her way. He studied the backyard, and whispered.

"Easy."

Maggie's nose worked triple-time, sniffing for scent. Scott smiled at her obvious desire.

Mrs. Earle had a small, raggedy lawn, but most of the yard was filled with a clutter of rose beds, shrubbery, and fruit trees. Bird feeders hung from the fruit trees, which attracted squirrels, who picked through the fallen seed.

Maggie loved to chase squirrels. She knew squirrels were fruit tree regulars, and usually appeared in the morning, so each day began with a hopeful search for a squirrel.

"Got one, Maggie? You got one?"

Scott saw no squirrels, and decided the coast was clear. He clipped her to the thirty-foot lead, and opened the door.

"Get'm!"

Scott got a kick out of watching her charge to the tree. Head up, ears pricked, she was totally into the hunt. She hit the base of the tree, seemed surprised that no squirrels were present, then lowered her nose and trotted in high-speed circles, searching for scent.

Mrs. Earle called out from her door.

"Did she get one?"

Mrs. Earle was a straw of a woman in her eighties, bundled in a terry cloth robe.

"No, ma'am. Not today."

"I'd love to see her get one. Do you know the difference between a squirrel and a rat?"

Scott didn't know many jokes, but this was an old joke. He was pleased he remembered.

"A squirrel is a rat having a bad hair day."

Mrs. Earle frowned.

"I don't understand."

He couldn't tell whether Mrs. Earle was confused, or putting him on. He decided she was serious.

"A rat has a skinny tail. A squirrel's tail is fluffy. You know how when you have a bad hair day, your hair sticks out and won't do what you want? A squirrel is a rat having a bad hair day."

"That's not what I meant. Rats and squirrels both eat my oranges. These tree rats have been stealing my fruit for years."

Scott felt a tug on the lead. Maggie had widened her search.

"Mrs. Earle? I know Maggie's been barking a lot, what with all the officers coming and going. I'm sorry. They won't be around much longer."

She waved a hand, dismissive.

"A person can't have too many policemen. I've never felt safer."

Scott felt another tug.

Maggie was circling something in the flower bed. She leaned forward to sniff, then backed away, circled a few steps, and leaned forward again. Scott saw an object but couldn't make out what it was.

Mrs. Earle said, "Don't let her pee-pee in my flowers. These girl dogs kill grass."

"She found something. Maggie!"

Maggie's head snapped up. Scott took up the lead, and walked over to see what she'd found.

Mrs. Earle called from her door.

"What is it, a rat? If it's a rat, don't let her touch it!"

"It's a raccoon."

Raccoons, opossums, and skunks were common in Los Angeles. Scott often saw the nocturnal creatures when he patrolled the city at night, and when he arrived home at the end of his shift. And twice, Maggie had gone berserk when opossums waddled slowly past the French doors, safely out of reach behind the glass.

Adult raccoons could grow pretty large, but this raccoon wasn't much larger than a cat. Scott's first thought was rabies, so he pulled Maggie away. The animal's coat appeared glossy and clean, but its eyes were a vivid red, and thin blood and bile matted its rear end and mouth. As he studied it, a blood bubble grew in its mouth, and the animal made a soft hiss.

"Aw, damn. Poor thing."

Then Scott saw what appeared to be gray crumbs flecked with

red and blue, and realized the raccoon had thrown up ground meat. Only the red and blue didn't fit. He probed through the mess with a twig, and saw what appeared to be fragments of red and blue pills.

Scott put Maggie into the guest house. He covered the raccoon with a large plastic pail, and was trying to decide what to do when he spotted the gray ball. It was dirty and lopsided, and stood out on the hard-packed soil under a rosebush.

Scott moved closer, and saw red and blue flecks. He broke open the ball with a branch, and saw it was made of raw hamburger. Red and blue flecks were mixed with the meat, along with something that looked like white powder.

Scott found a third meatball next to the guest house, and this ball was partially eaten. The raccoon.

Scott covered the balls to mark their location and protect the evidence. He alerted the duty officers out in the patrol car, and called Carter to report his discovery.

A DOZEN RADIO CARS blocked Scott's street and the street above. SID rolled out criminalists to collect the samples and the raccoon. Mrs. Earle's yard was searched, as were the properties on either side, and the property directly behind. A boot officer named Leslie Day found a fourth meatball caught between agapanthus three feet from Mrs. Earle's back door. No additional lumps of meat were found.

Scott stood with Maggie in the yard, watching the officers search. He had tried to keep her in the guest house at first, but she wouldn't stop barking. Once she was outside and leashed up with Scott, she was as calm as she was at any other crime scene.

Carter, Stiles, and a third task force detective rolled out, along with two detectives from North Hollywood Station. Carter and Stiles spoke briefly to Scott, then set about coordinating a door-knock to question the neighbors.

Scott stayed out of the way. He watched the action, and thought about the man in the sport coat, and Cole's offer.

Carter snagged the criminalist as he was leaving.

"How long has the meat been here?"

"Fire up the grill. You could eat'm."

"Give me a frame. Time in the weeds."

The criminalist thought for a second.

"Moderate oxidation on the exterior, the inside's still pink. No ants to speak of. Cool night like we had, I'd say they've been here at least ninety minutes, and not more than six hours."

"Sometime between midnight and sunup."

"That's my call."

Stiles said, "What about the poison?"

"A central nervous system component for sure, and a fast-acting anticoagulant. Maybe an acid. Something nasty. Blew out the raccoon in no time."

"I'd like a source list, and a list of the countries where these things are sold."

"Even if they're available here?"

"Even so, and if it turns out these items aren't sold in the U.S., would you call me? Don't even take the time to type a report."

Stiles followed the criminalist out to his van. Carter seemed to notice Scott, and came over. Carter hadn't mentioned yesterday's incident, and neither had Scott.

"You call your boss?"

Meaning Lieutenant Kemp.

"Not yet."

"I'm required to notify your division commander, and he'll call your boss, so you might want to give him a call. Let him know what's going on, and all that. As a courtesy."

"Good idea. Thanks."

Carter watched the uniformed officers searching the weeds and the flower beds. An officer with a ladder was searching the roof.

Carter said, "Not my business, but you might want to think about a change of location."

"I have to figure out what to do about Mrs. Earle."

"The old lady in here?"

Scott nodded.

"Either she's gotta go, or I have to go. This is her home."

Carter looked uncomfortable, and Scott wished he would leave.

"So you know, we're increasing our presence. We'll have two cars out front, two on the next block, and both streets will be residents-only for the next two days."

"Even if I leave?"

"Even if you leave. If you stay, we'll maintain the closure as long as necessary."

"I'll leave."

"Good. I think that's wise."

Carter stared at the ground, and still didn't leave.

Scott said, "I'll see you downtown."

"Don't bother. You have to find a place."

"I'll look through mug shots. Maybe we'll get lucky."

Carter finally turned to leave.

"Up to you."

Scott watched Carter walking away, and touched Maggie's ear.

"Detective Carter."

Carter glanced back.

"He tried to kill my dog."

"I understand. I'll see you downtown."

Scott watched Carter leave, and gazed down at Maggie. He touched the soft fur of her head, and smiled when her tail wagged.

Carter didn't understand yet, but he would.

Elvis Cole

THE WOMAN I didn't know met me at a supermarket in West Holly-wood on Santa Monica Boulevard. I bought two hot espresso drinks, arrived thirty-six minutes early, and parked behind a tow truck in a gas station across the street. I checked in with Pike and Jon Stone, and set back to wait.

The Mystery Meryl arrived twenty minutes early. She parked among a loose scatter of cars and trucks, and did nothing out of the ordinary. She seemed comfortable with waiting, like someone who thought nothing could go wrong.

I copied her tag, and called my DMV friend.

"Shows a silver Lexus SUV registered to a Meryl Lawrence. We checked this name last night, didn't we?"

"You found four. Three up north, and one in Pasadena. Belle-fontaine."

"I remember. The Lexus shows the same."

"The Lexus shows the Bellefontaine address?"

"Correct."

The woman who wasn't Meryl Lawrence was driving a Lexus registered to a Meryl Lawrence who supposedly lived at the real Meryl Lawrence's address, only the real Meryl Lawrence didn't own a Lexus. Impressive.

"Last night, you found a Cadillac and a Porsche registered to Meryl Lawrence. You didn't mention a Lexus."

Her voice grew hazy.

"Yeah, I remember. This is weird."

Weird was a bad sign.

"When I search her name, I get the Caddie and the Porsche, but not the Lexus. When I search the tag, I get the Lexus, but not the Caddie and Porsche."

I said, "Weird."

"Must be a glitch in the system. I'll get back to you."

Driving a vehicle registered to the real Meryl even though the real Meryl didn't own the vehicle sounded like more than a glitch. I wondered how she did it.

I sat behind the tow truck until I was ten minutes late, then backed away and circled the block. I was turning into the parking lot when Scott James called. I wanted to answer, but let it go to voice mail. The imitation Meryl Lawrence had my undivided attention.

I parked, and got into her car.

"Nonfat, no-whip mocha and a skinny vanilla latte. Take your pick."

Her expression hovered between a smile and a frown, as if she didn't know what to make of the coffee. She chose the vanilla.

"You must have good news."

I sipped the mocha. Cold.

"The florist remembered Charles."

She eyed me over the vanilla, waiting.

"Is he the man in your drawing?"

"No. They couldn't offer much in the way of a description, but he's not the man in the sketch. That's definite."

I couldn't tell if she thought this was good news or not.

"But they remembered him?"

"You don't like the coffee?"

"I don't give a shit about the coffee. What do they remember?"

"Mid to late forties, brown-on-brown, suit. A generic business type. He told the clerk the flowers had to be impressive. Sounds like the kind of turd you thought he'd be. Trying to take advantage."

I sipped more mocha, and pushed her with Lerner.

"The good news is, I'm closer to Lerner. I got a line on Jacob's old friends. They'll know Lerner for sure, and someone will know how to reach him."

Her nostrils flared, as if she resented the subject.

"Let's go back to Charles. Did you speak with Amy's neighbors?"

"I didn't go back to her house. I won't find anything new, and asking her neighbors about Charles is only a waste of time."

"Your time has been paid for. Maybe one of her neighbors saw him. Maybe she gossiped about him."

She was definitely all about Charles.

"Speaking of which, my time is something I want to discuss. We need to reconsider our arrangement."

"Excuse me?"

"I quoted a price based on what you told me, which didn't include a murder and a police investigation. The police are all over me, and I'm working around the clock because you're in a rush. Two thousand dollars doesn't cut it. I want another three."

"You're trying to screw me."

"I'm getting close, Meryl. Amy and Charles are in the crosshairs."

"It doesn't sound like you're close. It sounds like you're ripping me off."

"The flowers weren't delivered to Amy's home. Charles sent them to a house in Silver Lake. I think she's living there. Maybe with Charles."

"Where?"

"Three thousand."

"You're making this up."

"You hired me because I'm good. You want to part ways, fine, we can part. I'm close."

She didn't seem as angry as I expected. She was breathing fast, but she looked hungry and excited.

"I'll give you another thousand."

"Twenty-five hundred."

"A thousand tomorrow, and another if you find her in the next two days. If you find her today, you'll get both plus a five hundred bonus."

"Sounds good."

She dropped the latte into the parking lot.

"You'd better find them, you sonofabitch. Get out."

I got out, and went to my car. She backed up fast and drove hard to the nearest exit. She was angry, but I thought she was also scared. I waited until she was gone, then tapped Joe Pike's number.

Pike said, "I'm on her."

The woman who would be Meryl Lawrence had secrets, but my secrets were better.

41

SCOTT JAMES left a message that was short and direct.

"If you meant it about helping, call me. I'm on my way to the Boat."

I was surprised and relieved. The liar Meryl had pushed me harder than ever to find Charles, and find him quickly. Charles had told Amy their deal would close in a couple of days. I didn't have to be the World's Greatest Detective to see the connection. The secret Meryl knew about Amy's upcoming deal, and wanted to find Charles before the deal closed. Since she knew about Charles, the deal, and the Echo Park house, it seemed likely she knew about the man in the sport coat. I wanted the man in the sport coat, and so did Scott James.

I tapped the callback, and Officer James answered.

"Did you mean it, when you offered to help?"

His voice was low, and tense, as if people were listening.

"I meant it."

"I want the man in the sport coat. Do you know who he is?"

"No."

"You know something."

"I know things, but not who he is. I want him, too."

"Okay, listen. The ATF analyzed the bomb from my car. You know what taggants are?"

"Detection markers."

Taggants had been required in plastic explosives since the nineties.

"The explosive from my car and the stuff we found in Echo Park don't have taggants."

I took a breath and let it out. Plastic explosives were light, stable, and as easy to shape as pizza dough. A brick of polymerized explosive could be rolled into long, thin strings or pressed flat into sheets or braided like hair. This shape-changing malleability and stability made it ideal for lunatics to sneak aboard airliners. Taggants were added to make the material detectable. Amy's material would be perfect for the people she wanted to reach.

"Has Carter put Etana with the explosives?"

"Not yet, but they're digging. Etana had three brothers. His oldest, Ricardo, was found in a canal down in Venice last night. Carter thinks their deaths are connected."

I jotted the name, and crunched the numbers. Carlos Etana was too young to have been connected to Juan Medillo, but an older member of his family might have been.

"Have they checked for a connection between the Etanas and Juan Medillo?"

Scott sounded surprised.

"You know about Medillo?"

"I'm magic. I also know he's been dead for seven years, and someone's been paying the property tax in his name. Maybe someone named Etana."

"I'll try to find out. They only learned about Ricardo this morning."

The Amy file was behind my seat. I took it out and flipped through my notes from Eddie Ditko and the title company. Nothing explained the connection between Walter Jacobi and Juan Medillo, or how Medillo had come to own Jacobi's house. I paged to the memorial announcement. *Beloved brother and son. Loving sisters and father.*

"Who's working the house?"

"Doug Stinnis and Edie Quince."

Stinnis. The detective who called Solano.

"Did they talk to Medillo's family?"

"They talked to the father yesterday. Stinnis didn't like him, but they thought he was credible."

"Meaning he has no knowledge or involvement?"

"They believed him."

"What about the sisters?"

"They haven't found the sisters."

I glanced at their names in the memorial. Nola and Marisol.

"What's the big deal?"

"Married and left town. The father says he doesn't know where they are."

"He doesn't have contact info for his daughters?"

"They had a falling-out after Juan's murder. Stinnis says it must've been bad. All these years later, the old man did nothing but trash talk. He says they probably knew and were ripping him off, but he hasn't heard from them in years. Claims he doesn't even know their married names."

Beloved brother and son. Loving sisters and father.

"They got married, moved, and he doesn't know their married names?"

"I've gotta go. Detective Stiles is looking at me."

"One more thing."

"I'll call you back. I'm supposed to be looking at mug shots."

"Has the lab work from the house come back?"

"I don't think so. The asshole you chased sprayed the place with bleach."

"Try to find out. See if a woman's DNA was in the house."

Scott was quiet a moment.

"Why are you asking about a woman?"

"Find out. Let me know."

"I knew you knew something. You totally know something."

"I know things, but not enough."

I hung up and reread the memorial announcement. Seven years after Juan Medillo's memorial, the loving sisters had vanished, and the loving father did nothing but trash talk.

Families.

The memorial announcement pictured a cross, angels, and a heavenly beam of light. It was written by Nola Medillo, and included the name and address of an Eastside church.

I dialed Information, and let the computer connect my call.

A woman named Ms. Cortez answered. I told her I was trying to reach Nola Medillo regarding a property owned by her brother. Ms. Cortez stopped me before I finished, and couldn't have been more helpful.

"Nola's a friend. Let me put you on hold, and I'll call her."

Nola Medillo's married name was Terina. Eleven minutes later, I was crossing the city to meet her. No callbacks. No waiting. The karmic books were finally balanced.

42

Nola Medillo Terina and her husband lived in a neat frame house a few blocks north of the Pomona Freeway, less than one mile from her father. She was a trim, plain woman in her early forties. She answered the door with an awkward smile, pushing strands of hair from her face.

"This has to be a mistake. You're confusing my brother with another Medillo."

"No, ma'am. Juan Adolfo. Your Juan."

I showed her a copy of the property title. She looked more amused than suspicious when she studied the document.

"Juanito couldn't afford shoes, let alone a house."

"You didn't know he owned the home?"

"I had no idea. Please, come in. Is it mine now?"

Her expression and body language screamed sincerity.

I followed her into the living room, where she perched in an overstuffed chair. Her home was simple and comfortable. A gas fireplace with an ornate mantel filled the end of the room. Small vases and bowls that might have been in her family for generations dotted the mantel along with pictures of herself and her husband and siblings.

"I don't know, Ms. Terina. I'm not here to distribute his property. I'm hoping you know how he came to own it."

"I'm sorry, I don't."

"Do you know the name Walter Jacobi?"

She shook her head.

"No, sir. I'm sorry."

"He was Juan's cellmate up at Solano."

Her face darkened, but only for a moment.

"Juan wouldn't talk about his life in the jail. When we saw him, he wanted stories from home."

"The house belonged to Jacobi. The title changed hands while they were cellmates."

"This is illegal?"

"No, ma'am, but someone has been taking care of the house and paying the taxes in Juan's name."

She looked curious.

"Pretending to be Juan?"

"In a way. The problem is, the house is being used as a place to do crime."

She darkened again and glanced at a hutch in the corner.

"This is silly, Juan with a house. Absurd."

The hutch was narrow and dark. A framed color photograph of a boy sat alone on the middle shelf. It stood on a thin box, as if on a pedestal. The boy appeared to be in the fourth or fifth grade, and wore a short-sleeve white shirt with a tie and his Catholic school emblem. The boy could have been her son, but I knew he was Juan, young and smiling before drugs and crime and prison. She noticed me staring.

"You see the smile? Look at his happy smile."

I looked away from the smile.

"Ms. Cortez told me you and your sister and Juan were close."

"The three of us, yes. Maybe me more than Marisol, but I'm the oldest."

"Owning a house is a big deal. I'm surprised he didn't tell you."

She stared for a moment, and glanced away. Embarrassed.

"My brother was an addict and a criminal. Maybe he was ashamed, how he came to have it."

"Your father told the police he didn't know about the house. Was he telling the truth?"

Her eyes lost their soft warmth when I mentioned their father.

"I wouldn't know."

"He told them he thinks you and your sister know. He says Juan would have told you, and you and Marisol are ripping him off."

She tensed and drew herself taller.

"My father is an asshole."

"I probably shouldn't say this, but the police think he's an asshole, too."

I thought she would smile, but she didn't.

"A horrible man. Hateful. Juan's life was hell because of that man."

She glanced at the smiling boy again, but now her eyes held no joy.

"For my sister and I, Juan only showed the beautiful smile and happy eyes. This is who he was to us, but not our father."

"Someone knew about his house, Ms. Terina. If Juan wouldn't tell you, who would he tell? Friends? A girlfriend?"

She pushed at her hair again, and went to the hutch.

"The prison sent us his things. Unfortunately, the package was sent to our father."

She stared at her brother's picture.

"There were letters. Some, from a special young man. My father destroyed them. He burned them in the yard like a madman."

I saw the scene, and understood the estrangement.

"I'm sorry. It must have been ugly."

"One, I read. Most of it, not all, before the madman took it."

She set Juan's picture aside, and brought the box it sat on to the couch.

"He came to the memorial. He came out of love, but my father is such an unfortunate man."

Nola Terina opened the box, and took out the registry from her brother's memorial. A silk ribbon marked the page where the people who attended signed their names. She ran her finger down the list, and stopped at a signature in the middle.

"Here. You see? Hector something."

The handwriting was scrunched and difficult to read.

"Pedroia?"

"Yes. He was so nice to come."

I copied the name as she continued.

"A sweet boy, I thought, and our father repaid his kindness with cruelty. Marisol and I, our hearts broke. We resigned as his daughters that day."

"Hector Pedroia."

"This was seven years ago, but he worked at a restaurant, the El Norte Steakhouse. He was a cook."

She phoned the restaurant for their address and gave me directions.

Hector Pedroia had left the steakhouse years ago, but the owner knew where to find him.

43

Hector Pedroia's Original Taco Cuisine food truck was parked near Chinatown not far from Union Station. The tacos were expensive, but the line was long. Pedroia was working the register while two younger cooks prepared food. The truck was painted a bright, happy aqua, and sported a handwritten menu offering tacos made with lamb shank, Cuban *lechón*, *birria*, and other designer selections. The *birria* was stewed goat. Not a popular meat in Anglo markets, but simmered with *guajillo* and *ancho* chiles, it was one of my favorites.

I got into line and waited.

Pedroia gave the woman ahead of me a pick-up number and change, and flashed a hurried smile.

"Yes, amigo, what would you like?"

"Two *birria* and a lamb."

"Anything to drink, my friend?"

"I'm good. When the line slacks, I'd like to talk. Nola Medillo sends her regards."

Pedroia didn't slow or change expression. He barked my order to the cooks and rang up the tab.

"Habañero crema with the lamb? A drizzle topped with cilantro? The *birria*, a few slivers of radish?"

"Perfect."

My number was forty-two. I waited with the crowd on the sidewalk, and watched the three men work. The grill cook turned out a steady supply of hand-pressed corn tortillas, grilled meats, and vegetables. The line cook, whose station was next to Pedroia, assembled each taco with flair, placed them in aqua cartons, and called out pick-up numbers. Pedroia took several more orders before he glanced my way, and said something to the grill cook. The grill cook took over the register, and Pedroia moved to the line. He filled a carton with tacos, held up the box, and gestured for me to meet him behind the truck.

Pedroia offered the carton and a handful of napkins when I arrived. He had to be in his mid-thirties, but his face was lined beyond his years.

"I didn't mean to pull you away. I would've waited."

He shrugged, as if such concerns were pointless.

"The *birria* was my grandmother's. She claimed my family has made it this way for a thousand years, but she was given to fancy. I made a few changes."

I took a bite. Spicy red juice ran down my fingers.

"Delicious."

"Not too hot?"

"Transcendent."

He pulled a towel from his apron and wiped his hands.

"How do you know Nola?"

"I'm looking into something involving her brother. She told me you were close, so I'm hoping you can help."

"Is this what she said, we were close?"

"My word, not hers. Sorry. She spoke well of you. Not so well of her father."

He smiled, but with more sadness than pleasure.

"The lamb. Don't let it get cold."

I took a bite of the shank.

"Sir, this is superb."

He was pleased with my compliment.

"Juan has been gone for years. What could involve a dead man?"

"He came to own a house when he was up in Solano. Turns out Juan's name is still on the title, and someone using his name has been paying the taxes. I'm hoping you can tell me about it."

Pedroia made a tired snort.

"Of course. Colinski's house."

I ate more lamb, and tried to look calm.

"Juan told you about it?"

"Of course. Juan told me everything. He told me everything *about* everything, whether I wanted to hear or not."

"It was Jacobi's house. Juan got the house from a man named Jacobi, not Colinski."

He wiped at his hands again, and now there was anger in the rubbing.

"He got the house from Jacobi, yes, but he did this for Colinski. The Great Colinski wanted the house."

He rolled his eyes when he said it, and my ears filled with a growing hum. The sound of something far away getting closer.

"Who was Colinski?"

He glanced away. Embarrassed.

"An older boy from the neighborhood. One of those trashy boys Juan used to run with. A criminal. Juan's crush."

He fell silent, and wiped at his hands.

"Juan would do anything to please him."

"Does the Great Colinski have a first name?"

"Royal. Such a name, don't you think? Royal Colinski from East L.A."

The burner vibrated in my pocket, but I was learning too much to stop.

"Why did Colinski want the house?"

"Who knows? A place to hide, cut dope, stash cash, party. Stupid, I said, how are you going to clean up, being involved with a man like this, but the Great Colinski had spoken."

"Jacobi and Juan were both addicts. Did Juan trade drugs for the house?"

"Yes! This was Colinski's brilliant idea."

"Do you know where he is now, Colinski, or what he's doing?"

He flipped the towel.

"I had no interest in the people Juan ran with. I'm clean now, but not then, and I wanted to be clean. We wanted to get clean together, and Juan tried, I do believe he tried, but he would see his old friends, and fall into the old patterns."

I asked him to hold the carton, and took out the sketch.

"What do you think?"

He studied the image.

"Colinski?"

"I'm asking."

His uncertainty wasn't inspiring, but I knew he was trying. Juan's crush. The Great Colinski.

"Could be."

"Three nights ago, a man was murdered at Juan's house. This man left the scene."

"I think this is him, but I am not sure."

I put the sketch away.

"One more thing. Three weeks after Jacobi signed over the property, he died of a drug overdose."

"I remember. Juan told me."

"Did Juan kill him?"

Pedroia looked surprised.

"Juan was weak and needy, but not cruel."

"Eleven days after Jacobi died, Juan was murdered."

"A prison brawl. Brown and black. Juan was caught in the middle, they said. Not even involved."

"He was stabbed sixteen times."

Pedroia clenched when I said it, as if the knife were punching into his back.

"Are you saying Juan was murdered because of this house?"

"I don't know. But with Jacobi and Juan dead, no one was left to connect Colinski to the house."

Pedroia glanced at the uneaten tacos, and dropped the carton into the trash.

"He wouldn't listen."

"Nola thinks well of you. She respects what you felt for her brother. She didn't ask me to say this."

He nodded.

"The *birria*, not too much kick?"

"Not for me. I like spicy."

"One always wonders."

Pedroia climbed back into his aqua truck. I walked back to my car, and checked my phone. The incoming caller was Pike, so I got back to him right away.

"Medillo had help getting the house. I got a name. He might be the man in the sport coat."

"I got a name, too. Your fake Meryl is a problem."

The heat in my chest cooled.

"Who is she?"

"Her true name is Janet Hess. She's the Special Agent in Charge of Homeland Security, the L.A. Field Office."

I climbed into my car, and started the engine. Pike was right. My fake Meryl was a problem.

44

The Los Angeles River flowed southeast across the bottom of the San Fernando Valley to Griffith Park, where it made a hard right turn past Dodger Stadium, Chinatown, and Downtown L.A. to the Long Beach Freeway like a fated lover anxious to find her mate. The river and the LBF dropped straight through the heart of the city to Long Beach, where the river ended its forty-eight-mile trek to the Port of Los Angeles. There, at the end of its journey, the *Queen Mary* and the Aquarium of the Pacific flanked the river's mouth. The L.A. Field Office of Homeland Security waited across the street.

"She went to Long Beach?"

"Yes. The SAC. Want me to stay on her?"

"No. This changes things."

"Thought it might."

"We have to talk to Jon. Come to Silver Lake, and we'll figure out what to do."

I pulled into traffic, but stopped two blocks later, and Googled her name. Her official DHS portrait was easy to find. Janet Hess looked a couple of years younger than the woman I knew as Meryl Lawrence, but Meryl was Hess, and her CV was impressive.

Janet Hess currently serves as Special Agent in Charge (SAC)/ Director of Intelligence, Homeland Security Investigations, U.S. Department of Homeland Security, Los Angeles, California. Ms. Hess is responsible for all aspects of the ICE/HSI investigative mission in the Los Angeles metropolitan area, Las Vegas, and southern Nevada. Prior to her current appointment, she served as ASAC/Field Intelligence Director of the Los Angeles Human Smuggling and Trafficking Unit (HSTU), and as Supervisory Special Agent/Group Supervisor of the Orange County National Security Group and Anti-smuggling Investigations Unit. Prior to working with DHS, Ms. Hess served with the Department of Justice, Immigration and Naturalization Service (DOJ/INS) as a Special Agent with the National Security Investigations Unit and Joint Terrorism Task Force (JTTF).

Hess had the full force, authority, and resources of her agency at her disposal, yet she hired a civilian under false pretenses, and exposed herself and her agency to a liability nightmare. She must have expected to gain something by using me she felt she couldn't get from her agents, and this was likely a secret thing she wanted no one else to know.

I took out the Amy file, and studied the sketch. Scott felt it was a good likeness of the man in the sport coat, but Hector Pedroia couldn't pin the tail on Royal Colinski.

I put the sketch aside, steered back into traffic, and phoned Scott as I drove.

"You still at Major Crimes?"

"Yeah."

The low voice.

"I need two things. Can you talk?"

"Not really. Stiles is close."

"The surveillance teams went away. Did you know?"

"Uh-uh."

"Try to find out why. Be subtle, but try to find out."

"Okay. She's gone. Now we can talk."

"I need you to run a name."

"Running a name isn't as easy as it sounds. Who is it?"

"Thing is, whoever this turns out to be, you can't tell Carter or anyone else. You have to sit on it until I give the word. Agreed?"

"This sounds shifty, Cole. I don't like shifty."

"He might be the man in the sport coat."

Scott was silent, but I heard him breathe.

"I'm not saying it's him, but it's possible. He's the true owner of the house."

"I'll run it."

"This stays between us?"

"Yes. Give me the name."

"First name Royal, R-O-Y-A-L. Last name Colinski."

I spelled Colinski.

"He'll be in the system. Print his full sheet and his mug shot. We'll need it."

I reached Silver Lake a few minutes later, and found Jon's Rover above the construction site. I parked uphill around the curve, walked down, and climbed in. Jon had the driver's seat pushed back, and his laptop propped on the console.

I said, "Did you get to her car?"

"Negative. She hasn't budged."

Amy was stretched on the couch, reading a magazine. Her computer and phone were on the coffee table. She was motionless. Jon stared at the screen, just as still.

I watched Jon watch Amy. Jon Stone had been cooped in the Rover for twenty-eight hours, but he appeared sharp, alert, and freshly shaved. If he could lie on rocks above the tree line in the Hindu Kush for a couple of weeks, I guess spending the night in a Range Rover wasn't so bad.

"This spook of yours, the one who told you the Internet chatter led nowhere, do you trust him?"

Jon glanced at me, curious.

"Yeah. Why?"

"He told you Homeland couldn't ID the person making the posts, so they kicked it back to Washington."

Now he frowned.

"Yeah."

"The woman who hired me is a federal agent with Homeland Security. She is, in fact, the Special Agent in Charge of the L.A. Field Office, Janet Hess."

Jon shifted for the first time.

"You know this for a fact?"

"Pike followed her to the Field Office."

I brought up her image from the Homeland Security website, and showed him.

"Hess."

"The Special Agent in Charge."

"That's what it says. The highest-ranking officer in the Los Angeles Field Office."

Jon settled back.

"And why would the SAC want you involved in her case?"

"Why would your spook tell you their case was closed?"

Jon moved like a panther leaving his bed, and took out his phone.

"Let's find out."

Jon tapped a button, and held the phone to his ear. After a moment, he spoke.

"Obadete mi se vednaga, vuv vrusca c posledniat ni razgovor. Predishnata vi informatcia se okaza pulna glupost."

Jon put his phone away and saw me staring.

"Sorry, dude. Security. He'll get back to me."

I stared, and he shrugged again.

"What, you don't speak Bulgarian?"

Amazing.

Amy sat up, put aside the magazine, and went into the bedroom. Jon noted the time.

"Read nonstop one hour forty-one minutes."

He brought up the bedroom camera. Amy appeared in the upper corner of the image and went into the bathroom. We could see the open door, but not Amy.

"Can we hear if she makes a call?"

"Maybe. Shh."

He ramped up the audio. We heard silence, followed by the tinkle of water.

The toilet flushed, water ran, and Amy went into the closet. She backed out a few seconds later with the fringed jacket and a large, bright-colored purse. I remembered the jacket from the night before, but didn't recall the purse. I wondered if the Ruger was in it. She tucked her phone into the purse, followed it with the picture of Jacob, and left the bedroom. Jon changed cameras as she entered the living room, and started the Rover.

"She's leaving. You want out, go now."

Amy added her computer to the purse, and put on the jacket. The layers of long, dangling fringe swayed like hair in water. She hung the purse on her shoulder, adjusted its weight, and went to the door.

"In or out, dude. I'm staying with her."

I buckled the seat belt.

"I'm in."

We watched as she let herself out.

45

Amy locked the door and made her way down the steps. She held tight to the rail, as if she were afraid of falling. A certified terrorist threat.

We called Pike to fill him in. Jon used the Rover's speakerphone so all three of us were on the call.

Pike said, "I'm twenty out. Does she have the explosives?"

Jon answered.

"Don't know. I couldn't reach her vehicle."

Amy backed out in fits and starts, inching her way into the street.

Jon said, "This is excruciating."

She finally made it into the street, and waited for the door to close. Four cars stacked up behind her, and we were the fifth.

Jon said, "This isn't starting well."

When we stacked up again at the bottom of the hill, we were so far behind we wouldn't be able to see which way she turned. I jumped out and ran past the line of cars in time to see her turn. I ran hard back to the Rover.

"Left. She turned left."

Jon jerked the Rover into the oncoming lane, powered past the cars ahead, and pushed through the turn. I rolled down the window, and stood tall in the wind.

"I don't see her, Jon. I can't see her."

Jon muscled around cars, and the Rover's turbocharged mill screamed. The blue water blurred as we raced up the edge of the lake. I glimpsed her Volvo, climbing into the hills.

"Got her! She's leaving the lake."

Jon pressed, and closed the gap.

The streets north of the reservoir led through the hills to the Golden State Freeway and a pleasant community called Atwater Village. I felt better as we approached Atwater. It was a lovely spot for lunch.

I said, "Lunch."

Jon said, "Lunch."

Then Amy turned away from Atwater, got on the freeway, and once again pulled ahead.

Jon powered forward, and I called Pike.

"She's on the 5, northbound at Atwater."

"Twelve minutes behind you."

We clawed through sluggish, late-morning congestion, glimpsing the Volvo, and losing it.

Pike's voice came from the speaker, quiet and calm.

"I'm on the 5."

"She's approaching the Ventura."

Jon jockeyed us closer.

"Crossing the Ventura. Burbank."

Pike said nothing, but Jon cursed.

"Bob Hope Airport. She's going to the airport."

"Maybe."

"It's the airport."

"Get closer."

We could ride Amy's tail all the way to Seattle on the 5, but if she had a boarding pass and photo ID, Amy Breslyn could board the next jet out, and leave us at the security gate.

We were six cars behind when Amy left the freeway and turned toward Bob Hope Airport.

"Closer, Jon. Tighten."

Pike's voice: "Eight minutes."

Pike was pushing it, too.

I sat taller, using the Rover's height to see past the cars ahead.

She was four cars away when her blinker flashed and she turned toward the airport.

"Joe?"

"I'm here."

"We're not letting her get on a plane. Jon?"

"Say it."

"Drop me at the terminal. Follow her to the parking structure, but don't park. Text me when she gets out, and circle back. She might be picking up someone. I'll walk in with her, but if she flashes a boarding pass or joins a security line, I'm pulling her out."

"What will you do if she screams?"

"Pull faster."

"Meaning I should wait outside for you and the kidnap victim."

"Yes."

We were three cars behind when Amy passed the airport, and continued higher into the Valley.

Jon grinned.

"Negative airport. Northbound to nowhere."

Pike's voice: "Off the 5. I'm close."

We dropped back again, and followed her to a low-end industrial area at the eastern edge of the Valley, where strip malls and mobile-home parks cowered beneath gang tags. Hancock Park was a world away. We were close, and we sensed it. Jon marveled at the surroundings.

"She isn't coming up here for lunch, dude."

"Blinker. She's turning."

Jon eased off the gas.

Two blocks ahead, Amy turned across traffic into a sprawling, drive-in storage operation called Safety Plus Self-Storage. A billboard on the corner read HOME BOAT RV—24 HR SECURE—100+ UNITS. Jon's grin flashed from the far side of the Rover.

"Ground zero, brother. The Death Star."

"Catch up. Go."

Safety Plus was serious about security. A cinder-block wall topped with spirals of concertina wire protected the storage units. All we saw were the roofs of long metal sheds, the tops of shrink-wrapped RVs, and CCTV cameras atop stout metal poles. East Valley taggers had Kryloned the wall so often, their paint looked like urban camouflage.

We roared forward, braked hard, and stopped outside a nursery across the street to peer through the entrance. Inside, we could see a rental office with a glass front and a small parking area, but that was about all. A chain-link fence crowned by more razor wire barred the public from the RVs and sheds. An automated gate in the fence let customers with key cards drive to their units. The parking lot was empty except for a shiny blue pickup and a golf cart beside the office. Amy would have had a key card. She and her Volvo had disappeared into a maze of all-weather sheds and plastic-wrapped motor homes. Charles could be inside. The man in the sport coat might be with him. The place could be crawling with lunatic terrorists, but we saw nothing but wall.

"Tell Pike where we are. I'll try to find her."

I slid from the Rover, jogged across the street, and walked past the office to the gate. I was hoping to see Amy's car, but didn't.

"Excuse me! You can't go in there!"

A beefy woman with a belt bulge and surly eyes stood in the office door. She pointed at a sign on the fence.

"Tenants only."

I gave her a disarming smile and turned away. Mr. Friendly.

"Just looking. Sorry."

The woman went back into the office. A CCTV camera sprouted from the roof, giving her a view of the parking area. Another camera covered the gate. Safety Plus had cameras everywhere, and the cameras would feed to a monitor in the office.

I walked over and went in.

The woman was watching a movie at her desk behind the counter. Boxes, bubble wrap, padlocks, and packing supplies filled shelves, available for purchase. A sign on the counter said FRIENDLY SERVICE— REASONABLE PRICES.

"I'm moving, and I need to store some furniture. Could I take a look around?"

The CCTV monitor sat on her desk, but she had pushed it aside to watch the movie on her laptop. I couldn't see the screen, which meant I couldn't see Amy or Amy's unit.

She pointed at a stack of brochures.

"Prices are in the brochure. Help yourself."

I took a brochure.

"I need a pretty big space, but I can't say how big is big enough. I should take a look, so I'll get an idea if my stuff will fit."

She waved toward the brochure without looking up.

"Tells you the sizes."

I unfolded the brochure and pretended to look.

"I'd rather see the units. So I can visualize. How about a quick tour?"

She paused her movie as if I had asked for a kidney.

"Ronnie gets here at two. I can't leave the desk."

"Oh, sure, I understand. No worries. I can take a peek by myself."

"Against the rules. Liability."

She un-paused her movie, and resumed watching. I heard gunfire and screeching tires.

I pointed at the security monitor.

"How about this? Could I take a quick peek at the video feed? So I can see what the inside looks like."

"Two. Ronnie will take you around."

She turned up the movie's volume.

"What happened to friendly service?"

"Two."

"What if I told you this was a matter of national security?"

She paused the movie again and picked up her phone.

"I'd tell you to leave, or I'm calling the cops."

"The woman who just drove in is storing explosives on your premises. Which is her unit?"

She punched 9-1-1.

"I don't know, and it doesn't matter. The cops are coming."

I was fighting the urge to pistol-whip her when the automated gate opened and Amy's Volvo nosed to the street. Amy was behind the wheel and appeared to be alone. I left the office as she turned, and ran to the street.

Joe and his Jeep were outside the nursery when I reached the entrance. The Rover screamed through a tight turn, and Jon shouted.

"Did you find it?"

"No. Stay with her. Go. I'll find it."

Jon powered away, and I ran to Pike.

"It's here. This is as far from her life as she could get. It has to be here."

I studied the walled fortress across the street. 24 HR SECURE— 100+ UNITS. And an eight-cubic-foot box of plastic explosives could be in any of them.

Pike said, "How will we find it?"

"Magic."

I took out my phone, and called Scott James.

46

Scott James

SCOTT SAT IN AN EMPTY CUBICLE, watching the detectives as he decided what to do. The cubicle's data terminal and phone were missing. None of the detectives wanted a cubicle without a terminal, so Stiles put Scott in the empty. Now he needed a terminal.

The room was busy with working detectives. Stiles moved back and forth between the conference room and the squad area. Each time she came out, she looked at him, and twice she walked over to ask how he was doing. Carter was in the conference room when Scott arrived, but now he was in the commander's office with Mantz, a lieutenant from the Intelligence Section, and the deputy chief who ran the Counter-Terrorism and Special Operations Bureau.

Three workstations in the squad room appeared to be unused. The surrounding workstations were occupied, but Scott had little choice. Stiles was back on the phone in the conference room, so he went to the workstation farthest away.

The department's data system required his name, badge number, and password, after which the system would record his every keystroke for later review. This threat of oversight was to discourage the sale of information to lawyers and private eyes. If later questioned, Scott told himself he could honestly say he was running down a possible connection with the Echo Park house.

Scott slouched low behind the partition, typed in Colinski's name, and entered the search request. He checked to make sure Stiles was still on the phone, looked back at the terminal, and saw the man in the sport coat.

Scott's chest burned with a rush of adrenaline.

Royal Colinski was the man in the sport coat. Younger, not as lined, longer hair, but Colinski was the man in the sport coat.

Scott glanced up, and the burn grew stronger. He looked at the faces of the detectives around him, and Stiles, who was thirty feet away, all of them trying to identify and find the unknown suspect he now knew was Royal Colinski.

Thanks to Cole.

Scott stared at Colinski's face, and cursed himself for agreeing not to tell. If he gave the word, Colinski's picture and warrant would pop up in every radio car and roll call in the city, and ten thousand cops would be on the search.

Scott took out his phone to call Cole.

"Hey."

Scott startled, and found the gray-haired detective in the next cubicle peering across the partition.

The detective said, "Deets is on his way."

"Sorry?"

"You're at his desk. Just letting you know."

Scott set about clearing the terminal.

"Sorry. I hope he won't mind."

"Nah, it's fine. I'm just letting you know. When he gets here, he'll need it."

"Sure. Thanks. I won't be much longer."

Scott punched in the search again, and quickly skimmed Colinski's record. The file led off with Colinski's identifying information, which was followed by a lengthy criminal record. Scott was surprised that Colinski's most recent arrest had occurred sixteen years earlier, and that no warrants were outstanding against him. His prior history showed two stints in prison and multiple felony and misdemeanor arrests, most involving theft, armed robbery, and violent hijack.

Scott glanced up, and froze when Stiles emerged from the conference room. He got ready to shut down the terminal, but Stiles went to the commander's office, and joined the meeting inside.

Scott tapped the partition.

"Ah, Detective."

The gray-haired detective turned.

"Where's the printer?"

"Coffee room. To the right, around the corner."

Scott touched the print key, then signed out of the system, and went to the coffee room. He was relieved to find the room empty. He collected the rap sheet, quickly folded the pages, and returned to his original cubicle. He took out his phone to call Cole, but Cole beat him to it. His phone buzzed, and showed Cole's number in the window. He instinctively lowered his voice.

"You got him. Colinski's the guy."

"Did you tell anyone?"

Scott felt a flash of frustration.

"No, I didn't tell anyone, Cole, but let's think about this. Carter can have ten thousand policemen searching for this animal. We'll put him down fast."

"Carter's out. We'll tell him later, but not now. Get something to write with."

Scott looked up, checked the room, and ducked down.

"Carter's right about one thing. You're up to the butt in this, and you have been since the beginning. There's no way you could've found Colinski this fast if you weren't. You know things nobody here knows."

"That's right. Like the address here. Copy it, and we'll both know."

Cole rattled off a Sun Valley location, and followed it with a question.

"Your dog found the explosive on your car?"

"What does this have to do with Colinski?"

"If it was made with the same material you found in Echo Park, everything."

Scott wondered where Cole was going.

"They were the same. Why?"

"Two hundred kilograms of this stuff may be here. We need to find it, and we have to find it under the radar. Carter can't know."

"Are you serious?"

"I identified the person who made it. I followed that person to this facility, but they have a hundred storage units. We need your dog."

Scott sank lower in the cubicle.

"Dude, listen. If you're right, if you have that much explosives in a public business, we have to tell Carter. We have to get the Bomb Squad up there."

"No, Scott, we don't. Trust me. Not everyone working with Carter is being straight with him."

"Who isn't straight?"

Scott knew he had spoken too loud. The gray-haired detective was staring when Scott glanced up, but quickly turned away. Scott hunched farther into the cubicle and lowered his voice.

"What were you doing in Echo Park? What do you know about those stolen munitions?"

"Did you print the rap sheet?"

"How did you find Colinski so fast?"

"If you want this to end, bring the dog."

"Who isn't being straight? What does that mean?"

"Bring the dog. I'll tell you everything I know, and I'll give you Colinski."

"Her name is Maggie."

"Bring her. Don't tell Carter, or anyone else. You gave me your word."

Cole hung up.

A door opened on the far side of the room. Carter and Stiles came out, followed by the deputy chief and the suit from the Intelligence Section. Carter and Stiles spoke for a few seconds, then Stiles turned back to the others and Carter went to the conference room. The deputy chief said something funny, and Stiles flashed the big smile.

Not everyone working with Carter is being straight with him.

Stiles started back to the conference room, but suddenly turned and came to Scott.

"How're you doing with those mug shots?"

Scott handed her the binder.

"Struck out. He isn't in here."

"Then I'll get you started on the next two hundred."

Scott eased to his feet.

"Gotta take a rain check. I have to find new digs for tonight."

"I'm so sorry about all this. You go take care of that dog. We'll get you more pictures tomorrow."

"Thanks."

Scott watched her walk back to the conference room. Carter was inside, on the phone. Carter had been watching them, but now he turned away.

Bring her, and I'll give you Colinski.

Scott gathered his things, and left to get Maggie.

47

Elvis Cole

THE RATTY BLUE TRANS AM pulled up behind us forty minutes later, and Scott got out. He left the dog in his car. The dog was big, and built strong, and filled the front seat like a black-and-tan wolf.

I said, "Isn't it dangerous, letting her ride in front?"

Scott shoved the rap sheet at me, and stared at Safety Plus.

"Colinski. This the place?"

"Yeah. The woman in there is a problem, so we'll need a plan."

"Before we plan, tell me what you know, and how you know it. And let me say this upfront, if what you tell me sounds like bullshit, my dog and I are leaving."

I gave him everything, beginning with Amy and Jacob Breslyn, how Jacob died, and that Amy was trying to learn who killed him by reaching out to al-Qaeda.

I said, "A man named Charles appears to be helping, so he's probably the person who set up the contact. The house belongs to Colinski, so he's hooked into the deal, either as a middleman, or through a connection with the buyers."

Scott stared across the street.

"The buyers being al-Qaeda terrorists."

"The people who killed her son in Nigeria are aligned with al-Qaeda."

Scott shook his head, and looked at the dog.

"Perfect. The asshole who put the bomb on my car is a lunatic al-Qaeda terrorist."

"I don't know who built it, but you wanted to know what I know. Now you know."

Scott went to his car. The window was down, and the dog was leaning out. Scott touched her nose, and scratched the sides of her head.

"Carter doesn't know any of this. No one on the task force is talking about any of this. Who isn't being straight with him?"

I took out my phone, and showed him the official HSI portrait of Janet Hess.

"Know who she is? Special Agent in Charge Janet Hess."

Scott studied the picture.

"Uh-uh. Never met her."

"What about an agent named Mitchell?"

"He's been around the office."

"When Carter and Stiles came to my house, Mitchell was with them. Hess is Mitchell's boss."

I held up my phone again, showing her picture.

"Hess hired me to find Amy Breslyn two hours before you and I met, only she didn't identify herself as a federal agent. She pretended to be a friend of Amy's. She told me someone named Thomas Lerner could help, and gave me his address."

Scott glanced at her picture.

"Hess sent you to Echo Park?"

"Yes. This is why I was there, and what I was doing."

"Stiles says he doesn't exist. She thinks you made him up."

"She's half right. Lerner doesn't exist, but Hess made him up, not me. And if Carter and the task force don't know any of this, it's because Hess and her boy Mitchell haven't shared the wealth. Hess knows everything I've told you, and more."

Scott frowned hard and scratched the dog again.

"Does she know Colinski is the man in the sport coat?"

"I don't know, and I don't know which side she's playing. She knew about Amy and Charles, and they're involved with Colinski. She sent me to the house, and the house belongs to Colinski."

Scott stared at the dog, only now she wasn't relaxed and happy. Her ears were up, and she looked like she wanted to bite.

"This is bullshit. We should tell Carter. Let him bust Hess and this thing wide open."

"If we tell Carter, Hess will find out. Hess doesn't know what I know, so she thinks she's invisible. If Colinski is taking shots at you, he thinks he's invisible, too. I don't know if they're connected, or how, but they don't know we're here, Scott. If we keep it this way, they won't see us coming."

Scott glanced at the entrance.

"Colinski."

"The deal happens tomorrow. When Breslyn is safe, we'll get Colinski, and all the rest of them. But first, we have to secure these explosives."

Scott nodded, and turned to get into his car.

"Let's do it."

"Slow down. We need a plan. The woman in there hates me."

"Here's your plan. Pike, in front. Cole, get in back."

"With the dog?"

"You'll be harder to see, and Pike looks more like a copper. Get in."

I climbed over the bucket past the dog to the tiny back seat, and Pike slid into the shotgun. The dog wedged herself on the console, but most of her spilled into the back.

Dog hair covered the seat, and the floor, and the armrests. Fur clung to the doors and the roof and piled under the seats and along the rocker panels in drifts like snow. Fur swirled and hung in the air, and settled on me like dandruff.

The dog sniffed me.

If the dog looked big in the window, she looked even bigger an inch from my nose.

I smiled, and tried to look friendly.

"Remember me? You met my cat."

The dog panted hot breath in my face as we drove across the street.

48

WE PARKED BY THE TRUCK outside the little office. Scott let Maggie out, and the two of them went inside.

"I hope he knows what he's doing. This woman is a battle-ax."

Pike said, "Mm."

Five minutes later, Scott, Maggie, and the ax came out. The ax smiled at Pike, and eyed me pleasantly.

"Why didn't you say you're a policeman instead of pretending you were a customer?"

Scott spoke before I could answer.

"Undercover coppers are like that, Hannah. That's why he makes me drive this crappy car."

Hannah.

"Thank the lady, Maggie. Shake."

Hannah beamed when the dog lifted its paw.

"She's such a sweet girl."

Scott dimpled like a poster boy.

"If you're one of the good guys."

Hannah giggled and returned to her office. The dog jumped in beside me, and Scott slid in behind the wheel.

"I asked if we could use the place to train."

"And just like that, she went for it?"

Scott glanced in the mirror.

"People love dogs."

We rolled through the gate and took a quick tour.

Safety Plus Storage was laid out along a grid of alleys like a rectangle cut down the center and across the middle. The alleys were lined with dusty, beige sheds, which were partitioned into different-size units. Customers provided their own locks to ensure their security.

Scott decided to follow a clockwise search pattern and parked near the gate. Hannah watched from the office door and waved. Scott and I waved back. Pike didn't.

Scott said, "I'm going to work Maggie off leash, so stay a few steps behind us. If she sniffs you or bumps you, don't pet her."

"You said she doesn't bite."

"When we work, she's all business. Right, Maggie? Am I right, pretty girl?"

Scott spoke to the dog in a little kid's voice, and something between them changed. She dropped to her chest with her butt in the air, as if she knew what was coming and desperately wanted to play.

He unclipped her leash and pointed at the nearest shed.

"Find it, girl. Maggie, *seek!*"

She swirled away with effortless power, and followed his point. The corner of Pike's mouth twitched.

"Marine."

Scott let the dog range ahead. She sniffed along the base of five or six units, then he crossed her to the opposite side. Pike and I followed, contributing nothing.

We reached the first corner, and turned. A camera tree stood overhead, sprouting a bloom of cameras. I wondered if Hannah was watching. Her movie had to be more interesting than three men following a dog, but the movie hadn't shaken her hand.

We reached the far back corner, and turned again. The dog crossed, and re-crossed, and was approaching the central intersection when she backtracked, and grew agitated. Her head swung low to the ground, and her pace quickened. She reversed herself, reversed again, and abruptly lay down, facing a door.

Scott said, "Damn."

"She found it?"

"This is what she did at my car and the house. That's her alert."

The dog gave Scott a sloppy, German shepherd grin, and Scott called her away.

The nearest camera watched from the corner behind us, and another watched from the far corner. The ax had an unobstructed view, but we would be small in the frame, and far away.

Pike moved close to block the camera.

The lock was a beast, with a shrouded shackle, a drill plate protecting the core, and a security rating too high for my pick gun. Scott fidgeted when I took out my tools.

"Dude. That's a four-fifty-nine. Burglary."

"Watch the office. If she comes out, let us know."

Scott didn't move.

"What if you can't open it?"

Pike said, "Keep watch."

Scott clipped up his dog, and hurried away.

I inserted the tension bar, and went to work with the rack pick. The lock opened three minutes later.

Amy's unit was the size of a small room, with a table in the center set up as a workbench. Scissors, spools of thread, and a roll of black fabric covered the table, along with two battery-powered lamps. Inexpensive shelving units hugged the wall behind the table, and were crowded with boxes, bags, and white plastic bottles. A tailor's dummy wore a fringed leather jacket in the corner, admiring itself in a mirror propped against the wall. Amy's unit was more like a tailor's shop than a cache of explosives.

Pike and I quickly moved to the shelves. The explosives could be in a single box, or cut into pieces for easier storage.

A shopping bag from a local hobby store contained kits for making buzzers and doorbells. Jugs of liquid resin and rolls of plastic food wrap sat beside the bag, and a mini-loaf baking pan was wedged between the jugs. Plastic sewing kits were stacked next to X-Acto knives, and so many arts and crafts supplies Amy could open a hobby shop.

The next bag held a heavy, two-quart plastic food container filled with a white material like modeling clay. I pressed my thumb into the surface, and left a depression.

"Joe."

Pike looked, and tossed me a smooth, white block. The putty I'd found was heavy and pliable, but the block was light, and hard.

Pike said, "Resin?"

The shape and size reminded me of the baking pan. It was cut into six cavities, each about an inch deep, three inches wide, and seven long. The resin block fit perfectly.

"Yeah. She made it."

I flashed on a snapshot I'd seen in her home. Amy with Jacob and his high school newspaper friends, holding a tray heaped with dark rectangles. The cakes could have come from this pan, and probably had. Maybe Amy was still making cakes for her son, only now with a less happy intent.

I was searching the shelves again when Scott ran up to the door.

"Hannah came out. Did you find it?"

"A few pounds. We're looking."

"Look faster. If she sees what we're doing, we're screwed."

"Stall. Buy us five minutes."

Scott hurried away.

The next shelf brimmed with more rolls of cloth, crayon-colored spools of insulated wire, and a tool kit with all the tools necessary for do-it-yourself appliance repair.

Pike said, "Look."

He held out another resin block, as smooth and white as the first until he turned it over.

Faint steel eyes peered from the resin. I knew what they were even before Pike showed me the bag of ball bearings.

Ball bearings had been layered in the mold before the resin was poured. The steel eyes were as cold and merciless as the eyes of a crab, but a bag I found on the bottom shelf frightened me more.

Silver tubes bulged in a Ziploc bag. Each was the size of a short pencil, and twin wires sprouted from an end. I knew what they were from my Army days, only the wires back then were longer. These had been cut and stripped, and were ready for use. I looked under the Ziploc, and lifted the bag to the table.

"Electric detonators, and more explosives."

Neatly wrapped bricks of plastic explosive were stacked beneath the detonators. Each was identical in size and shape to the resin block.

Pike came closer.

"How much?"

"Thirty or forty pounds. More like forty."

I took a block from the bag, and turned it over. Eyes. I checked another. Eyes. A third. Eyes. Pike and I glanced at each other, and turned to the jacket.

The lovely leather jacket with its generous fringe was large for Amy, but otherwise identical to the jacket she wore.

Scott pounded up with the dog at his side.

"Did you find the rest?"

I touched the fine leather. It was soft, and the fringe was as light as air.

Pike said, "Just the two bags. Get your car."

Scott moved closer.

"This isn't four hundred pounds."

"Get the car."

Scott cursed, and pounded away.

I opened the jacket. Rows of pockets were sewn under the arms, down the sides, and across the lining, each joined to the next by neatly stitched lines of brightly colored wire. The resin block with its ugly steel eyes fit the pockets perfectly.

My head filled with a steady hum, like a fluorescent light beginning to fail. I saw Amy, past and future, what she intended and what she had done, as if her ghost were beside me.

Amy had shaped her putty in the mini-loaf pan. She wrapped each block carefully, and taped the seams as neat as a birthday surprise. The wrapping would make them easier to handle, and use. I didn't count the bricks or the pouches, but their number would be the same, and the weight of their special surprise would be about forty pounds, same as a four-year-old boy. Amy probably swung Jacob in circles when he was four. She knew she could carry the weight, and would carry it again, with just as much love.

Once the blocks were in their pockets, she'd press a tube into each, and daisy chain them together with crayon-colored wire, making for a festive display. These rainbow wires would twine to a switch, a switch she, herself, had built, which would send an electric kiss to each silver tube, instantly, simultaneously, causing everything thereafter to happen so fast Amy would not feel the furious explosion, as it shattered the air and the people around her with an agonized mother's roar.

I said, "Oh, Amy."

Scott's car pulled up fast, and he ran to the door.

"Tell me you found it. Tell me we got the stuff."

Pike said, "Just the bags."

I stroked the soft leather, and loved Amy Breslyn so much my heart broke. Everything Charles and Janet Hess and I believed about her was wrong. Amy outsmarted us.

Scott came closer, looking angrily from me to the jacket.

"What is this? What's she doing in here?"

Pike closed the jacket, and picked up the bags.

"A suicide coat. The woman's."

I said, "She plans to wear it, Scott."

Pike pushed me toward the door.

"Go now. Move."

I wanted to burn the unit. I wanted to torch the fine leather jacket and the wire and scissors and thread, and cloud the sky with smoke, but we didn't. I slipped the jacket off the mannequin, and folded it over my arm.

We locked Amy's unit, and quietly drove away.

49

WE SWUNG IN behind Pike's Jeep. Pike and Scott got out, and I climbed over the seat while Pike stowed the bags and jacket in his Jeep. Scott met me on the sidewalk.

"Okay, it isn't here. *Now* what?"

I wasn't sure what. The only thing I knew was that quitting on Amy wasn't an option.

"Keep pushing. Jon's on her. She'll lead us to it today or tomorrow."

"Cole, let's think it through. This poor woman isn't looking for answers. She wants to kill these people, and she'll kill herself to do it. She's a fifty-one-fifty."

Fifty-one-fifty was the LAPD code for a seventy-two-hour psychiatric hold.

"This is called helping her. She's safe for now. We still have time to figure out what Hess is doing, and take down Charles and Colinski."

"Maybe we don't need to wait. She's a middle-aged, middle-class lady who lost her son. She'll give up Charles and Colinski and the rest of it the second we grab her."

Pike said, "Won't happen."

"Meaning what?"

I picked up the answer.

"Meaning that person died between here and Nigeria. Amy's smart, and stronger than anyone knows. If she lawyers up, even for only a day, the deal will fold, and Colinski and Charles will vanish."

I took out my phone and called Jon Stone.

"What's she doing?"

"We bought gas, hit the drive-thru at In-N-Out, and bought some flowers. Now we're at Forest Lawn."

"The cemetery?"

"Jacob. She's been at his grave for about twenty minutes."

Saying good-bye. Or confessing.

I told him what we'd found.

"She never intended to sell to these people. That's why she's pushing to meet the buyers. The explosives are bait to get them into the kill zone."

Jon was silent a half second too long.

"She's making it for someone else."

"It's for her. It looks like the jacket she's wearing now, the same jacket she wore last night. Identical. She probably wears the twin so they get used to it."

Jon made a long hiss.

"Tell me you got the putty."

"Forty pounds and the detonators. The rest isn't here."

"It's not in her car, bro. I looked when she bought the flowers."

"If she comes back to the storage unit, we're done. If she comes back—"

His voice cracked like a whip when he answered.

"I know what to do."

I put away the phone, and turned back to Scott.

"Maybe she's crazy, and maybe she's a fifty-one-fifty, but this woman has been through enough. They took her son, the government can't tell her squat, and here's Hess, the big federal agent, doing what? Maybe this is all some Top Secret, deep-cover, high-level operation, but I don't care. My interest is Amy. I'm going to take care of this woman. I'm going to find out what Hess is doing, and if I don't like it, I'm going to take her down just like Charles and Colinski."

I rattled to a stop, and found them both staring.

Pike said, "He gets on a roll."

Scott seemed tired and sad.

"So how's it play out?"

"Sometime tomorrow, they're supposed to wire-transfer money. When Amy gets the confirmation, she'll take Charles to the explosives, and the two of them will deliver the material to the buyer. The way it sounded on the phone, Colinski will be with the buyers."

Scott nodded, and looked at his dog.

"One more night."

Scott took a plastic bag from his pants, squeezed out a greasy cube, and offered it to the dog. Her delicate care surprised me. She picked the meat from his fingers as gently as a girl would touch a butterfly.

"He knows where I live. He tried to kill her last night."

I didn't understand what he was saying, and then I did.

"Colinski?"

"We found a dead raccoon in the yard, and poisoned meatballs. Raw hamburger, loaded with poison."

He tucked away the bag.

"They couldn't get close with the barking, I guess. That means they were trying. We have to stay somewhere else tonight."

"You're welcome to stay with me. Both of you."

He laughed.

"Carter would love it. Me bunking with you would make his day."

"Carter didn't find poison in his yard. I'm serious."

"I'll stay with my girlfriend, or one of the handlers."

He petted the dog, and shook his head.

"Al-Qaeda. Your garden-variety American killer isn't enough."

I wondered if Scott was scared. I had been hunted by dangerous men. They scared me every time.

"If we keep the deal alive, everything ends tomorrow. You won't have to worry about Colinski, and I'll make sure Amy gets proper help."

"I'll keep Carter out of it, Cole. I gave you my word."

He considered me for a moment, as if he were having second thoughts.

"Are you going to bring in the police, or is this strictly DIY?"

"When she's safe. Might even call Carter."

Scott's phone buzzed with an incoming text. He frowned at the message, and tapped out a quick reply.

"Speak of the devil. They want me downtown. Mug shots."

I put out my hand.

"Thanks for the help, and for keeping your word."

We shook.

"You're a strange dude, Cole. Not as strange as Pike, but strange."

Scott slid into his car, and drove away. I looked at Pike.

"Are we strange?"

Pike went to his Jeep without answering, and brought me back to my car.

50

Scott James

SCOTT DROPPED MAGGIE at Glendale before he rolled to the Boat. The parking lot was empty except for a single K-9 car, but this was typical. Most handlers worked out at the Academy gym before their shift. Since everyone was together, Leland held roll call in the parking lot, after which everyone drove a couple hundred yards to an ex-SWAT training field behind Dodger Stadium nicknamed the Mesa.

Scott parked beside the K-9 car, let Maggie do her business, and got her squared away in one of the runs. He gave her his last chunk of baloney, told her he'd be back as quick as he could, and went to the office.

Mace Styrik, the senior sergeant-supervisor, was kicked back at Leland's desk, poring over training logs.

"Hey, Sergeant. I'm leaving Maggie. Back in an hour or so."

Styrik waved without looking up.

Scott left through the kennel to give Maggie a scratch, and went to his car. He hesitated when he reached his car, and studied the distant surroundings. Colinski had watched for him here. This was where they found him, and followed him to Runyon Canyon. Scott wondered if Colinski was watching him. The man might have a high-power rifle, with the crosshairs centered on his chest. Scott raised his middle finger.

Eighteen minutes later, Scott parked at the Boat, and rode the elevator up to Major Crimes. Stiles met him at the door, but her usual smile was missing.

"Did you find a place for tonight?"

"Yeah. It's going to work out."

Scott followed her toward the conference room. Ignacio, Carter, and a uniformed lieutenant were waiting inside. He was surprised, but the surprise turned to worry when he saw Mitchell and Kemp. They looked as grim as five funeral directors. Kemp's eye ticked, the way it did when he was trying to control his anger.

Stiles held the door until he was inside, then closed it and stepped to the side. Scott looked at Kemp, trying to get a read, and knew it was bad.

Ignacio gestured at a chair.

"Have a seat. You know everyone here except Lieutenant Van-Meter. Lieutenant VanMeter is with Internal Affairs."

Lieutenant VanMeter was a woman in her forties with rough skin and dyed black hair. She nodded to acknowledge the introduction, but said nothing.

"She's here at my request, as is Lieutenant Kemp."

Scott nodded. Mitchell's presence felt strange. Here he was, a federal agent, keeping secrets from Carter and Stiles and the others, and only Scott knew. Scott's throat was dry, but he thought he should say something.

"Why are we here?"

Ignacio glanced at Carter.

"Detective, show the officer, please?"

Carter picked up a tablet computer from the table and showed Scott a picture of himself with Cole and Pike outside Safety Plus Storage.

The picture rocked him like a blindside truck. Carter and Stiles had him followed, and now he was screwed.

Ignacio gestured at the picture.

"Recognize yourself? This would be you, an hour or so ago, with Mr. Cole and his associate."

Scott wedged his hands under his thighs.

"Yes, sir. That's me."

Ignacio grunted.

"You don't appear to have a drug or alcohol problem. Can we assume you recall the direct order I gave you to stay away from Mr. Cole? Do you recall this order?"

Scott glanced at Kemp, hoping for help, but found no encouragement.

"Yes, sir. I remember."

Ignacio glanced at the IAG lieutenant.

"Lieutanant, please."

VanMeter read from a notebook.

"From the Manual. Two-ten-point-thirty. Compliance with lawful orders. Obedience of a superior's lawful command is essential for the safe and prompt performance of law enforcement. Negative discipline may be necessary where there is a willful disregard of lawful orders, commands, or directives."

Ignacio was putting on the show to set the stage. They wanted something. Scott thought he knew what they wanted, and it left him feeling queasy.

Ignacio nodded.

"Here's the deal, Scott. Detective Carter believes Mr. Cole has information crucial to his investigation, and you probably know the true nature of Mr. Cole's involvement. After your little field trip today, I'm pretty sure he's right. So here we are, and I'm giving you another lawful order. I order you to cooperate, and answer his questions."

Kemp cleared his throat. He pulled a chair from the table, turned it, and sat facing Scott.

"Eight-twenty-eight. It's a violation of department policy for an employee to make false or misleading statements."

Kemp's expression was as hard as Ignacio's, but Scott sensed the LT was warning him. *Whatever you do, don't lie.*

"I'd like to speak with a League rep or an attorney."

Stiles sighed.

"This is so wrong, Scott. Why are you doing this?"

Carter stepped forward as if no one had spoken, and asked his first question.

"What were you and Cole doing up there?"

Scott looked at Ignacio.

"Commander, considering the situation, I'd like to speak with a League rep, or an attorney."

Scott's thoughts were racing. He wasn't going to lie, but he wouldn't give up Cole. He looked at Mitchell. Scott wanted to give up Mitchell. He wanted to tell Carter that Mitchell's boss brought Cole into the case.

Ignacio said, "Lieutenant."

VanMeter read another.

"Eight-oh-five-point-one. Cause for disciplinary action. Employees shall be subject to disciplinary action for acts of misconduct. Misconduct defined. Violation of Department policies, rules, or procedures, to wit, disobeying a lawful order, or making false or misleading statements."

Stiles said, "Don't do this, Scott."

Carter picked up the tablet again, and showed him a picture of Pike carrying the bags and jacket to his Jeep.

"What's in the bags?"

Scott shook his head.

"He took them out of your car. This is your car, right, the piece of shit Trans Am? They were in your car."

Scott wanted to say something, but he didn't know what to say.

"I'd like to speak with a rep or an attorney."

Ignacio's face was stern, but Scott sensed the man didn't want to go through this mess.

Mitchell spoke for the first time.

"If charges are eventually brought, those charges will be federal."

Ignacio glanced angrily at the fed.

"No one is talking about charges. This is an administrative matter."

Ignacio conferred with VanMeter, and read from the notebook.

"I'm required to read this admonition. Your silence can be deemed as insubordination and lead to administrative discipline, which could result in your discharge or removal from office. You understand what this means?"

"Yes, sir."

Do what we say, or we can fire you.

VanMeter placed a printed form and a pen on the table.

"This is an acknowledgment you received the admonition. Sign and date here. If you refuse to sign, I'll mark the space 'refused,' and sign as the witnessing supervisor. Up to you."

Scott signed.

Ignacio said, "I hereby order you to answer the administrative questions we've put to you, and give a statement for administrative purposes."

The rigid formality was frightening.

"I'd like a League rep, and an attorney."

Ignacio fired another angry glance at Mitchell, and turned back to Scott.

"To clear up any confusion, by being ordered to make a statement, nothing you say can be used against you. Is that clear?"

"I'd like a League rep."

Ignacio's jaw flexed. He took a printed form from the end of the table.

"Here's what's going to happen. This is the completed complaint form, signed by Detective Carter. The complaint alleges you willfully failed to obey a lawful order, and by doing so violated department policy. If you answer the man's questions, I'll trash it. If not, I'll hand it to Lieutenant VanMeter, and she'll open an investigation. None of us wants this to happen."

He put down the first form, and held up a second.

"One-sixty-one-double-aught, already signed by the chief. Temporary relief from duty. If you refuse to cooperate, you'll be placed on administrative leave, pending the outcome of the investigation. Do you understand what I'm telling you?"

Scott's mouth felt dry as an East L.A. sidewalk at noon.

"Yes, sir."

Kemp leaned forward.

"When you're placed on leave, you're required to return all city-owned property. This means everything, Scott."

Kemp leaned closer until his face was only inches away.

"Maggie."

Scott wanted to give them all of it. Tell them about the woman and Colinski and the Homeland feds who were screwing them, and what Cole was planning to do, but he couldn't make the words come out.

Carter asked again, and this time his voice was soft.

"What do you know, son? What's Cole doing?"

Scott felt numb in a way he hadn't felt since he lost Stephanie Anders. Kemp and Carter and the people in the room seemed a thousand miles away. His eyes burned, and he blinked, but the burning got worse. Carter's voice was an echo.

"What did he tell you?"

Scott heard himself speak.

"We can sit here forever, Carter, but I want a rep."

He wanted to see Maggie. He wanted to sit with her, and hold her, and explain.

Kemp sat back.

"Goddamn it, Scott."

Ignacio glanced from Carter to VanMeter, and shook his head. He was a tall man, and towered overhead.

"Dismissed. Get out of here."

Scott didn't rise until Kemp took his arm.

"Get up."

Kemp steered him out and away from the conference room. He turned Scott to face him, and leaned very close.

"Really? *Really?* You'll be gone in a month. Is that what you want?"

Scott shook his head.

"Where's your K-9?"

"Glendale."

"Sergeant Leland will arrange for her care. Do you have other city property?"

"I want to see her."

"The commander just sent your ass home. You lost her. Do you have other city property in your possession?"

"No."

"Get out of here, and go home. Whatever's going on with you and Cole, you'd better get that shit together. I'll save you if I can, but don't count on it."

Making his way to the hall took forever. Reaching the elevator took even longer. Scott felt trapped in someone else's life in a world he didn't create. He wanted to start over, but didn't know how. He wanted to take everything back, and return to the beginning, but here he was, and even pushing the button for the elevator seemed beyond him.

Mitchell stepped into the hall, and turned toward the elevator. He stopped when he saw Scott, frowned, and went back into the office.

A few seconds later, Stiles came out. She saw him, too, but she didn't hide in the office. She crossed the hall to the restroom. Scott remembered something Cole asked earlier, and the memory sparked a tickle of hope.

Scott went to the restroom, knocked twice, and walked in.

"Detective Stiles?"

Stiles was closing the door in a stall when he entered. A shock of angry surprise flashed on her face.

"Turn yourself around, and get out of here."

Scott stepped back, and held the door to the hall open. He didn't want her to feel threatened.

"I'm sorry. I need to ask you something. One thing."

The surprise passed, but she was still angry.

"What?"

"Why did you pull the surveillance off Cole?"

Her mouth tightened as if this was an unpleasant topic.

"This wasn't our decision. Our friends at Homeland preferred to handle Mr. Cole, whatever that means."

"Mitchell."

"He encouraged the surveillance. This came from above."

Hess.

Stiles came out of the stall, and made an exasperated sigh.

"Would you please come to your senses, and talk to Brad? You can save yourself."

"Maybe you're right."

Scott returned to the elevator, and went to his car. The tickle of hope grew to a flame. Hess was the key. Hess was his last, best hope to make everything right.

51

Dominick Leland

SERGEANT DOMINICK LELAND sat in his office at the Glendale training facility, remembering Dakota. The rest of the Platoon was up at the Mesa, so Leland had the place to himself. Chewing tobacco was forbidden by regulations, but Leland didn't give a damn. He spit the juice into a Styrofoam cup, and sipped an orange soda. The soda tasted worse than the Red Plug, but wasn't against the rules.

Over his thirty-two years as a handler, what with his time spread between the military, the Sheriffs, and the Los Angeles Police Department, Leland was blessed with nine certified K-9 partners. Five German shepherds, three Belgian Malinois, and a Dutch shepherd. Two were killed during service, two died of unexpected illness, two wore out their hips, and three gave the full measure until they were too damned old, at which time Leland adopted them. At home, which he shared with his wife of thirty-six years, whom he called the Missus, the walls of his study were hung with pictures of his children, his grandchildren, and portraits of himself and each of his nine K-9 partners.

Dakota was his favorite. She was a slender, black German shepherd, right at seventy pounds. This put her on the small side for a GSD, but with that jet shep face and ears like horns, the bad guys must've thought she was Satan's own hound. Truth was, she was a sweetheart. Smart as a whip, no quit in her, and superb with the kids and the Missus.

So, anyway, the day she was retired, Leland brought her home, same as any other day, let her hop out of the car, and gave her a good scratch.

"Welcome home, dog. From this day forward, you're on vacation."

Hopping out when they got home that night was normal, but when Leland went to his black-and-white K-9 car the next day, leaving her behind was a nightmare. Dakota expected to go with him, just as she had every morning for the past eight years. She whined, cried, barked, shivered like a Chihuahua, and tried to chew through the fence. Leland had never seen a more pathetic face, like an abandoned child pleading with her best friend and daddy not to leave her behind. This went on every morning. Leland felt a terrible guilt, and an even more terrible shame. Truth was, Dominick Leland could have trained that behavior out of her, but he didn't want to lose the fierce love and true loyalty that burned in his partner's heart.

Leland left the house earlier the next day, and took Dakota for a ride. He did this most mornings thereafter, and, when he got home after work, if he wasn't too beat, and on his days off, he took her out in the car. And sometimes, for a treat, he'd pop the siren and lights, and rip down the highway rolling Code Three. She loved to go fast.

A few years back, Dakota went End of Watch. Leland missed her, and their rides, and thought of her often, especially when he was reminded of the pain a man can visit upon the delicate heart of a dog.

Sitting there in the quiet, Leland heard a car pull up, and the kennel door open. He thought about Dakota, and the way she carried on that morning. He gave them a few minutes before he got up, blew his nose, and went to the kennel.

He opened the door, but didn't go in. Scott was sitting in the run with his dog.

"Officer James, go on home. She's mine."

Leland closed the door, and went back to his office. He heard the kennel door a few minutes later. When Scott's car left the parking lot, the dog cried. She carried on, and it was terrible.

Leland broke off a bite of the Red Plug. He chewed, and listened to the dog, and thought about the rides with Dakota, each and every one precious. He got to wondering if a ride would make Maggie feel better. Might not, but Leland gave it a try.

52

Elvis Cole

PIKE STAYED IN SILVER LAKE to wait for Amy and Jon, and I drove home with the putty explosives and Amy's terrible jacket. Jon called as I climbed the hill.

"We're home."

"She stop anywhere the explosives could be?"

"She stopped for Italian. Looks like we're in for the evening."

"I'll come up later. Can I bring anything?"

"Nah, I'm good. I heard back from my guy. He stands by what he told me."

"C'mon, Jon. They're on it."

"I asked him to check again, and got the same answer. Unresolved, pending future developments. HSI kicked the case."

"He's lying."

"Lying to someone who does what I do isn't smart, and this dude is smart. He's so smart, he crunched a few numbers, and decided the L.A. office has too many quality cases that go nowhere."

A quality case was a case with a high probability of success.

"How many is too many?"

"Three this past year, and four the year before. All involved explosives, munitions, or computer technology."

"Cases derived from the Internet?"

"No, not all. What they had in common was the quality of the intel. The leads were solid, he says, but L.A. kicked them back. My guy finds this suspicious."

I was finding it suspicious, too.

The A-frame was peaceful and calm when I pulled into the carport. I let myself in and drank a bottle of water, then brought the jacket and the bags inside. I didn't like having forty pounds of high explosives in my home, so I carried them outside, and down the slope, and hid them under my deck. I didn't like having them under my deck, either, but it was better than keeping them in the kitchen.

Colinski's rap sheet described a hard-core professional criminal with a history of violent crime, but nothing in his record linked him to explosives or extremist political groups. With the most recent entry dating from sixteen years ago, nothing in his sheet gave me a likely way to find him. I called Eddie Ditko, and asked him to help.

Eddie hacked up a phlegm ball.

"Sixteen years doesn't mean shit. A guy like this, they're keeping tabs. Whadaya wanna know?"

"The tabs. I want to put eyes on him."

Eddie thought for a moment.

"Hijacking, armed robbery, all the stuff with the guns. Got a friend at Robbery Special I can tap."

"Great. And see if anything ties him to explosives or radical extremists."

"Radical extremists?"

"Al-Qaeda."

"You gotta be shittin' me. A crook from East L.A.?"

"A lot can happen in sixteen years."

I scrambled three eggs with jalapeños, ate at the sink, and went up for a shower. I let the hot water beat my shoulders and neck, and wondered if Colinski and Charles were worried, or confident, or setting the stage for tomorrow. I wondered if Hess was one of the good guys, or a bad guy. It didn't matter. Nothing mattered except Amy.

When the shower ran cold, I toweled off and put on fresh clothes. I was walking downstairs when the phone rang. Eddie.

"Pucker up, baby. You're gonna want to kiss me on the lips."

"Don't toy with me."

"Colinski dropped off the world six or seven years ago. Nobody knows where he is."

"He was in Echo Park."

"No one's saying he isn't here, only that he dropped off the grid. If we can find him, my guy wants to talk to him."

"About what?"

"A couple of armored-car capers up near Palmdale, and another out in Palm Springs."

"They think Colinski pulled the scores?"

"Nah, nah, nah. They want a thief named Eli Sturges for the scores. They're thinking Colinski got into the fencing side. The big sixteen-year absence, the way he vanished? Here's a guy who's playing it smarter. He puts the scores together, and lets other people take the risks. Here's the part where you pucker."

"Can't wait."

"If the guards don't open the armored car, Sturges blows'm open. Military stuff. He's used RPGs to stop'm or knock'm over. He cracked a car with an IED that left a crater the size of a swimming pool. If Colinski was selling that stuff in Echo Park, who do you think he's selling it to?"

I wasn't sure what to think.

"I have reason to believe the explosives were intended for radical Islamist terrorists."

Eddie laughed.

"Eli Sturges is a stickup hood from the Valley. He doesn't have time to be a terrorist. He's too busy taking scores."

"Can you get me a picture?"

"I'll get one. I'll email it."

I lowered the phone and stared across the canyon. I went outside, and stood ten feet above the explosives. I tried to see them through the cracks in my deck, but couldn't. Just as well.

Amy reached out, and Charles reached back. Charles knew he could sell the explosives to Colinski, only Amy was adamant about dealing with al-Qaeda, so Charles told her what she wanted to hear. Maybe Colinski was playing along, or maybe Charles was lying to everyone, but the end result was the same. They needed Amy to believe the buyers were al-Qaeda terrorists only until they had her explosives. Then Amy Breslyn didn't matter.

"They're ripping you off."

I went back inside, drank a beer, and was still thinking about it when the sun went down and a car stopped outside my house. When I went to the door, I was surprised to see Scott James.

"Aren't you worried Carter will see you?"

"Doesn't matter. He saw me with you at the storage. They followed me."

Officer James looked pale and lifeless, as if he'd just checked out of a hospital.

"Did you tell him what we were doing?"

His eyes flashed with an angry life that quickly faded.

"I kept my word to you, Cole. I told him nothing."

I looked past him to his car, and saw the front seat was empty.

"Where's your dog?"

"They took her. I'm suspended, pending a review board."

I let him in, and locked the door. He drifted into the living room like a man in a fog.

I said, "So what happens?"

"About what?"

"You and the dog."

"Her name is Maggie."

"Maggie."

"You have a nice place up here."

He didn't want to talk about the dog.

I grabbed two Falstaffs from the fridge. He was still where I'd left him when I got back, staring into the great black empty beyond my deck.

"Here. Try this."

He studied the can.

"Falstaff. Never heard of it."

"They haven't made it in years. Snagged a case off eBay."

Scott held the beer, but didn't drink.

"It was Hess. Hess pulled the surveillance. Carter wanted it, but Hess made him pull it."

"You sure it was Hess?"

"Stiles told me."

"Did Hess say why?"

He smiled, but he wasn't smiling at me.

"Whatever Hess told them was a lie. She pulled the crew to hide whatever it is she's hoping you'll find."

"Amy."

He smiled again, and shook his head.

"Not Amy. This doesn't have anything to do with Amy. If Carter tripped over Amy Breslyn right now, he wouldn't know who she was, so who cares if the surveillance team saw you asking about Amy Breslyn? It wouldn't have meant anything."

I began to see where he was going, and wondered where it would lead.

"Not to Carter or Stiles or the task force."

He considered the Falstaff again, and took a sip.

"Nope, not them. No one on the task force knows about Amy Breslyn, so there has to be someone else, right? Hess didn't want that person to know you were looking for Amy. She wanted to keep that person in the dark, so she turned out the lights."

Everything about what he said felt right.

"This is making sense."

The burner chirped again. I knew who was calling even before I checked the window.

"Hess."

He smiled even wider, but he didn't look happy.

"Answer. I have a few questions. It'll be fun."

I sent her to voice mail.

"Later. Talk to me. You're onto something."

I sat in the chair, and Scott took a seat on the couch.

"Hess is crapping on the task force, and Carter, and the department. She's withholding something, which means she's hiding something. Kinda like you."

I shrugged, and had more Falstaff as he continued.

"And if she's hiding something, she has something to lose. We can use that. We can get my dog back."

He suddenly stared at me.

"I'm not going to break my word to you, but later, after, I'm going to give them Hess. Maybe they'll let me stay."

He blinked, and blinked harder, then turned to face the black. I got up. I didn't want him to feel embarrassed.

"I'm gonna cook some dinner. Make yourself at home."

The burner chirped again when I was in the kitchen. I thought it was Hess, but it was Jon Stone.

He said, "Are you ready?"

"What? Is everything okay?"

"Charles is here. The sonofabitch brought flowers."

I went back to the living room, and motioned to Scott.

"Charles. Where's Pike?"

"Backyard. He's set to enter the dining room if something gets weird, but it won't. Charles is all laid-back. They're talking."

"She called him by name?"

"Yeah. Charles. I'll send you a screen grab."

Scott spoke loudly so Jon would hear.

"Are they talking about Colinski?"

"Who's that?"

"Scott James."

"No one's mentioned that name. He's prepping her for tomorrow."

"If they leave before I get there, follow them."

"If he leaves, but she stays, I'm staying with her."

"Then tell Pike to follow him."

My cell phone dinged as we talked, and Jon heard.

"That's me. The screen grab."

"Hang on."

The screen grab showed Amy on one end of the couch, and a man in a blue business suit on the opposite end. The picture was so small I had to expand it to see their faces, but when I saw Charles, I smiled. We hadn't found the missing explosives, but finding Charles was better.

"Jon? Pike doesn't have to follow Charles."

"He doesn't?"

"Uh-uh."

I showed the picture to Scott.

"Want Hess? Meet Charles."

Scott studied the picture, and wet his lips. He reminded me of a hungry dog.

We didn't need to follow Charles because we knew where to find him. Charles had visited my home with Carter and Stiles. His true name was Special Agent Russ Mitchell.

The pieces snapped together with audible clicks, building a perfect picture. I understood what Hess was doing, and how to help Amy. I might even be able to help Scott.

The world was suddenly simple. Janet Hess would help me, or she would arrest me.

53

RED NEON FISH slid across her SUV as Hess drove toward me. White fish and green fish, cast by headlights, traffic lights, and pulsing Hollywood Boulevard streetlights, swam over gleaming paint. Janet Hess stopped with the nose of her car so close our vehicles kissed. I wondered what she drove in her real life, and if she was married with children. I wondered whether her life would be ruined after tonight, or if she would ruin mine.

I got into her car as I had each time before, only this time I carried my laptop.

"I'm your best friend. Learn to love me."

"Did you find them?"

Them. Not Amy.

"Here. You can see for yourself."

I held the laptop so both of us could see.

"Kinda like we're at a drive-in, isn't it?"

"Is the show-and-tell necessary? What is this?"

"Watch."

The video was cued up and ready. Amy was seated on the left side of her couch, feet flat on the floor, palms on her thighs, staring at nothing.

Hess frowned as if she wasn't quite sure.

"Amy."

"Yes."

"Where is this?"

"Watch."

"Where did you get this?"

"Watch."

Amy sat without moving for twenty-five seconds, then looked toward the door two seconds before we heard three fast, light knocks. Amy stood, and went to the door. She momentarily disappeared on the bottom left side of the screen, then reappeared as she stepped back to open the door. I froze the image.

Hess glanced up, confused.

"What happened? Why'd you stop?"

"Charles is about to come in. I didn't want you to see him."

"Stop acting stupid. Show me."

"If you see him, you'll recognize him, Janet. He works for you."

"What did you call me?"

I nodded at the video.

"Only this isn't part of his job. He's on his own time here. Like you."

I closed the laptop, and tucked it under my leg.

"I called you Janet. As in Hess. See?"

I showed her a print of her government Web page, and the pictures Pike took on the day he followed her. I had one picture left, but I saved it.

"This would be you, on your official Homeland Security Web page. And here's us, together in this vehicle. And here you are again, swapping this vehicle for your G-ride in Long Beach. Note the public parking lot, so you can swap cars without anyone from your office seeing you."

I slid the prints onto the dash.

"You hired me to find Charles, not Amy. And I'm not ready to give him to you."

A shadow cut her face in half, masking her eyes. A car swung past, and the mask was swept away by its lights. Her eyes were thoughtful and calm. She was studying me when the shadow returned.

"You would be wrong, Mr. Cole. I'm conducting a special operation."

"No doubt. You think the director will buy it?"

"Of course. It's the truth."

"I'm thinking about telling him a truer truth. Namely, that seven hard cases involving explosives and high-value technology vanished here in his L.A. Field Office during the past two years. And then I'll tell him about the unknown subject who came along, offering explosives and explosives technology to al-Qaeda, which would make this case number eight, because it went away, too. Which was when the SAC—this would be you, Janet—began to suspect an agent in her office was involved, and the SAC—you, again—decided to violate protocol, and bring in a civilian investigator—this would be me."

Hess stared.

"How do you know this?"

"Magic."

She glanced at the prints, and the corner of her mouth curled. A smile.

"Looks like I hired the right man."

"One lie too many, Janet. Thomas Lerner. Really?"

"Stop playing games. Who is he, and where are they?"

"You screwed up, Janet. Making up Thomas Lerner? Did you think I was stupid?"

"What I thought was you'd find an empty house and maybe some stolen goods. I sure as hell didn't think you'd walk into a murder and a cache of stolen munitions."

"You knew Amy was trying to contact al-Qaeda?"

"I didn't know Amy Breslyn's name until two weeks ago. The real Meryl Lawrence called. Amy's behavior had her concerned, so she wanted us in the loop. I put it together from there."

"And realized you had a problem."

"That's one way of saying it, yes."

"Al-Qaeda isn't part of your problem. There aren't any terrorists."

"Of course not. Al-Qaeda! Please, the new bogeyman. The buyer's a hijacker named Eli Sturges. ATF heard Sturges was getting his crew together, so the SAC gave me a shout. It was happening fast. Sturges has been linked to a fence named Colinski, and Colinski's been linked to the house, so I needed an agent on the house or I'd miss my chance."

"Me being your agent."

"C'mon, Cole, I have a rotten agent. I didn't have time to mount an internal investigation, and I sure as hell didn't want him to suspect I was onto him."

"Did Amy embezzle money?"

Hess glanced away, almost as if she were embarrassed.

"No. I wanted to put a bug in your ear about Charles."

"Do you know what she's selling?"

"She offered al-Qaeda her expertise, and a quantity of material. I don't know how much."

"Two hundred kilograms of a plastic explosive. These particular explosives are not marked by taggants."

She rolled her eyes, and maybe looked worried.

"Do you know where it is?"

"I'll find out tomorrow, and take it."

"You're not going to do anything, Cole, except tell me where these people are."

"No, Janet, I'm going to do plenty. I'm going to drop you dead-center in your director's lap, unless I get what I want."

She rolled her eyes again.

"A shakedown. Please."

I patted the laptop.

"Or maybe I won't do anything. Maybe I'll lose this, and leave you stuck with a rotten agent. Then you can go to work every day, and wonder which one."

"Whoa! Whoa-whoa-whoa, Cole, this is a federal investigation. You're in no position to threaten me."

I leaned toward her, and didn't smile.

"No, ma'am. It's a Janet Hess investigation. So what's actually going to happen is, you're going to call the U.S. Attorney. By eight tomorrow morning, I want a written agreement granting immunity to Amy Breslyn from all charges—"

She slapped the prints on the dash. She was angry, and her voice was loud.

"These prove nothing. I discussed an investigation with you. I sought your expertise in a complex local matter, and, brother, you came through. This kind of thing is done all the time."

"Not by a Special Agent in Charge. You might've been a shit-hot street agent back in the day, but now you're management."

"I'm the SAC. The SAC can send whoever she wants."

"Seeing as how she sent herself, I'm betting the director doesn't know. You're working off the books, kind of like Meryl Lawrence. You're off the reservation, Janet, and you're breaking the law."

We stared at each other for what felt like a couple of hours until she sighed.

"What do you want?"

"A written agreement granting immunity for—"

She interrupted.

"No way, Cole. The woman offered her services to foreign terrorists. I appreciate the trauma she's suffered, but I cannot ignore what she's doing."

"You don't know what she's doing. You have no idea."

"She offered support and weapons to fucking lunatics. Terrorists."

I showed her the last picture. It was the picture I snapped of Amy's workroom with the fine leather jacket.

"That's what she wants them to think, Janet, but that isn't what she's doing."

"What is this?"

"She's planning to wear it tomorrow when she meets the people she thinks are al-Qaeda. See the pouches in the lining? She isn't helping them, Janet. She's delivering a bomb. She's going to kill them."

Hess stared at the picture, glanced at me, and turned away.

"I hate this."

"Full immunity by eight A.M., subject to her agreement to cooperate and testify, and present herself for a psychiatric evaluation and counseling, if so ordered by the judge. I get the notarized paper, you get the agent."

She was still staring, but her eyes were softer.

"I don't know if I can get it done that fast."

"No paper, no agent. And one more thing."

"I'm not saying I won't. I might not get it done in time."

"No paper, no agent. You're going to call the chief of police. Call him tonight."

"LAPD?"

"Yes. They suspended a K-9 officer named Scott James for helping me."

"The cop from Echo Park?"

"You're going to take the bullet for Officer James. You're going to tell the chief James was working for you, and with your assurance his involvement was legal, and in the national interest. You'll say you recruited him because he met the suspect, and you used the power of your position to convince the officer to conceal his involvement, even though you knew this to be against LAPD policy."

"I'll look like an asshole."

"You'll apologize, and you're going to convince the chief to make this right."

"Jesus, Cole, I get it."

She frowned at her watch. I knew she was feeling the pressure, but I also knew she would give it a shot.

I said, "Agent Hess?"

She looked at me, and I patted the laptop.

"I got him for you. You can have him."

"And then what? Nothing here will be admissible."

"The truth is what we agree to."

She stared at me, waiting, and maybe I waited, too.

I said, "Thomas Lerner exists. I met him exactly as I stated to Carter."

She leaned back, and watched me.

"You didn't hire me. I became involved while trying to find Lerner, exactly as I claimed in my statement, and, being me, I investigated. I discovered a link between the house and Colinski, and a possible connection with an employee of Woodson Energy. Since Carter had accused me of being involved, I didn't bring this information to the police. I brought it to you, which is how you and I met. You immediately looked into these things, and discovered the criminal involvement of one of your agents."

I stopped, and waited some more. I knew she was thinking, but I couldn't tell what.

"This thing happens tomorrow, Janet. Help me save Amy, and you'll get your agent, and whoever else happens to be there."

Hess nodded, and her face looked softer, there in the shadows.

"This is why I hired you, Mr. Cole."

I opened the door, slid out, and looked at her.

"Get the immunity, and take care of James. You have my cell. The next time you call, I'll answer."

I closed her door, went to my car, and drove back to Silver Lake.

True Things We Value

54

Jon Stone

Jon cleaned his weapons while Amy Breslyn slept. The two .45s and the M4, though he didn't expect to use them. Ritual. He cleaned them in the dark, sitting in the Rover's back seat.

When the guns were away, he fired the engine to recharge his power packs. The power packs supplied juice for the laptop, his satellite transceiver, and cell phones. While the power packs charged, he slipped out of the Rover with his toiletry kit, and stood in a dark pool of shadow. Three minutes after four in the a.m., the little street was sleeping.

Jon stretched deep from the hips, getting his hamstrings and spine, and twisted to warm his core. He clicked off a hundred push-ups, stretched, and knocked out a hundred lunges. He finished up with a hundred burpees, and a nice little sweat. Wasn't much, but he did what he could.

Jon shaved and brushed his teeth, then took off his clothes. He cleaned himself with wet wipes and a bottle of water, and put on the fresh clothes Cole brought from his home. Breakfast was trail mix, a banana, and two protein bars. By then, the sky was beginning to lighten, so Jon took his place behind the wheel.

These cops Cole brought were a pain. This woman Hess? An idiot. The government agents who tagged along? Fuckups waiting to happen. Delta didn't allow fuckups. Fuckups got people killed.

Hess rolled in like she was in charge, and laid out her plan to approach Ms. Breslyn. The 'first contact' team would consist of two women and an older, but non-threatening, man. The team would include herself, another woman, and the man, the other woman being a shrink in her forties, and the man being a U.S. Attorney with a gentle, assuring presence. First contact, like Ms. Breslyn was an alien. Hess was explaining how their 'first contact' had to be staged when Jon interrupted.

"Forget the team. I'm going to approach her, and I'll be alone. Thanks."

Hess and her suits lit up like flares, so Jon turned off his radio.

A little while later, they called his phone, and asked if he'd wear a wire.

"No."

Jon sat in the Range Rover cocoon, listened to Amy sleep, and knew people were beyond the edge of the darkness. Talking and planning, positioning cars at egress points to cover the house, and setting up at the storage facility. No one knew how Amy would react, or which way this would go, so they had to be flexible. Jon resented their intrusion.

The deep blue canopy paled, and lights went on in a couple of houses. Construction workers come early to beat the morning crush arrived, parked, and leaned back to catch a few last-minute zees.

The image on Jon's laptop grew visible as Amy's room lightened with the dawn. At five fifty-one, her arm moved. At five fifty-two, her leg. She checked her watch at five fifty-eight, and sat up stiffly, the way people do, after a long sleep.

Jon pressed the push-to-talk.

"She's up."

Pike said, "Rog."

Cole said, "Need anything?"

"Yeah. Keep those people away from me."

Cole didn't answer, and neither did Hess. Stone knew she was listening.

Amy did her business, then went to the kitchen. She stayed for several minutes, came out with a cup of coffee, and returned to the bedroom. She selected an outfit, laid it out on the bed, and went into the bathroom with the coffee. He heard the sink, and then the shower. Seeing her clothes laid out made him think of a mortuary, the way morticians laid out clothes as they prepared to dress a corpse. Jon tried to stop thinking about it, but the image stayed with him.

He wondered at her inner landscape. In a few hours, Amy would put on an explosive device, and end her own life, yet she had slept soundly. She appeared calm and relaxed before she went to bed, and seemed comfortable and at ease now. Maybe she was at peace with this terrible end. Maybe she was relieved.

Amy came out naked, and went to the bed.

Jon touched her image.

"Not on my watch."

She dressed, poured herself a second cup of coffee, and sat on the couch in the living room with her computer. Jon watched for signs of messaging, but decided she was reading the news.

At two minutes after seven, she put the coffee cup in the kitchen, returned to the bedroom, and took the large purse and fringed coat from the closet.

Jon pressed the push-to-talk.

"Five or less. She's getting ready."

He shut the Rover's engine, and pocketed the keys.

Hess spoke from the two-way.

"Don't fuck up."

Bitch.

Amy stopped in the living room to put on the jacket, and hung the big purse from her shoulder.

Jon left the Rover and walked toward her house. He'd wanted to meet Amy and talk to her since he learned about Jacob, and now here they were. Groovy.

Hess had no idea. She was clueless, and here for the wrong reasons.

Amy was locking the front door when Jon reached the steps. She gripped the rail as she always did, and started down, one step at a time, watching her feet as if she were afraid she would fall. She didn't see him.

Jon climbed a few steps, and waited.

She took another step, and another. She finally saw him, and startled, as if he'd given her a fright.

Jon smiled, and held out his hand.

"My name is Jon. I'm here about Jacob."

She seemed startled again.

"How do you know him?"

"I don't, but I've been there, where he died. I'd like to tell you about it. Let's go up. We'll talk."

Jon followed her up to the house, where he sat with Amy Breslyn. He said things he couldn't have said if he had worn the wire, but they made her feel better, and gave Amy hope.

55

Elvis Cole

THREE HOURS and twenty minutes after I left Janet Hess in a Hollywood parking lot, we met again in a different parking lot, this one in Silver Lake. A street agent couldn't have made it happen, but Hess was the SAC. She presented me with a signed, notarized agreement from the U.S. Attorney's office. The agreement stipulated in writing the assurances and protections I'd asked for. Amy Breslyn was safe.

Despite everything between us, I found myself liking her.

"You're all right, Hess."

"Don't get carried away."

"What about James?"

"Done."

I found myself liking her a lot.

Hess wanted to see the video, but she hadn't come alone. She arrived with six ATF agents in three cars, and an ATF Crisis Response Team. The CRT team was the ATF's version of SWAT, and rolled up in a large, black Suburban. We were surrounded by agents in a parking lot.

I said, "Here?"

Hess led me away from the others to her G-ride. I opened my laptop, and resumed the video from the pause.

Amy stepped back as she opened the door, and Mitchell walked in. Hess recognized him instantly, even when all she saw was the top of his head.

"Fucker. Russ, you bitch."

"You'll see his face in a few seconds."

"I know who he is. Asshole."

When we reached a point in the video where Mitchell mentioned Rollins, she stopped me.

"Rollins is Colinski?"

"I think so. He's the man James and I saw at the house."

She shook her head, angry and disgusted.

"Stupid Russ. You idiot."

"You can't have the laptop, but I'll give you the video. He lays himself out, how he set up the deal, what they're selling, everything."

She turned away.

"I want it as soon as possible."

"You got it."

We got into an ATF car with the CRT commander. One of the ATF agents drove, and Hess sat in front with the driver. They wanted to see Amy's house.

I sketched out what I knew as we drove up, mostly repeating what I'd heard Amy and Mitchell say, and describing Safety Plus. The CRT commander bombed me with questions about Amy's storage unit, and ordered a second CRT team deployed to Safety Plus. He told Hess to roll out a Bomb unit.

I said, "The explosives are gone. I took them."

"Where are they?"

"Under my deck. I took them home."

We cruised past Amy's house and Jon's Rover. The CRT commander eyed the Rover as we passed.

"We'll have to get him out of here."

I said, "He's watching out for her. He'll stay."

"This is for his safety."

"He's staying. Me, the Rover guy, and my partner, we're downrange on this, and we're calling the shots. Make your peace."

Hess turned to the CRT commander, and backed me.

"They're downrange. Let's go a step at a time."

Back in the parking lot, Hess and I got into the Suburban with the CRT commander, a CRT crisis negotiator, and a red-haired ATF agent named Darrow. Amy's willingness to cooperate would dictate how they dealt with Mitchell and Colinski. We couldn't work out a plan until we knew whether Amy was willing and able to help, and we couldn't know this until we faced her. Amy's response was critical. Hess looped in Pike and Stone via radios, and laid out how she wanted to approach Amy. Jon cut her off, told her he would deal with Amy, and hung up.

Hess said, "What the fuck?"

I said, "Temperamental."

SACs aren't used to being cut off.

I touched her arm.

"We got you this far, Janet. Trust him."

I left them a few minutes later, and drove back to Amy's. It was still dark. I parked three houses below, facing uphill. I could see Amy's house, but not Jon's Rover. Pike was higher, looking down from above. I wondered if Amy was dreaming.

The sky was lighter when Hess arrived. A second ATF car appeared, and parked below me. The sun rose, neighborhood residents left their homes, and the dawn brightened into a full-on day.

A few minutes after seven, the radio popped.

Jon said, "Five or less. She's getting ready."

Amy was about to leave the house, drive to her storage space, and finish a device with which she would end her own life. I wondered what she was feeling.

Hess spoke from the radio, responding to Jon.

"Don't fuck up."

I wondered if Amy felt anxious or scared, and if she was having second thoughts. The Amy I knew wasn't. My Amy didn't want to die. She was smart, strong, and determined, and she had arrived at a course of action that seemed rational to her. A broken heart could do this.

Jon appeared, walking down from the Rover. He stopped at the steps, and looked up toward her house.

I couldn't see Amy because of the angle, but she would be outside by now, and on her way down. Amy needed to finish the jacket quickly, so she was probably running through a mental checklist of the remaining work.

Jon started up the steps, and then he was gone.

Amy wouldn't see him at first. She'd be lost in her thoughts, checking off the rational steps that led to her rational death, and each of those steps would make perfect, inevitable sense.

Until she saw Jon.

Everything would change when she saw him. Jon would offer a different path.

56

Jon was with her about fifty minutes before he called.

"C'mon up. We're good."

Hess and I went, along with the red-haired agent, Darrow, and a tall, athletic agent named Kelman.

Here we were, all these strangers, some with badges, invading her world, and hitting her with the cold-water truth that much of what she'd been told and believed were lies.

Amy was emotional at first, but she seemed to take comfort in Jon. He sat near her on the couch. Hess and I sat opposite them. Darrow and Kelman searched the house while we spoke.

Amy didn't appear suicidal or unstable. People with such problems often don't, but her responses were clear and intelligent. She understood what was happening, and was processing the new truth of her situation.

I showed her the sketch of Royal Colinski and his mug shot.

She said, "That's Mr. Rollins. He was at the house."

Hess showed her a picture of Mitchell. Amy identified him as Charles Lombard.

Hess told her about Eli Sturges and his relationship to Colinski, and asked about the missing explosives. Amy's answer surprised us.

"I don't have any more. The material you're talking about isn't real."

Jon leaned back so she couldn't see his face, and flashed a huge grin. She'd already told him.

I was more doubtful.

"The material in Echo Park was real. The putty I found with the vest is real."

She nodded.

"Yes, that material is real. I had forty-eight pounds of live material. The remainder is material we make for training purposes. It looks and feels the same, but it's chemically inert."

Jon grinned.

"Play-Doh."

Darrow was back in the room.

He said, "Did you think you could fool these people?"

"No, sir. I could've taken more of the live material, but I didn't want to risk so much falling into the wrong hands."

Jon laughed aloud this time.

Hess said, "Where is this material, Amy?"

Amy glanced at me.

"In the unit next to the one you were in. I have two units. Side by side."

She gave Hess the key card and a lock key. Hess dispatched two agents and a CRT team with orders to secure both units and their contents. I realized Amy was telling the truth when she told us the missing material was harmless. Maggie would have alerted at the second unit if the explosives were real. She hadn't been trained to find bombs that couldn't explode.

Hess checked her watch. Time was a factor, and the clock was running.

"Okay, Amy, help us out here. How do we get from here to Colinski and Sturges? How does the deal unfold?"

Amy sketched out the steps. They matched with what I already knew. Rollins was supposed to transfer funds into a foreign account this morning. He would notify Mitchell when it happened, and Mitchell would notify Amy. When Amy confirmed the transfer, she'd take Mitchell to the hidden stash, and Mitchell would arrange the handoff to Colinski and his buyers.

I said, "How do you check the account? Your computer?"

"Charles is supposed to call."

She still called him Charles.

Hess said, "Let's see. Maybe you're rich."

Amy opened her computer, and signed into her account. A few seconds later, she shook her head.

"No. Not yet. You can see."

Darrow sat beside her, and studied the screen.

Hess leaned toward her again.

"What did you mean, you'll take Charles? Are you supposed to pick him up?"

Amy frowned vaguely, as if they'd never discussed it.

"No. He'll pick me up. He'll come get me, and I'll tell him how to get there. He doesn't know. I didn't want him to know, in case he got ideas."

Jon grinned, and shook his head.

"Awesome."

I thought about Mitchell for a moment, and turned to Hess.

"Will Mitchell go hard or easy?"

"Easy. He'll flop like a fish. I want him off the board fast."

Jon said, "Be advised."

Loud.

Everyone turned. Jon was wearing his Delta face.

"Just so we're on the same page, Ms. Breslyn isn't on the board. She will at no time be exposed to these people when they aren't in custody."

Hess said, "Absolutely not."

Darrow's phone buzzed. He pushed to his feet when he saw the message, and hurried to the windows.

"White male. Approaching the house."

Hess and I moved to the windows, too, and Kelman moved to the door. Jon was on his feet with his pistol out faster than any of us, and helped Amy up.

"Let's us go in back. C'mon."

Amy seemed confused.

"Charles didn't call."

I peeked past the edge of the drapes, and saw Russ Mitchell climbing the steps. A bouquet of red and white carnations was in his right hand. I recognized him the same time Hess said his name.

"Mitchell. You asshole."

Jon and Amy had retreated into the dining room. Jon stood so she was behind him.

"Amy, does he have a key?"

"Absolutely not!"

"Jon."

I touched my lips to show him what I wanted.

He whispered something I didn't hear, slipped behind her, and covered her mouth gently with his hand.

Hess set Kelman to open the door, and Darrow at the flank. She stood across the living room by the hall, and I stood by the entrance to the kitchen, all four of us with our guns out. Hess was the first agent he would see. She pointed at Kelman and Darrow.

"Take down, prone."

I said, "Try not to kill him. We need him."

Hess smirked.

"He's not going to fight."

A shadow passed the drapes, and disappeared behind the door. The house bell chimed, followed by two quick knocks. Kelman watched Hess. She shook her head. The bell chimed again, and this time Hess nodded. When the door opened, Mitchell took half a step inside. He stopped when he saw Hess, and immediately raised his hands.

Hess said, "Hands out to the sides. On your knees."

Mitchell's face was bright red, like a man fighting tears.

"I give up. Jesus, I'm sorry."

Hess shouted.

"Step in. Get on your fucking knees, Russ."

He spread his arms wider and higher, and worked even harder not to cry.

"I want a deal. Whatever you want. I'll cooperate."

"Get down!"

He dropped the bouquet, and the flowers fell.

"Whatever you want."

Mitchell broke, and ran. Darrow and I moved fastest, but Mitchell pulled up short before we reached the door. He stood frozen on the porch for an instant, and his gun went off with a high-velocity crack. Russ Mitchell's body folded beneath a red mist, and fell.

57

Hess was livid.

ASSHOLE!"

She turned from the body, and hurried to Amy.

"What will Colinski do if he can't reach Mitchell?"

Amy was trying to see the body but the agents blocked the door. The street agents from below ran up when they heard the shot, and were on their phones with the agents who remained in the parking lot.

Amy said, "Did you shoot him?"

Hess blocked Amy's view.

"Stay with me, Amy. Focus. He's gone."

Jon said, "Easy."

Hess fired a glance, but gentled her voice.

"You said Colinski is going to call Mitchell about the money. If he can't get Mitchell, will he call you?"

"I've never spoken to him on the phone. I barely spoke to him the one time we met."

"So he doesn't have your number?"

"Not unless Charles gave it to him."

"And you don't have his?"

"Charles dealt with him. Charles handled all that."

I pushed past the agents and went to the body. Someone had cleared Mitchell's gun, but his body was otherwise undisturbed. I checked for a wallet.

Kelman said, "Hey. You're not supposed to do that."

"Okay."

I turned over the body, and went through Mitchell's pockets. I was hoping for a scrap of paper with Colinski's address or a treasure map, but I came up with his phone, wallet, and keys. I tossed the car fob to the closest agent.

"Check his car. Phone numbers, addresses, contact information."

Mitchell and Colinski would have spoken and texted as they worked out their deal, which meant Colinski's number would be in Mitchell's phone. I took the phone and wallet inside, gave them to Hess, and went to Amy. She was back on the couch with Jon. Darrow took the phone from Hess, and examined it.

"Could you speak with Colinski if you had to?"

"I don't have his number."

"If we could reach him. If we could call him, would you be okay talking to him?"

She studied me as if she thought I was asking a trick question.

"Why wouldn't I?"

"He's a scary man."

"I'm a scary woman."

Jon smiled, but he didn't laugh.

I said, "If I was Colinski, and you called, you know what I'd be thinking?"

She answered without hesitation.

"Where's Charles? Why is this woman calling, and not Charles?"

Jon nodded, encouraging.

"What would you say?"

She glanced to the front door, where the agents hid the body she had not yet seen.

"I'd tell him Charles is dead. I'd say I shot him, and I hope you won't let this affect our business."

I glanced over, and saw Hess listening.

"She can do this. She can make it happen."

Hess wet her lips like she was getting hungry.

"We'd have to plan the moves. Keep it simple. We have a lot of moving parts."

Mitchell's phone rang. Darrow was still checking the phone when it rang. He startled so badly he almost dropped it. The Caller ID read WINSTON MACHINES.

I held out my hand to Amy.

"Answer or voice mail?"

Hess took the phone, and held it toward her.

"You don't have to. Only if you can."

Amy took the phone, and answered.

"Hello?"

Hess and I leaned close to hear the other side, but all we heard was silence.

Amy said, "Mr. Rollins?"

Silence.

"Mr. Rollins, I'm here with Charles, and I have a problem."

A male voice spoke. Gruff.

"Who is this?"

"Amy. We met at your house. With Charles."

Colinski warmed, and his voice softened.

"Hi, Amy. I remember, of course. Please let me speak with Charles."

"Charles is dead. I shot him. I'm afraid I had to shoot him."

Colinski fell silent again, and at the same time Darrow waved his arms, and pointed at the computer. He mouthed the words 'the money' and gave a thumbs-up.

Colinski had made the transfer.

Amy said, "Mr. Rollins, are you there? I don't want this to interfere with our business."

Silence.

I leaned closer, and whispered.

"Offer to send him a picture."

I ran outside to the body, but only Kelman pitched in to help. We dragged Mitchell's body into the living room, and rolled him faceup.

Amy went to the body without missing a beat.

"Here, I'll show you. I'll send a picture."

She snapped a pic of the head, then frowned at the camera.

"I took the picture, but I need your number to send it."

Hess plucked at my arm, and whispered.

"We gotta get her off. We have to figure this out."

Amy said, "All right, yes, thanks. Here we go."

Amy tapped in the number and texted the picture.

I leaned close again.

"You're worried someone heard the shot. You have to check. You'll call him back."

I stepped back, and watched.

I didn't hear what Colinski said, but Amy's voice turned cold.

"He was disrespectful. Let's leave it at that. I do not tolerate disrespect. As I said, I hope this doesn't create a problem."

She listened for a moment, before interrupting him.

"Wait, I hear something. I think the neighbors heard the shot. I have to check. I'll call you back."

Amy played it well. She was believable and convincing, and then she hung up.

58

Mr. Rollins

CHARLES WITH A CRATER in his head the size of a lemon and his eye all bugged out and bloody looked like the kid in the house, the dipshit Eli sent who started this mess. Mr. Rollins wanted to send Eli the picture, and say, y'see, motherfucker, this is *your* fault.

But he didn't.

Mr. Rollins was angry, but the rules helped him stay true. He thought through his next move carefully.

"I'll cover the two hundred thousand, Eli. I'll take the hit to cover the loss, but it's time to walk away."

Two hundred thousand being the amount Eli paid for the explosives.

Eli, that asshole, furious.

"What loss you mean? The loss I take tomorrow because I cannot do my job?"

"Be reasonable. Let's think this through—"

Eli, all over him.

"I would see four to six million tomorrow. Is this the loss you will cover?"

"A thing like this happens, here we are, the last second, you have to take notice. Like a warning, Eli."

"Here is a warning. You knew my timeline. You knew the truck would have this money. Four to six million. Not today, not the day after tomorrow, only tomorrow. We need this explosive."

"She's lying, Eli. I'm telling you. We should walk."

"You cover the four to six million?"

"There'll be other trucks."

"No. I am telling *you*. We get the material. My timeline ends *now*."

Eli hung up.

59

Elvis Cole

HESS PACED THE ROOM like a feral cat as Amy described their conversation.

"He said this didn't have to affect our relationship. He seemed very agreeable."

I said, "You have two hundred thousand dollars of his money, Amy. He's wrestling with it. We'll see."

Hess stopped pacing, and looked at us.

"If he goes for it, this happens only two ways. They come here, or she goes to them."

Jon shifted.

"Do I need to repeat myself?"

Hess ignored him, and went on with her pacing.

"The Sturges crew, Colinski, these animals are gunned-up killers. I don't want them rolling into this neighborhood."

Kelman shook his head.

"They wouldn't go for it. Sturges and Colinski would take one look at this little street, and blow. Sturges might send a couple of his crew, but then what?"

I said, "The storage place. You already have people there. You'll need more, but they can start locking it down."

"What's it like up there?"

I laid out a description of the entrance, the parking lot, and the gate, all of it surrounded by the wall.

Jon didn't wait for me to finish.

"It's sweet. A perfect kill zone."

Hess frowned at him.

"You're just lovely, aren't you?"

Time was passing, so I pushed us forward.

"The material they want weighs four hundred pounds. That works for us. Amy can't move it herself, so if they want it, they'll have to come get it. She can tell Rollins to meet her in the parking lot with the buyers."

I sat beside Amy, and walked her through the rest.

"Tell him what kind of car you drive. You've met, so you'll recognize each other, right?"

She nodded.

"Say so. Don't mention the cameras, but tell him about the gate and your gate card. When they arrive, you'll open the gate and take them inside to your unit. Sound good?"

Amy nodded again.

"I understand."

Hess came over and tried to be encouraging.

"You're okay with this?"

"It isn't rocket science."

Jon laughed again, and I laughed, too, but my laugh sounded nervous.

Hess held out the phone.

"All right, Ms. Breslyn. Get some payback."

Amy glanced up, and their eyes met. Anger flashed in Amy's eyes, a volcanic fury that lived inside her and wanted to come out. I knew we were seeing the rage that she carried, and I thought maybe Hess now sought to release it.

I said, "Let's call."

Amy dialed, and sounded even more natural and convincing. Colinksi seemed reluctant at first, but Amy sold him.

She said, "Mr. Rollins, I hate to ask, but when our business is finished, after you have the material, would you help me get rid of his body?"

Hess quietly raised her hand, and gave me a silent high five.

Colinski agreed to the meet, and when Amy hung up, we raced to the location. Darrow drove Amy's Volvo. Amy went with Jon, and Pike and I rolled together.

We arrived first, but first didn't help.

60

Scott James

SCOTT HAD NEVER been to the tenth floor of the Police Administration Building. The chief of police lived on the tenth. The three assistant chiefs and eight deputy chiefs were on the tenth. Down on the street and at the Academy, the tenth floor was known as Heaven, and the rulers of Heaven were God; the Father, the Son, and the Holy Ghost; and the eight apostles.

The tenth-floor halls were surprisingly plain. Most of the doors required key cards or codes to open, but Ignacio had a card and knew the codes, so opening the doors wasn't a problem.

Scott was surprised when Ignacio called that morning. He ordered Scott to report to the Boat, in uniform, now. He called at seven-forty A.M., and offered no explanation.

Ignacio only made one comment.

"You must have an angel."

Ignacio met Scott in the lobby, took him up to the tenth, and introduced him to an apostle. Ignacio left after the intro.

Deputy Chief Ed Waters was a graduate of the University of Notre Dame. He had a Ph.D. from USC, and a list of law-enforcement accomplishments and credentials that went on for pages. Waters had testified before the Senate and the House many times, and was a likely replacement for the present chief when his term expired.

Waters currently topped the Counter-Terrorism and Special Ops Bureau, which put him above Metro Division on the LAPD Organization Chart. Since the K-9 Platoon was part of Metro, this placed Scott in Waters's line of command.

Waters had smart eyes, a ruddy face, and a stern demeanor. He asked Scott to sit, and described a conversation between Hess and the chief. Hess had made it sound as if Scott helped save America from a national disaster, and took responsibility for any and all of his misdeeds.

"The chief and SAC Hess have to work together, so forget this business with the complaint. It's dead."

Scott felt uncomfortable, but managed a nod. Most of what Hess told the chief was lies.

"Thank you."

"I'll send out paper to the Metro C.O. and the commander of Internal Affairs. Your boss will be notified sometime this morning. When you report is up to him."

Scott nodded again, but felt even more uncomfortable. He wondered if Waters believed all this bullshit.

"Great news, Chief. Thanks."

He wanted to pick up Maggie as soon as possible. He wanted to turn out for roll call, and get back to work, but Waters didn't dismiss him.

The deputy chief leaned forward, and laced his fingers.

"The SAC went out of her way to save you. I guess she knows she stepped over the line, and she's embarrassed. Whatever the case, she went to bat for you, and delivered the goods."

Scott felt himself flush, and wanted to leave, but all he managed was another nod.

"Still, I don't know that I would've gone along with her, the way you did. I'd like to think my oath was more important, and my obligation to the department. But maybe that's just me."

Waters fell silent, and seemed to be waiting. Scott thought the man was probably measuring him.

"Sir, everything Carter charged in his complaint was true. I disobeyed Commander Ignacio's order, and I withheld information from Detective Carter. These were my choices, and not the choices of SAC Hess or anyone else."

The deputy chief's expression didn't change very much. Only a little.

"Why?"

"Because a sonofabitch was trying to kill me and my dog."

Waters finally stood, and offered his hand.

"Welcome back, Scott."

61

Mr. Rollins

MR. ROLLINS met Eli and his crew in the parking lot of a Pizza Hut, three blocks from the storage place, way the hell up in East Jesus a thousand miles from civilization. Eli, sitting there in his classic bronze 1969 SS396 with two of his guys. This freaking beautiful car was like wearing a sign: SEE ME!

Mr. Rollins had a rule. Draw no attention to yourself. Mr. Rollins was driving a stolen white Camry, the plates having been swapped with an identical Camry he found at UCLA. Toyotas and Hondas were the most common cars in Los Angeles. Silver and white were the most common colors.

Mr. Rollins leaned on Eli's door. Eli was one of those tall, lanky guys with a mop of curly black hair.

"I told her what you drive, so she knows the car. She's in a beige Volvo. You'll see her when you turn in."

"You are not coming with us?"

"I'll be in my car, but we're not going yet. Wait until I call. I'm gonna scope it out, make sure we're cool."

"Okay. We wait."

"If it's cool, we'll pick up the gear, and maybe go take care of the body."

Eli leaned sideways to peer up at him.

"You want to clean her garbage, clean. I am not a garbage man. Make more of your meatballs."

The two idiots in his car broke out laughing.

Mr. Rollins walked away.

"Yeah. Laugh."

Ten minutes later, he was on the roof of a nursery across from Safety Plus, studying the Volvo with his Nikon binoculars. A woman sat behind the wheel, but with the glare and glass reflection, he couldn't see her. The woman he met in Echo Park was round and short. The woman in the Volvo sat low behind the wheel, which maybe meant she was short, or a tall chick, scrunched down.

Mr. Rollins decided to see. He gave Eli a call.

"We are sleeping over here, you take so long. We ordered the pizzas."

Morons yucking it up.

"Looks good. Go meet her. And remember, you're terrorists."

"Where are you?"

"Going to my car. I'll be right behind you."

Mr. Rollins called the number he had for Charles. She answered before, and answered again.

"We're here. Is that you inside?"

Amy said, "Yes. I'm here. I've been waiting."

The woman in the Volvo waved.

"Great. See you soon. Ten seconds or so."

Mr. Rollins put away his phone, and watched. Eli showed up a few seconds later, turned through the entrance, and stopped. Neither car moved for another ten seconds until Eli got out and spread his hands, his gesture saying, what, are you just gonna sit there?

Then Eli turned to climb back into his car, and all hell broke loose. Mr. Rollins didn't stay to see it play out. He eased off the roof, returned to his anonymous car, and recited his list of getaway rules.

Go slow.

Stay in the right lane.

Brake early.

Mr. Rollins followed the rules, and got away.

62

Elvis Cole

THE HEAT in the rental office built quickly with so many people crowded into a small space. The CRT team commander and Kelman were up front, near the glass. The CRT commander was miked to talk to the deployed elements. Darrow was closer to us, wearing a radio headset so he could speak with Hess. Special Agent in Charge Hess was in Amy's Volvo.

The agents almost mutinied when the SAC announced she would be in the car, but Hess held tough, and told them to watch her back. The SAC sends who the SAC wants. She was beginning to make me smile.

Joe and I stood with Jon and Amy in the rear. Amy was draped in a bullet-resistant vest heavy enough to stop a rhino. Jon had ripped it from the CRT team vehicle.

Amy was in the office because she held the phone. If Colinski called, he'd expect Amy to answer. She needed to see the field of play to know how to respond.

When the phone finally rang, everyone in the office looked at Amy except for the CRT commander. He kept his eyes on the Volvo.

"Hello?"

Amy listened.

"Yes. I'm here. I've been waiting."

Amy raised her hand, and Darrow whispered to Hess.

"Wave. They see you. Wave."

Inside the Volvo, Janet Hess waved.

Amy lowered the phone.

"They're coming. He said ten seconds."

Darrow repeated the information to Hess, and the CRT commander mumbled into his mike.

A bronze SS396 turned through the entrance, rolled forward, and stopped. Both agents lifted binoculars, and Kelman immediately called out identifiers.

"Sturges, driver. Front passenger, Remi Jay Wallach, he's their blaster. One male in rear, can't make him out."

I squinted through the glass.

"I don't see Colinski. Colinski isn't in the car."

I snapped at Darrow.

"Tell her. He isn't with them."

Darrow told her and asked what to do.

"What do we do, wait? He isn't here."

Sturges got out of his car. He stared at the Volvo for several seconds, and spread his hands, asking what she's waiting for.

I pulled Darrow close, and spoke into his mike.

"Don't get out, Hess. Colinski is watching. He'll see you're not Amy."

Sturges turned to get into his car, and Darrow shouted, relaying Hess's order.

"Take down! Now! Gogogo!"

I was a spectator. I watched from a glass box as others did the work.

On the command, CRT operators rushed forward from hides along the wall and behind our office, and an amplified voice shouted commands at the people in the car. Sturges dove behind the wheel, and hit the gas. I guess he thought he could get away, like they do in the movies. The car fishtailed sideways, the rear tires throwing smoke. Flashes reached from the back seat, a few at first, then a long crazy stream scribing a pointless arc. The front passenger door flew open. The passenger fell out or maybe he jumped, but either was just in time. The operators went to work with their M4s, killing the car and the people within. I knew the moment when Sturges was hit. His foot left the gas, and the slipping, sliding tires stopped spinning. His car lurched forward, and slammed into the Volvo with a dull thud.

The operators swarmed the car, proned the passenger who had fallen out, and secured the scene. I ran outside to check on Hess, but she was out of the Volvo and laughing before I reached her. I was proud of her. She really did well.

It was a good day. Amy was safe, and would get the help she needed. Hess came through for Scott. His suspension would go away, and he would return to the job he loved.

It was a good day in many ways, but it could have been better.

I promised Scott I would give him Colinski.

I didn't.

63

Scott James

Eleven days later

THEY KNEW FROM Remi Jay Wallach, the lone survivor of Sturges's crew, that Royal Colinski was present at the storage facility. Colinski was probably suspicious after Mitchell's suicide, stayed back as Sturges walked into the trap, and fled. Scott didn't fault Elvis Cole for this. Stuff happened.

Colinski's whereabouts remained unknown. Three people could now offer testimony to link the man with capital crimes. Remi Jay Wallach, Amy Breslyn, and Scott. Since Scott was no longer the lone witness, and Colinski's face was splashed on the evening news, Carter, Stiles, and the other detectives believed Colinski had fled the city. Even Cowly and Cole agreed. The only concession Scott made to Colinski's escape was his weapon. Scott had never been one of those cops who slept with his gun on the nightstand, but now he did. He kept his pistol handy.

A patrol car remained outside Scott's house for three days following Colinski's disappearance. During that time, and in the eight days since, Maggie made no middle-of-the-night raging alerts. After the third silent night, Scott asked that the guards be canceled, and they were.

Eleven days after Colinski escaped, Scott had the day off. Late that afternoon, he and Maggie were heading to the park when his phone rang.

Cole said, "Hey, dude. I know it's the last minute, but how about some dinner? You can bring that dog."

"Maggie."

"Maggie. Sorry."

Scott was learning to like Cole, and enjoyed his company.

"Rain check? Joyce and I were planning to grab something."

"Bring her. Pike's coming. I'll fire up the grill."

"What about Jon?"

"Parts unknown. He does that."

"Lemme call Joyce. Can I let you know in an hour?"

"No problemo."

Scott left a message on Cowly's phone, and smiled at Maggie.

"If we go up there, stay away from that cat."

Maggie wagged her tail.

A soccer game was breaking up when they reached the park. Scott was glad the teams were clearing the field. He'd brought along a bag of baloney cubes and the tug toy for after their run.

Scott left his gym bag in an open location so he could keep an eye on it, and circled the park at his usual slow pace for thirty minutes. Maggie stayed glued to his left, like always, with her long shepherd tongue dangling like a pink rope.

"You must be the most patient dog in the world, following my slow butt around this park so many times."

Wag.

Maggie was never bored when she was with Scott. Being with Scott made her happy. Made Scott happy, too.

Scott finished their final lap back at his gym bag. He unlocked the bag, took out her collapsible water bowl, and filled it. Maggie emptied the bowl quickly, so he filled it again, and watched her drink. Leland had taken him aside the day he returned to the roster.

Every second we have with these fine animals is a blessing. No creature, human or otherwise, will love you with such devotion, or trust you so fully. Remember this, Officer James. These dogs will lay their precious hearts bare to you, and hold back no part for themselves. Can anyone else in your pathetic excuse for a life say the same? Such trust is a gift from God Almighty above, so best you be worthy.

Scott ran his hand over Maggie's back, long strokes, the way Leland taught him.

"I almost lost you, baby girl. It won't happen again. I promise."

Maggie wagged her tail and happily curled against him.

Scott put away her bowl, and took out the baloney. The instant she saw the bag she snapped to attention.

"Wanna chase a baloney ball, Maggie-girl? Wanna show me how fast you can run?"

Scott fished the first chunk from the bag and threw it as far as he could. The hefty cube flew a good thirty-five yards, and skittered into the clover beyond the parking lot. Maggie chased down the cube before it stopped bouncing.

"Good girl, Maggie! Atta girl!"

As Maggie trotted back, a man got out of a white Camry with a basketball. He bounced it five or six times, but Scott ignored him. The basketball courts were on the opposite side of the parking lot.

Maggie stood at attention when she got back, anxious to run down another treat. Scott showed her a piece of baloney.

"This one, and one more, and then we have to go, okay?"

Explaining, as he would to a child.

Scott threw a bullet. The baloney arced far past the parking lot, bounced off a sidewalk, and landed in a sandpit surrounding the swing sets more than fifty yards away.

The man with the basketball watched Maggie sprint past, tucked the ball under his arm, and walked toward Scott.

Scott inwardly groaned when he saw the baloney roll into the sand, and shouted a command.

"Maggie, down! Stay!"

Maggie's head whipped around so fast she almost fell over. She was only a few feet from her prize, and torn.

"Maggie, down! Down!"

She gazed forlornly at the lost treat, and dropped to her belly. Scott hated to call her off, but he didn't want her eating a mouthful of sand. He picked up his gym bag and trotted after her.

The man with the basketball was closer. Something about him was familiar, but sunglasses and a low Dodgers cap covered his features. They were the only two people at this end of the park, but the man was coming toward him.

Scott stopped.

The man tossed the basketball aside, and reached under the sweatshirt. Scott saw the flesh-colored vinyl gloves.

"Remember me, asshole?"

Colinski.

"Yeah. You tried to poison my dog."

Colinski drew a pistol, and come toward him faster.

Maggie

Maggie dropped to her belly reluctantly. She glanced over her shoulder at Scott, and quickly turned back to the baloney. A happy flood of saliva drooled from her mouth. Maggie didn't care about the sand and grit. The hefty cube glowed with salty scents of pork fat and chicken, and her tail thumped the ground with anticipation.

Maggie fidgeted, and glanced hopefully at Scott again. Scott was jogging toward her, but suddenly stopped and stared at the man with the basketball. The man had meant nothing until Scott stopped, and now Maggie read the change in Scott's posture from fifty yards away. Something was wrong.

Her ears flicked upright and swiveled. Her mask darkened in concentration.

Patrol dogs and Military Working Dogs were trained to protect their handlers. If the handler was attacked, and unconscious, or fighting for his or her life, the dog had to know what to do without being told. As Leland said, *These animals aren't robots, goddamnit! They think! You train her up right, this beautiful dog will watch your back better than a squad of goddamned Marines!*

The man approaching Scott threw the basketball aside with a sharp, snapping move, and the signs of aggression were as clear to Maggie as a point-blank gunshot. Then the man pointed a gun at Scott, and Maggie broke her stay.

Scott threatened.

Pack threatened.

K-9 Maggie accelerated to a full-stretch sprint in less than half the time possible by the world's fastest human sprinter. Scott and the man with the gun were half a football field away, but Maggie could cover this distance a full second and a half faster than the fastest professional football players.

The pain in her wounded hips didn't matter.

The weapon the man turned toward her didn't matter.

Maggie stretched and pulled. She stared at the man as she ran, and saw nothing else.

Only Scott mattered.

A growl sawed from her chest like teeth gnawing bone.

Scott

Maggie was coming. Maybe she had read a threat in the man's carriage or aggression in his approach, but Scott would never know. He loved her so deeply in this moment his eyes blurred.

Colinsky didn't see her. Maggie was forty yards behind him, and coming at a dead sprint.

Scott nodded at his dog.

"Missed your chance, Royal. She's got you."

Maggie was still thirty yards behind them, and Scott knew the man had a decision. Shoot Scott first, then the dog, or the dog, then Scott. Scott was fifty feet away, so Colinski had plenty of time to shoot Maggie before Scott could reach him.

Scott spread his arms, the gesture saying, take your pick.

Colinski smirked.

"Stupid mutt."

When Colinski turned to bead-up on Maggie, Scott took his

pistol from the gym bag. He didn't shout a warning or order Colinski to throw down his weapon. Scott pulled the trigger.

Colinski hunched when the bullet struck him. Scott shot him twice more before he fell.

When Colinski dropped and lay still, Maggie broke off her attack as she'd been trained, and circled the body. A man on the far side of the parking lot shouted.

Scott hurried over, secured Colinski's weapon, and clipped Maggie's lead. People gathered on the basketball courts and at the edge of the soccer field, but no one came closer.

Colinski made little hiccupping sounds, and blood burped from his mouth. He mumbled something, but Scott couldn't make it out.

"Stop talking. Save your strength."

Scott took his phone from the gym bag and called the emergency operator. Colinski gripped his leg as Scott dialed, and said something about rules.

Scott pulled his leg away, and stepped back.

When the emergency operator answered, Scott identified himself, and requested an ambulance and the police. The operator wanted him to stay on the line, but Scott hung up, and put his phone and pistol back in the gym bag.

Royal Colinski died before the ambulance arrived.

Scott led Maggie a few feet away, and sat on the brilliant green grass with his arm around his dog. He felt her breathe. Her heart beat strong and true. Her breath was filled with life.

64

Elvis Cole

Sixteen days later

Two RED-TAILED HAWKS floated above the canyon like sleepy sentinels. They hung in the sky like fish in water, with no discernible effort, as much a part of the air as a cloud.

Pike said, "They'll go soon. Getting dark."

We were on the deck. The grill was fired, and the coals were close. My plan was to grill four beautiful lamb porterhouse chops for myself, an eggplant, and a mixed bag of veggies we could share. A vegetarian bean casserole was in the oven. The casserole was for Pike, him being a vegetarian, but I liked it, too.

I held up my empty Falstaff.

"Two left. Want one?"

"Sure."

I ducked inside for the last two Falstaffs, and tossed him a can. We popped the tops and drank. We'd been on the deck for most of the day. Drinking for most of the day, too.

I said, "Jon still gone?"

"Uh-huh."

"When's he get back?"

"Never says. You know."

Pike used to make trips like this, too.

I raised my can.

"To Jon."

"Jon."

We drank. These weren't our first.

I said, "Saw Amy."

"How's she doing?"

I wasn't sure how to answer.

"Sees this shrink the court told her to see. It's only been a couple of weeks. The shrink asks a few questions, they talk, the shrink makes notes. She says he's okay."

Pike tipped his can toward the sky.

"Look."

The male hawk folded his wings, turned on his side, and fell like a dart. He pulled around in a long curving turn, opened his wings like parachutes, and streaked past my deck. His tiny hawk head moved as he passed, checking us out.

I said, "He's showing off for his girlfriend."

Pike nodded.

I was inside getting the lamb and veggies when the doorbell rang. I was surprised when I opened the door.

I said, "The SAC."

"I guess it's better than being called a bag."

Hess came in without being asked, and saw Pike on the deck.

"Oh. You have company. I should've called."

"Yeah. You should've."

She took in the room and the view the way people do, and saw the food on the counter.

"Look, I owe you an apology and an explanation. I could've called, but I was scared you'd hang up."

"You don't act like the scared type, Hess."

She glanced away, nervous.

"Of some things."

She was kinda cute when she acted shy, but I'd been drinking.

"I was about to cook. C'mon out. Say hi to Joe."

I grabbed the food from the kitchen, and took it outside. Hess came out behind me.

"It's the SAC."

"Please stop calling me that."

Joe stood, and offered his hand.

"Hello, Janet. You did well there, in the parking lot."

I dropped the lamb on the grill, and heard a nice sizzle.

"She loves parking lots."

Hess turned red and squirmed, but like that day at Safety Plus, she held her ground.

The corner of Pike's mouth twitched. A small twitch, barely noticeable. He looked at Hess.

"Hope to see you again."

Pike went inside, and out the front door.

Hess stared after him.

"Where's he going?"

"He's leaving. He figures you came to see me, and now we're alone."

She flushed again. Darker.

"I came to apologize."

"So apologize. This oughta be something."

"Have you been drinking?"

"Yes. Do you like lamb?"

I arched my eyebrows at her, waiting.

Hess studied me for a moment, and nodded.

"Sure."

"Good. Where's the apology? I don't have all night."

"Can I have a beer first?"

I pointed inside with my elbow.

"Fridge. Help yourself."

Hess went inside, and helped herself.

65

Jon Stone

Dear Ms. Breslyn,

I hope this note finds you well, and offers a measure of peace. An associate informs me the person behind the Abuja attack has been identified as one Sambisa Yemi, a known member of an Islamist terrorist group in northern Nigeria. Witnesses were present when Mr. Yemi personally fixed the weapon package to a young woman named Asama Musa, and instructed others to transport Ms. Musa to the targeted café. For her part, I should tell you Ms. Musa was also a victim. She was stolen from her family by Mr. Yemi, and kept as his slave and hostage for apprx four years. My associate tells me Mr. Yemi admitted his role at least twice during private conversations, and, when interrogated, gave a complete confession.

I have forwarded this information to the appropriate authorities. The wheels of justice will turn, but without Mr. Yemi. He was shot to death last evening near the village of Yana. His death was likely the result of *tribal conflict, but we may never know. As yet, no person or group has taken credit.*

When I return from abroad, I hope you'll allow me to pay my respects. I would love to hear more about Jacob.

Your friend,
J. Stone